THE MEET-POOP

A NOVEL

Also by Noelle Salazar

The Flight Girls
Angels of the Resistance
The Roaring Days of Zora Lily
The Lies We Leave Behind

Published in the United States

Noelle Salazar Inc.

ISBN: 979-8-9999392-0-3
Ebook ISBN: 979-8-9999392-1-0

Printed in the United States of America

www.noellesalazar.com

Book cover design by Ali Shearer (@juniper.charm)
Edited by Dan Hanks (www.danhanks.com)

THE MEET-POOP

A NOVEL

NOELLE SALAZAR

Author's Note and Content Warning

Dear reader,

I am so excited for you to meet Lior, Graham, and Brontë!

Thank you for giving my debut romcom a chance.

If you, like me, prefer to know ahead of time of some potentially sensitive topics or trigger warnings, then I feel obliged to tell you there is a pet's passing in this book. Why would I include such a thing? Because to live is to die. And because once upon a time I had my own sweet girl, who, like Brontë, ended up with a bit of an incontinence problem at the end of her life. Which led to some mishaps of our own. And a lot of laughter. Laughter through tears, one of my favorite phenomena.

I tried to be considerate of feelings, but if you feel you'd rather not read that bit, I understand and respect that completely. Please skip chapter 28.

For Daisy Mae Clementine Space Avenger
The goodest dog there ever was

CHAPTER 1

Lior

I t was a truth universally acknowledged, at least by me and my dry cleaner, that if I wore a designer dress to a party, it was going to end up with something spilled on it.

"Oh shit," a familiar voice said. "Please tell me you were doing your impersonation of the early catwalk years again."

I glanced in the mirror and laughed at the sly grin on the flawless face of my good friend and fellow fashion model Katya. She had just entered the bathroom where I was trying to rinse red wine from the front of my many-thousand-dollar frock.

"Hey, finding one's signature walk is *hard*," I reminded her.

She snorted and glanced into the sink, and then at my chest. My stained, nude, barely-there bra was on display for anyone who walked in the door.

"It wasn't even my fault this time," I said, watching the burgundy color cloud and swirl around the ivory porcelain as Katya disappeared into a stall.

I glanced at myself in the mirror and snorted laughter. I looked ridiculous, the halter top of the dress unbuttoned and lying damply in the sink, my stained bra and naked stomach revealed for anyone who opened the door to see. But it wasn't anything anyone out there hadn't seen before. Half my portfolio was me in sheer clothing.

"Someone turned around and walked straight into me," I said, defending myself

"It's like you have a sign on you," Katya called over the sound of her peeing.

"I'm afraid to know what it says," I muttered.

The toilet flushed and Katya appeared again, striding to wash her hands in the sink beside the one I was rinsing my dress in. I watched her turn her face this way and that in the mirror and then shrug and turn her attention to the fabric I was tending to.

We were at a birthday party for our friend, Petra, and it seemed like the entirety of today's 'It' girls and boys of the modeling world had turned out for it. After flying in from Paris the night before, I'd almost decided not to come. But an important new designer, Daniela Rossi, had been on the invite list and word around town, and from my agent Jen, was that she was dying to work with me. Not showing up could mean her gaze landed elsewhere. And so would her designs. Designs I loved and was dying to wear. They were soft. Feminine. But with a surprising edge to them. Flowing pale pink chiffons with black leather trimmed cut-outs. Celery green satin with charcoal beaded necklines and wrist cuffs. They felt like a fairy tale, but with a dark twist.

Thankfully Daniela and I had crossed paths earlier in the evening and she'd already left, so I didn't have to worry about her seeing what happened to clothes I was gifted by designers. This unfortunate Chanel number might not live to see another day, its beautiful cream fabric still a shocking shade of merlot, despite my rinsing. I lifted it and wrinkled my nose at the stain splattered across the wet and sheer material.

"It looks like one of those ink thingys," Katya said, leaning a slender, gleaming thigh against the counter and staring at the mess.

"A Rorschach test?"

"That's it," she said, snapping her fingers, her silver-painted talon-like nails flashing under the overhead lights. She peered closely at the stain. "I see... a disaster."

"Are you looking at the dress, or at me?"

She laughed and slid from the countertop. "Stop that and tell me how I can help you. Did you wear a jacket? Did you come with someone who can plaster themselves to the front of you?"

"No jacket," I said and then met her ice-blue eyes. "And I came with Oliver."

"Fuck."

Fuck was right.

Oliver Manning was a movie star who had dated his way through at least a dozen of Hollywood's latest leading ladies, and had since moved on to the model scene – starting with some of the lesser-known girls before setting his sights on a bigger fish.

Me.

I wasn't new to the celebrity dating game and the almost diabolical match-making schemes that people – and their agents and PR people – dreamed up for the sake of getting more bodies to a movie, to stream a show, or to buy a brand. I'd tolerated many a date set-up for the good of both parties getting their faces in magazines. But, despite being in the twenty-first century, the men still got applauded for being seen on my arm, while my face was the one plastered on magazine covers and social media sites alongside headlines like, "Lior Flynn Couldn't Hold Onto Another One" when it inevitably ended. It was a tale as old as time: men sleeping around equals hero, women even alluding to sleeping around equals slut. Bring on the scarlet letter. Jump onboard the shame train. Woot Woot! I'd never understand why a woman getting hers was a bad thing. We deserved nice things too!

Unfortunately, Oliver Manning had gotten it in his head that we were a great match, and had let the press know he was serious about me by making a spectacle out of his wooing. He'd even given an interview on a prominent nighttime talk show that he thought we'd make beautiful babies together. It had actually been printed in a notable magazine that I might be the luckiest woman alive to be wanted by a man like Oliver Manning.

Of course, nowhere did the article mention that he was lucky too.

As is the nature of things, him dating someone new meant magazines and talk shows brought up his past history with women... and a rumor that had plagued him for years. Somewhere along the way, whispers of him being into the "classic" sexual practice of caning had arisen. Not giving. Only receiving. Of course, no one ever asked him outright in interviews, and he never addressed it on his own, so it was up in the air if it was true or not. I'd never believed it myself. One, because I knew how it was to have untrue rumors get started, and two... caning? It seemed a stretch. And with as many movies as he'd been on, surely someone responsible for dressing him or doing his makeup would've said something about seeing bruises on his body?

So, despite a possible fetish that might eventually require me to whack the man repeatedly in the bedroom, I'd entered into the relationship with a curiosity – although I was totally up front about not looking for anything serious. A good time was all I was capable of having. Anything more was off the table.

Unfortunately, it didn't matter what I said. Oliver persisted like a dog with a raging bone(r), buying me a car I made the delivery man return on the spot, offering a vacation on a yacht I denied, and inviting me to the screening of a movie I badly wanted to see... but not badly enough to see it with him.

He wouldn't take the hint that this wasn't what he thought it was going to be, and I'd grown tired of his persistence. Asking him to do a solid and plaster himself to me would assure he'd make a spectacle of the situation and draw even more unwanted attention. As soon as the wine hit my dress, the options of getting out with the least amount of eyes on me ran through my mind. When I considered asking Oliver to help me, I realized I'd rather walk

through the crowd naked, call all the media outlets to alert them...
or eat nails.

And that's when I realized Oliver needed to go.

I sighed as I turned off the faucet and stared down at the
ruined front of my dress.

"I'm going to end it tonight," I told Katya.

"That seems a little drastic. It's just wine. Remember when
you lit that little Givenchy jacket on fire in Amalfi?"

I pursed my lips together, trying not to laugh at the horrible
memory and the ridiculous picture that had shown up online and
in all the Italian newspapers.

"I meant Oliver," I said, running my hand over the wet fabric
and flicking water at her.

"Hey!" she said, laughing for a moment before sobering. "Are
you sure? I know he's an idiot but there are *some* benefits"

There were. But none I needed. What I did need was to end it.
For my own sanity. Yesterday when I'd come home from a whirlwind modeling trip to Paris, I'd found my home filled with ridiculously large bouquets of flowers. My agent had run across town to
let the florist in, and then sent me several texts apologizing and a
box of gourmet donut holes to make it up to me. I'd texted a photo
of the ridiculous display to both Katya and my best friend Addie,
back in Seattle. Both had sent back the same image of a large
dumpster on fire.

It was my fault for letting it go on too long, but he had made
such an effort and, for the most part he was good fun to be
around, the sex was decent, and he was easy on the eyes. I didn't
want more than that though, and he clearly did.

"The relationship has run its course," I said, making air quotes
at the word "relationship" and then pulling up the front of my
dress, fastening the halter around my neck, and staring at my reflection. The damp fabric left little to the imagination. "It's time."

Katya opened her purse and handed me a tube of lip gloss and
I laughed.

"Is this... armor?" I asked.

"Game face, baby."

I swiped the gloss over my lips, nodded in approval at the sheer plum shade, and handed it back. I looked absurd with my dress pressed in damp, stained spots to my chest, yet it was probably only going to bring me more attention and adoration. "Lior Flynn, she's just like us!" People were so weird.

"Wish me luck," I said.

"Wait. You're going to do it here? Have you even found out if the caning rumor is true? Please tell me it's true." She clasped her hands in front of her chest, the corner of her mouth lifting in a mischievous grin. It was her most famous expression. Photographers always asked her to give them one of her famous smirks. It was her Tyra Banks equivalent of the "smize". Cindy Crawford's mole. Gisele Bündchen's "horse walk".

"He never asked me even once, and I found no evidence," I said, hanging my head in mock shame. "I've failed you. I'm sorry."

"Damn. Well, if it makes *you* feel any better, my last date was into pegging. While I was still reeling from this revelation, he brought out a small suitcase with a variety of sizes, shapes, and colors."

"Welp," I said, eyes wide and blinking as though trying to ward off that bit of information with the sheer force of my lashes. "Trying new things is... fun?"

She shuddered in response.

"What did you do?"

"Suddenly remembered I had an early shoot," she said and we laughed. That lie worked like a charm every time. "You sure you want to break up with Oliver here?"

"Go big or go home, baby," I said, and turned on my heel. "And I intend to do both. I'm too old for this shit anymore. Plus, he won't make a fuss with so many people around."

"Good point," she said, then leaned in to kiss my cheek. "Good luck."

As I suspected, Oliver took the break-up in stride. I was a bit surprised by his easy acceptance and lack of theatrics after all the effort he'd put in to try and woo me. Then again, there were tons of cameras around and a party filled with beautiful women. He'd be okay.

I took my leave, giving the birthday girl an air kiss on her cheek and quietly slipping out a side door. Smiling at my usual driver as he tucked me safely inside the car, I leaned back and let out a long exhale.

"Are we waiting for Mr. Manning, Miss Flynn?"

"We are not, Freddie."

He nodded his head, closed the door, got in the driver's seat, and pulled onto the street.

I was in bed an hour later, my ruined Chanel dress hanging over the side of the tub after another go at it with some soap. My text alert went off and with a groan I reached for the phone.

Katya.

When I opened the message I burst out laughing. It was a picture of Oliver making out with one of the newer models on the scene. A pretty Southern gal named Dallas.

"Back to the bottom of the barrel he goes," Katya said.

"And all is right with the world," I texted back.

I set the phone down and a moment later it went off again.

"Ditch the party for your pjs yet?" the message read.

Addie. Best friend extraordinaire. She knew me well.

I turned my bedside lamp on and took a selfie of me in my cat pajamas, my face freshly scrubbed, hair fanned out over my pillow. I hit send and waited for it to land to where she was probably in her own bed in Seattle with actual cats lying on her.

The pajamas had been a joke gift from her when I'd turned twenty-nine three months ago. Leading up to the big day, I'd proclaimed over margaritas one night that I was going to happily be a spinster cat lady after I retired from modeling.

"Called it!" she texted back.

I laughed. Adeline Warner had been my best friend since the first day of kindergarten. We'd taken one look at each other as we stood in line outside Mrs. Jacobson's class, dressed in matching blue puffer coats, and our fates were sealed. Besties for life. No one knew me like she did. No one had seen or heard my growing pains, both emotional and physical, like she had. And I'd been the one to witness all her transformations, discoveries, failures and wins.

When I grew six painful inches our junior year, leaving me gawky, clumsy, and unable to keep up with my new lankiness, she'd sat for hours in dressing rooms at the mall with me while I'd cried trying to find jeans that didn't hang off my body. When she made the cheerleading squad and then forgot her briefs, letting everyone get a glimpse of her strawberry-print underwear at her very first game-day performance, I'd bought us each a pint of Ben and Jerry's and we ate while she sobbed over the humiliation. We were together when we opened our acceptance letters to the University of Washington. I took her out to a fancy dinner a year later when she decided she wanted to be a veterinarian, dropped out of university and applied to a different kind of school. And when I got scouted for modeling two days into the following school year, she was standing beside me outside Dick's Burgers, shoving fries in her face and grinning like a loon and nodding, as if she'd always known this day would come. The juxtaposition of my life now, compared to those early days after high school, never failed to entertain us.

"Ruined a Chanel tonight," I messaged.

"I don't want to hear it. I need new tires and that dress probably could've paid for that AND new wiper blades."

"That dress could've gotten you a new car," I said, and promptly received the middle finger emoji in return. "Not that you can't afford one on your own."

Addie was the proud owner of the cutest veterinary clinic in West Seattle. Not that I'd seen many. My mother had been resolutely against having pets when I was a kid. But I assumed the little yellow house-turned-animal-clinic, with its white picket fence and animal-friendly plants lining the front walk was the most adorable in existence. And business was thriving thanks to my friend's combination of medical expertise and holistic approaches.

"Of course I can," she texted. "The difference is, you smile to afford a new car. I express anal glands."

"I don't want to hear any more about your sex life."

She sent a laughing emoji and then asked, "You dump Double Oh Ding Dong yet?"

Double Oh Ding Dong was her nickname for Oliver. He'd done a movie the year before where he'd played a spy. He'd clearly been going for a James Bond feel, but he didn't quite get there. It was like watching a door trying to order a martini.

"Done and dusted this very night."

"Amen to that. Now get some sleep. I can see your under-eye bags from here." The last bit was a direct quote from my mother when I was a mere seventeen years old.

This time I sent her the middle finger emoji, said goodnight, turned off my phone, and went to sleep.

CHAPTER 2

Lior

I made my way downstairs the next morning with a little bounce in my step, happy to be free from a relationship once more. I did my favorite online word games while standing at the kitchen island and sipping a cup of coffee, ignoring my phone as it did its usual morning blow-up of incoming texts and emails and other odds-and-ends alerts. Afterwards, I raced upstairs to change into a pair of baggy sweats I'd had since high school, a hoodie that had seen better days, and pulled my hair into a messy ponytail before hurrying back downstairs where I slid on my favorite, beat-up sneakers. Phone in pocket and headphones on, I headed out for a walk.

I'd been offered any number of contracts with famous workout brands wanting to see my figure running on their treadmills, stepping on their elliptical, or racing on their stationary bikes. "We'll set up an entire indoor gym for you," I'd been told at least a dozen times by as many companies. "You'll get free membership for life," famous health clubs had promised. But while I loved a good stretch at my local yoga studio, or a sweat-inducing kickboxing class at the boxing club around the corner, when it came to getting in cardio, I loved nothing more than a brisk morning walk around my neighborhood.

Rain, sun, snow, or sideways sleet, I was outside every day I could be. I loved seeing the familiar faces, the changes in seasonal decor, updates to an old house's facade, the smell of bread being baked, fresh brewed coffee filling the air, and the sounds of kids laughing and dogs playing that made up my life in Park Slope.

I side-stepped so a couple jogging together could go by, waved to the owner of the flower shop responsible for all the bouquets in my house, and then turned the corner to Prospect Park.

I had just come out the other side of Endale Arch when my phone vibrated with another alert. It had been going off all morning, which wasn't odd, but as usual I'd ignored it. I didn't have another job until next week so there was nothing pressing I needed to tend to. Anything coming in was either friends wanting to gossip about the party the night before, my mother texting with an article about a new cleanse she'd heard about, or my agent wanting to talk about my meeting with the designer I'd chatted with at the party.

The vibrating stopped and then started again. I realized it was a call coming in. No one ever called me before nine. I pulled my phone from my pocket and frowned.

It was Jen, my agent.

I tapped the accept button and the telltale sound of her exercise bike filled my ears. She was always calling from her bike or treadmill.

"Hey, Jen," I said. "Don't worry. I talked with Daniela last night and let her know I'm definitely interested in working with her. She said her team would get in touch with you next week."

"I know," she said in her usual brisk way. "They already called. That's not why I'm calling you. Have you been online yet this morning? I'm assuming you haven't since you didn't blow up my phone first thing with expletives."

A sinking sensation filled my gut.

"What's happened?" I asked, stopping and moving to the side of the sidewalk so as not to block traffic.

"Oliver Manning. He's claiming you dumped him and he's broken hearted. Thought you were the one. Can't imagine moving on from this for a long time."

"What the fu..." I caught myself, not finishing the word as a young mother and her school age daughter walked by. "But he took it so well! Katya even texted a picture of him making out with one of the new girls an hour after I left!"

"He's gotta save his reputation though, doesn't he."

"For fuck's sake. What an absolute assho—"

"I have several news sites wondering if you want to comment?"

"Sure," I said and opened the text messaging app on my phone. I quickly found the photo Katya had sent and forwarded it to Jen. "There's my comment."

She was quiet for a moment and then her laugh came through the receiver like a gleeful ray of sunshine. "I think people will hear that loud and clear," she said, her voice filled with amusement. "Anything else?"

"Nope."

"I put the meeting with Daniela on our joint calendar. Enjoy the rest of your day."

We hung up and I strode toward the botanical garden, music blasting in my ears, fury streaming through my veins. I knew it. He'd lied. They all did. They just couldn't help themselves. Bring on the cats, knitting needles, and tiny hat patterns, I was done with dating.

I broke into a jog, determined to pound it out on the pavement, my old sneakers barely absorbing the shock of each step, reminding me of my growing pains of yore as my shin bones reverberated into my knees. My phone buzzed again. Once, twice, a third time. Another call.

"Fucking hell," I said, slowing to a stop and pulling out my phone again.

Addie. I grinned. Here we go. I couldn't wait to hear what she had to say about the news she'd undoubtedly seen first thing. She had Google Alerts set to anything related to me.

"Okay," I said, laughing as I answered the phone. "Go ahead. Get it out of your system."

"Lior?"

I frowned.

"Mama?"

Mama was Addie's mom. Mine was referred to as Mother.

"Honey, Addie's been in a car accident."

The words that followed were a blur. Head-on collision. She didn't know much more than that yet. On her way to the hospital now...

"I'll be there as soon as I can," I said and hung up, blinking in confusion at my surroundings. Where was I? What did I need to do now?

Home. Pack. Adeline.

I turned and took a step, my shoe immediately sinking and sliding in something wet. I looked down, barely controlling my gag reflex as the smell of fresh excrement reached my nostrils.

I'd stepped in dog poo. What's worse, the offending party – a ambling Golden Retriever – was still doing their business as they walked away, their owner not bothering to clean up after them.

"Hey!" I shouted, my emotions raw and too close to the surface.

And as the man turned toward me, I finally snapped. The wine spilled on my expensive dress last night. Oliver's lies and smear campaign all over social media this morning. And now my best friend was lying in a hospital bed on the other side of the country?

I'd had enough. I opened my mouth and, just like the man's dog, proceeded to lose my shit.

CHAPTER 3

Graham

I
t was one of those perfect Brooklyn mornings, the air hinting at the heat to come in the next days, the foliage overhead bright with life, and my trusted old gal loping slowly beside me, her gait not as spry as it had been even just a few weeks ago.

My gaze moved from my dog to the path in front of me, my mind re-focusing on the article I was working on this week. So, when I saw the lanky brunette shouting in broad daylight about something – her hands on hips, sweatshirt impressively stained – I was momentarily bemused. Until it registered that the person she was shouting at was me.

I glanced around at the audience of at least a half dozen people milling around us, who began looking from her to me, to my dog, then back to the her, as she continued to yell – all the while shuffling around trying to scrape her shoe on the pavement.

Minus the shouting, she was cute. Scratch that. She was stunning, with the backdrop of the park in bloom behind her, no hint of any makeup on her face, and her light olive skin glowing in the morning sunlight.

Though that was possibly from the screaming she was doing.

It was almost funny at first. *Almost*. And as soon as I realized what had happened – and saw the trail of shit Brontë had left the last twenty feet or so of our walk – I started to apologize. But the woman cut me off with a string of insults that grew in rage and volume the more she furiously scraped her shoe, her headphones slipping down her forehead, her hands clenched into fists.

Thankfully her diatribe was only aimed at me, because had she gone for Brontë, there would have been trouble. So I simply smiled awkwardly, waiting for it to be over, and then watched as she turned on her heel and walk-scuffed away, leaving her own trail behind.

I pulled a bio-degradable bag from my back pocket as people made a wide berth around me and my dog, and began to pick up Brontë's mess.

"Way to make me look like an asshole," I said to my sweet old girl with a chuckle as I retraced her smelly trail, knotted the bag, and we headed for home.

Twenty minutes later, I opened the front door to our house and watched her lumber slowly inside. With a long sigh I shut the door and leaned against it, peering through the bright white of the entryway at Brontë who had walked about ten paces and stopped. She clearly couldn't decide if she should keep going to the comfort of her bed in my office or lie down where she was.

"I know, girl," I said, kneeling beside her and touching my nose to hers. "It's a tough call when you're tired. But, hey, you did good today! You even took on a bully." I kissed her long snout and got to my feet. "Come on, B. You can do it."

Stepping around her, I encouraged her to the kitchen to where her bowl of water and a plethora of snacks awaited. I would do anything to get her to eat these days - including buying the dog equivalent of human junk food. But she wasn't even interested in that.

That's how I'd known we were in trouble.

"She's fifteen," Dr. Shepherd, our longtime veterinarian had said when I'd brought her in three days ago after she'd refused food and hadn't bounded up with me in the morning like she always did. Not that I had been doing much bounding myself lately. In fact, the past year had been pretty boundless. But she'd always been keen to get going in the mornings, and seeing her falter this past week was worrying. "She's an old lady, Graham," the vet continued. "She's done really well. Better than most I see in here. You've taken amazing care of her."

As he said it, she looked to me and gave two solid thwacks of her tail. I smiled softly. She'd only ever done that for me. Everyone else got one thwack. But me, two. I always felt like it was her way of saying, "You and me, pal."

Dr. Shepherd added quietly, "She's winding down, my friend."

I knew he was right, but I didn't want to admit it. We'd been through a lot together. And thinking of being in this mausoleum of a house without her was unfathomable.

"Is there something I can do?" I asked. "Is there a timeline? Vitamins? Do you think she's uncomfortable?"

He leaned down and put his forehead against hers, giving her ears a scratch right where she liked it best.

"Just love her. Let her lead the way. If she doesn't want to go for a walk, don't push her. If she's not hungry, don't force it. She'll let you know when it's time. I don't think she's uncomfortable. She doesn't seem to be in any pain. She's just worn out."

"I know the feeling."

He squeezed my arm. "I know you've had a rough few years. And this sure doesn't help. I get it. But you have a new book coming out soon, right? And your column is better than ever. My wife and I cracked up over this past Sunday's. That guy at the record store..."

Dr. Shepherd had then rambled on about the column before talking again about my books, the latest of which was nearly done. I didn't tell him I'd been a little distracted lately and had gotten behind on word count.

According to the internet, lack of attention span was normal when your wife left you. Even more so when she'd done it to hook up with one of her clients she'd been cheating on you with. And yet even more normal when you got left behind to live in the house you'd bought years before the two of you'd met, and that she'd redecorated to fit *her* needs and likes.

Most of my things had been relegated to storage because they were too "shabby and old looking." Granted, the house was beautiful, if you liked living in a showroom. The bright and spare aesthetic didn't quite go with my previous decorating style of "the more comfortable the better". And though Nadia, my ex, had picked out some beautiful pieces for my office, none of it felt like me. And even less so now that she wasn't around to convince me the odd-shaped, shimmering gray sofa in my office screamed successful author.

Regardless, after she'd left, I'd retrieved some of my old, beloved things. Specifically the desk I'd inherited from my grandfather with the burgundy leather inlay – and his and my grandmother's initials etched into the corner – that clashed in the room Nadia had painted *Evergreen Fog*. Whatever the fuck color that was. Green? Gray-green? Green-gray? The color of my soul as it left my body?

It was either leave things as they were, try to make it work for me the best I could, or move house.

That last one was getting more enticing by the day.

Watching Brontë in the kitchen, after I refilled her bowl with fresh water, I noticed her once spritely blonde body now sagging, her eyes cloudy.

"Hey you," I said softly, sitting on the floor in front of her and bowing my head so it rested against hers. "Sorry about the crazy lady in the park. You can't help it if you gotta go. We all have accidents sometimes. I'll bet she's pooped her pants before too."

Brontë exhaled and leaned into me.

"How about I get your bed and we work in here today. You don't move a muscle, okay?"

I kissed her head and then hurried to my office where I grabbed her bed, her beloved stuffed cat, my laptop, a notebook, and my favorite pen. Five minutes later she was snoring and I was tapping my fingers on the table, the laptop open before me, while I stared instead out the window at the little garden Nadia had also stripped of anything soft and welcoming. Instead, she'd favored black iron, chrome, and the stupidest clear plastic chairs I'd ever seen. She hadn't even let me keep a small patch of grass for Brontë, someplace nice she could lie on during sunny days.

"Grass is out. The upkeep is bad for the environment," Nadia had told me. She'd apparently heard this from some woman called Maddy Marshall, one of her holy grails of advice givers on TikTok.

"There are grass alternatives that don't need to be trimmed," I'd said. "Plus, it would be nice to keep a place for her to use the bathroom that's fenced in, so I don't have to take her out myself in the mornings or late at night."

"The gravel can be rinsed," Nadia had countered. "And if you want a pet, you have to pick up after a pet. Right away. Otherwise the messes and smells will linger." Her button nose had delicately wrinkled at the thought.

So Maddy Marshall won again. And while I found this particular piece of advice on the three-by-three square of grass I was trying to salvage for Brontë ridiculously stupid, in the end the argument just wasn't worth it.

Nadia, a socialite turned influencer turned public relations darling, who had never once had to pick up after her pets a day in her life while growing up, just didn't understand. And wasn't willing to try. Regardless, I'd loved her. It wasn't her fault the way she'd been raised. When she wasn't worried about how she was being portrayed by others, she was funny and could be very sweet. And when she shined her light on you, you felt special and seen. I figured any problems between us had to be because of my shortcomings, and I was determined to make it work. I'd hated having divorced parents, no matter how well they'd gotten along and how easy they'd made the split for me.

So I'd tried. I really had. But in the end, it turned out I'd overlooked several red flags in the pursuit of what I'd thought was love.

I looked down at Brontë now, who was breathing loudly into the side of her bed.

"You're the only girl for me, B," I said. She didn't open her eyes, but her tail thwacked the white tile floor twice.

My mind drifted to the incident in the park. I made a mental note to call the vet to discuss what had happened with B, and then found myself picturing the woman I'd encountered. The pink of her cheeks, her wide golden-brown eyes... Despite her being tall and lanky, there had been something sprite-like about her - which was why I'd been shocked about the ferocity of the shouting. It didn't seem someone so dainty and innocent looking could spew hellfire like she had. And damn, she'd let me have it. It had been funny... until it wasn't. And as I thought about it now, I grew angry again.

I should've spoken up. I should've taken back my apology. I shouldn't have let her get away with her display, leaving me to duck my head as I set to work picking up after my elderly dog while onlookers scurried past. I hadn't done anything wrong, and I shouldn't have reacted like I had.

"Old habits die hard, I guess," I muttered.

I glared at my laptop. I was sick of these women who kept coming into my life. Always bulldozing me. Always making me feel like I was the one in the wrong. It had been happening since I was in high school, when shy, sweet-looking Elizabeth Bristol let it be known through her best friend that she liked me. My nose constantly in a book, I'd never have asked her out unless she had made the first move. But I knew who she was and had always thought she was pretty and interesting, at least by the selection of books I'd seen her reading over the course of the school year. So we'd dated. And slowly, so I didn't even register it happening, she began to assert herself and her opinions on my life, until a few months later I was wearing a certain brand of jeans, a particular cologne, and had missed two author events I'd been excited to go to at our local bookstore because she'd "needed" me. Which meant she was in a bad mood and wanted me to sit on the edge of her bed and compliment her - before batting away every compliment, then eventually getting bored, wrapping herself around me and shoving her tongue in my mouth.

Two weeks before the Sadie Hawkins dance, she'd left me for Billy Martinez.

I'd only casually dated after that. Girls I'd take on one or two dates before scurrying off with claims of too much homework to get serious or some other bullshit excuse. Until I met Palmer Arrington my sophomore year of college. It took me two years to realize she was a more subtle version of what Elizabeth had been. After she'd dumped me at the end of our junior year, my younger sister shouted at the closed bedroom door I was suffering behind, "Stop being a doormat!"

But neither Elizabeth or Palmer was any match for Nadia, who had been the legitimate worst. I was pretty sure her list of accomplishments included a trophy for gaslighting.

For some reason in those early days I'd bought into her poor little rich girl cries. Her "Nobody knows the real me or is even interested" pleas. I was a little bit older, a little bit wiser (I'd thought), and had some success under my belt. I wasn't green anymore. I knew what I wanted and my eyes were wide open. Blind, it turned out, but wide open, my sight only coming back to watch the train crash that was our demise, splashed out in full color in several newspapers and magazines.

So this woman in the park with her angelic face, expensive headphones, and dramatic overreaction to a little dog shit... well, she could bite me. I knew her type. I was a certified expert. Be cute all you want, poo-shoe lady. You can't fool me.

I tapped my laptop awake, then opened a new blank document and typed in the title of my weekly column, *Around the Neighborhood,* that I wrote for the Brooklyn Tribune. I was a weekly contributor, providing commentary on things I witnessed or overheard in the neighborhood. A new coffee shop, a love story seemingly playing out in a beloved bookstore, two old men discussing their favorite place to get donuts while playing chess in the park...

They were observations. Bits of information. And the community loved it, oftentimes sending emails and letters of things they'd noticed themselves around town.

Peering at the cursor on the screen, I started to type, the story quickly taking shape with a description of my usual morning with B – who oft made appearances in the column as my trusty sidekick. I described the crisp smell of the air as we stepped out the front door, the warmth of the sun on my face, signaling summer was coming soon, the flowers lining the sidewalk. Down the street we went, saying hi and stopping for pats (B, not me... though sometimes me) from neighbors familiar with our faces, around the corner where several businesses were just opening up for the day, and down a few more blocks to Prospect Park.

It read like the beginning of a romcom movie.

But what followed was anything but cute and romantic as I gave a scathing reenactment of my encounter with Little Miss Poo Patrol.

I chuckled as the last line materialized in my mind, imagining my editor shaking his head and laughing... the reactions I'd get from the neighborhood... the sympathy for B and me from our horrid encounter.

"This was no meet-cute, my friends," I said aloud as I typed, looking over my shoulder to Brontë, who opened a curious eye. "This, tragically, was a meet-poop."

CHAPTER 4

Lior

I woke to wetness against my nose, followed by loud purring and a soft headbutt to the chin.

"Good morning, Gomez," I murmured to the male half of my best friend Adeline's two cats, my eyes still closed.

Another headbutt to my jaw and I sighed, not wanting to return to reality just yet, but slipping a hand out from beneath the comforter I was cocooned in to give him a pet. Opening my eyes, I gave a contented sigh at the sight of Addie's guest room, which was inspired by a hotel room she'd once stayed in during a trip to the English countryside. Wainscoting, striped cream-and-robin's egg blue wallpaper, and florals upon plaids upon paisley fabrics. She had a way of making spaces looked lived in but fresh, a contrast to the cold and bare hospital room she was lying in now.

My heart sank as I thought back to the night before, my oldest friend in the world looking small and beat up, screens beeping beside her as they monitored some bodily function or another. It had been terrifying to see her in such a state, but a small comfort when she woke for a moment to give me a bleary half-smile and diss my outfit before falling back into a medicine-induced sleep.

I stared up at the cat sitting on my chest.

"Where's Morticia?" I asked. "She's going to be jealous if she sees you flirting with me."

I heard a sniff and glanced toward the bedroom door where his lovely wife sat on the threshold, glaring at me in disdain. She couldn't be bothered with telling me she was hungry so, as usual, she'd sent her man.

Morticia and Gomez had been aptly named by Addie after the matriarch and patriarch of the Addams family.

"Couple goals," she'd said by way of explanation.

Gomez bumped his head against my chin again. I was taking too long.

"Okay okay," I said, pushing myself up and sending both cats skittering from the room.

Pulling on the moss-green robe I kept here for when I visited, I trudged sleepily out of the guest room and down the hall to the kitchen. The two felines, white-haired Gomez with his dashing black mustache, and black-haired Morticia with a tiny white beauty mark beside her nose, did figure-eights around the legs of the table while they waited for me to deliver their breakfast.

I'd gotten in the day before and had immediately gone to the hospital where I'd checked in on my friend, gotten an update from her folks, met the doctor — a young guy who stared at me a moment too long before remembering he was a doctor, and then used my key to let myself into Addie's house. It was a no-brainer I'd stay there and take care of the cats until she could come home, which, I'd been assured, would be sooner rather than later.

She had a black eye, a broken cheekbone, a broken arm, several cracked ribs, and more bruises than I could count. It looked like she'd gone ten rounds in a boxing ring with someone twice her size. Or was hit by drunk driver at five am, their car ramming into hers after they'd run a red light. Which, we'd learned, was what had happened.

The cats fed, I made myself a cup of coffee and then wandered around the house. Addie lived in the kind of home we'd always dreamed of when we were girls. Small, tidy, and so cute it looked like it belonged in a fairytale. She had an eye for what looked good and could make a space look like a showroom with just a few well-chosen pieces. It was a gift. The kind people always tell someone they should do for a living. But Addie hadn't wanted to be an interior designer. She only did that for fun. She'd wanted to be in advertising. Until she realized she didn't and headed to vet school instead.

I smiled as I noted the nods to our friendship around the house. A hair ribbon tied to the chain of a lamp from a dance recital the year we decided we were totally going to be ballerinas – until we found out we were expected to practice outside of practice and admitted we had only been in it for the tutus. A smooth white rock from a long weekend in Cape Cod. Sand dollars from the Oregon Coast. A hand-spun bowl from a trip to Costa Rica. A dried lei from our first trip to Hawaii. And photos. So many photos. Some framed, others carefully curated and put in a coffee table book, and still more stuck to a bulletin board in her home office with tacks in the shape of umbrellas.

I carefully removed one particular photo from the board and stared at it. It was taken moments before we'd said goodbye at the gate for the plane that would take me to New York and my new life. My mother, in a sentimental move that shocked us all, had bought Addie a ticket just so she could sit with me until it was time for me to leave. We had tears streaming down our faces in the picture and were laughing. It was us in a nutshell. My favorite memories of us were always some version of this image, and I had the same photo framed on a shelf at home.

I kissed it, then re-tacked the picture to the board just as an alert sounded on my phone. I glanced down to see a reminder. "Japan. 3pm."

I'd forgotten to delete the reminder of my flight after cancelling the job I was supposed to be going on this week. I did so now and then hurried down the hall to shower before returning to the hospital.

"She's got some color in her face," was the first thing Addie's mom said when I walked into the room and handed her a chai latte.

"I've got a rainbow of colors in my face," Addie said from where she was sitting up in bed, doing an impressive eye roll with her one good eye. "No coffee for me?"

I started to hand mine over but got mean-mugged by Mama.

Everyone called Addie's mom Mama. The tiny blonde was a force to be reckoned with and we joked that while her husband, affectionally known as Pa, could be knocked over with a kiss, Mama couldn't be taken down by a tank. Nerves of steel, that one. But filled with more love than one knew what to do with. That had been my experience anyways when I'd first met her at the tender age of five. She'd taken one look at my own mother – standing off to the side with a slightly horrified look on her face at all the small children that could so easily get germs or stickiness on her – and then swept me into a hug, whispering in my ear, "You ever need anything, Lior, even just a hug, you come find me."

And I had. Many times over the years. Because where Liliana Flynn, my mother, lacked, Mel Warner, Addie's mama, did not.

I glanced at my friend now with an apologetic look as I pulled the take-away coffee cup out of reach again.

"Sorry," I said. "Can't get on Mama's bad side."

"Suck up."

"So you look... good," I said, taking in the purple, black, and green marring the side of her face that had been nearest the driver's side window.

"You should see the other guy," she said, giving me a crooked smile and then wincing. "Hey Ma, can you ask them about the pain pills again?"

"I've got it," Pa said and then disappeared out the door.

"He hates seeing her like this," Mama said and I nodded. Me too.

"Here we are," Pa said, returning not even a minute later, a nurse on his heels holding a small cup with what I assumed were the coveted pills.

The three of us stayed for an hour and then Addie's folks stood to go with promises to be back after lunch.

"Feel better, girly," Pa said, leaning down to gently kiss the side of Addie's head that wasn't bruised and stitched. "We'll be back soon."

"With ice cream?" she asked, meeting my eyes with her one good one and then frowning. "Wait. What day is it?"

"Monday," Mama said.

I knew what was coming next before she said it because Addie kept better track of me than anyone else in my life. Including my agent.

"You're supposed to be going to Japan," she said.

"Why do you even remember that right now?" I asked, shaking my head.

"Because I wanted you to bring me back a daruma doll."

"For the love, Adeline," Mama said. "You could've been killed. Or paralyzed. You're worried about not getting a doll?"

"They're really cute! They look like grumpy little men and symbolize having a fighting spirit."

"It does seem like the perfect mascot for you," Mama said.

"I think it might be offensive to call them a mascot," Addie said.

"Spirit animal?" Pa said.

"No, Pa!" both Addie and I said at the same time while her parents exchanged glances and shrugged.

"We'll be back," Pa said, moving to stand beside Addie and taking her hand. "Get some rest."

"I will," Addie said. "But come back soon with snacks. Good ones."

After the elder two Warners took their leave I sat in the chair next to the bed that Mama had vacated.

"I can't believe you're missing Japan," Addie said. "I'm so sorry."

"Did you let that guy run into you on purpose?" I asked, hearing my phone buzz with a text alert and reaching for my purse. It was Katya, asking about Addie and sending a selfie from her hotel room in Tokyo, where I had originally been scheduled to meet her for a shoot the next day.

"I told you I needed new tires and wipers," Addie said. "Desperate times call for desperate measures."

"I'd have mailed you the ruined Chanel to pay for it all... once my dry cleaner got the stain out." I showed her the message and picture from Katya and she motioned for me to come closer. We took a selfie and I sent it.

Katya texted back a sad face emoji, followed by several questions about Addie's status. While I texted back, Addie shifted in the bed, sucking in a breath as she tried to move and resting her uninjured hand over her broken ribs.

"Ow," she said.

"Stop that," I said. "Or let me help. What can I get you?"

"A time machine? Psychic abilities to see the asshole before he mowed me down?"

"Fresh out of both." I reached in my purse and pulled out a tin. "Mint?"

"Absofuckinglutely," she said. "It tastes like I've been chewing on blood." Our eyes met. "Oh." She winked with her good eye while I rolled both of mine.

The nurse on duty brought Addie a snack and snuck me one too. We talked, swapped Jell-o, my green for her red, watched sitcoms while she drifted in and out of sleep, and then I kissed her good cheek and promised to be back in a few hours after tending to her cats.

With Addie's prognosis good – the doctor tentatively

announcing she'd be able to go home in a couple of days – I didn't feel too terrible telling her I was planning to fly out the following Sunday.

"Unless you want me to stay, of course," I said. "I have a couple jobs lined up but I can cancel if you need me. Seriously. They're not big names."

"Snob," she said. "But you don't have to stay even that long. Promise to come back soon though? This does not count as a visit."

"Agreed. You've been a shit conversationalist. Plus, Gomez won't stop staring at me and I think Morticia is jealous."

"You may be gorgeous but rest assured, Morticia is not jealous nor threatened by you. She is merely tolerating your presence and waiting for you to leave."

"Fair enough."

"Have you seen your folks?"

I recalled the brief phone call I'd had with my mother the day I'd gotten in.

"Just wanted to let you know I'm in town," I'd said. "In case someone sees me, takes a picture, and posts it online, I didn't want you to think I was avoiding you."

God how I wished I could avoid her.

"If Addie's in the hospital, surely you have time for a dinner with us, Lior," she'd said.

I'd taken in a long, measured breath and let it out slowly.

"My best friend for nearly three decades has been in a serious accident. I can assure you, I don't have time for a dinner. Next time, Mother."

She didn't bother hiding her sigh of annoyance.

"Fine. What hospital and room is she in? We'll send flowers."
She'd paused then, and when she spoke again the bite had left her voice. "I hope she's okay."

"Thank you."

As much as she irritated me and spoke like she didn't care, I knew, if need be, my mother would offer to pay for specialists for my friend should she need them. She was an odd combination of indifference and caring. One should cancel out the other – but somehow didn't.

"Addie-Boo," I said, patting my friend's hand and giving her a wry grin. "This trip was hard enough without seeing my mother's pinched face and ice-lady eyes scouring my body for things to pick apart."

"Liorzibet," she said and I snorted at the newest nickname. "I'd argue with you, but yeah. No one needs that when they've had to see this." She gestured to herself. "I ran into Cal a few weeks ago though. He looks happy as ever."

Cal was my stepdad and one of the most decent human beings I'd ever met.

"I will never comprehend how that man ended up with that woman," I said. "He must've done something truly horrific in a past life."

"Nah. He's just a saint. And possibly in it for the money."

I snorted indelicately. I knew for a fact my mother had insisted on an ironclad prenup. Any man who wanted to be married to Lilian Flynn better come with his own significant wealth. Her money was hers and she wasn't sharing – unless it was your birthday, an anniversary, or Christmas. And then she went all out, so no one could ever say she wasn't generous.

"By the way," I said, pointing to a ridiculously huge flower arrangement on the windowsill that was overtaking all others like a giant blossom-monster. "She sent that monstrosity."

"Did she buy out a florist?"

"Of course."

"I'll send one of the extra special thank you notes I keep on hand especially for her," she said.

"Make sure to include lots of x's and o's. Mother loves them."

Addie snickered then winced. My mother thought anything other than a respectful and classy salutation was juvenile.

"Don't break a rib on her account," I said, and then dropped a gentle kiss on her cheek and went back to her house to scrounge something up for lunch.

I left the following Sunday after getting Addie home, filling her fridge with foods she could easily warm up, and promising to be back in a few weeks. After packing my one bag, giving Gomez a kiss on his head and shouting goodbye to Morticia, who couldn't be bothered to see me off, I drove to the airport, dropped off my rental car, and went through the hassle that was getting to one's gate.

Once parked in a seat with a scalding hot matcha latte, I opened my phone and scrolled all the things I'd missed or put off. Social media, emails, texts... And then, having saved the best for last, my favorite Brooklyn Tribune column, *Around the Neighborhood*.

It took me seconds of reading to realize something about the article felt familiar. Somehow, I already knew what – and who – this story was about.

And in a moment of absolute shock and horror, I bolted upright, dumping my latte on the carpet in front of me.

"Meet-Poop?!"

CHAPTER 5

Graham

"Well, hello Brontë! And you too, Graham."

I looked up from my spot at the little bistro table in front of my favorite coffee shop, Morning Joe, and smiled at the owner, who had crouched down to give Brontë a scratch behind her ears.

"Mornin', Joe," I said, noting the older man's clothing. "New sweater vest?"

"The missus surprised me last night with it," he said, running a hand down the forest-green garment. He pulled a dog snack from his front pocket and held it out to Brontë. She didn't even bother to sniff at it before lying her head down on her paw and closing her eyes. Joe looked up at me with a frown.

"Yeah," I said. "She's uh... we're..." My voice caught and I shrugged. Joe sighed and gave me an understanding smile.

"Time can be a kick in the pants, can't it?"

I usually laughed at the sayings that came out of the old man's mouth. But time *was* a kick in the pants. A hard one. Right in the groin.

With some effort he stood again and took the seat on the other side of the table.

"Loved your article last week. Went right out that afternoon to check out the ice cream parlor."

"What did you have?"

"Coffee and Oreo. Didn't sleep all night." He patted his softly rounded belly. "Caffeine and dairy together are apparently not my friends."

I laughed.

"Perhaps stick with something lighter next time?" I said. "They have some nice sorbets."

"Eh." He waved a hand. "Sorbets are boring. Humans are meant to live a little. Even if that means spending the night on the throne. Anyways, that segues nicely into the rest of what I wanted to say. Your article in yesterday's paper had me laughing so hard I had a coughing fit. Poor Nita thought I was finally gonna kick the bucket. But, as the kids say – worth it. The meet-poop, eh?" He grinned and glanced down at Brontë. "I mean, after reading how that lady 'lost her shit', I felt she deserved a little poo on her shoe. I'm just glad she didn't yell at our girl here. If that had happened, I'd be out in that park with my pitchfork."

The responses to the article had started coming in within hours of the paper landing on people's porches and in their inboxes, nearly every one of them asking if I knew who the woman was, or if I could post a description so people could be on the lookout. I would never hand that information over though. No matter how heinous she'd been, she didn't deserve the whole of Brooklyn hunting her down. And for some reason, I still couldn't get those wide golden-brown eyes of hers out of my mind. The dark hair with hints of copper thrown into a messy bun on top of her head. Her tall, lithe figure covered by a baggy t-shirt and sweats that barely hid the curves beneath...

Fuck. I *really* needed to get laid.

Between daydreaming about a woman who had screamed at me in the park, and having nightmares about my ex-wife screaming at me to tidy the house – because Brontë's dog bed and toys were ruining the aesthetic she was going for in her latest video – I was pretty sure I was going crazy. So actually, maybe getting laid wasn't what I needed. That would involve another woman, and right now the only female I could stand had four legs, was sleeping at my feet on the sidewalk, and wouldn't be on this earth much longer.

Fuck.

I pulled my attention back to Joe and smiled.

"If she had yelled at Brontë, I'd have shit on her shoe myself."

Joe laughed, patted me on the shoulder, and started for the door of the shop. "Get ya anything?"

"Thanks but I'm just about finished and then it's back home to get some work done on the book."

"You'll let me know if you need any help?"

I grinned. Joe Castelluccio, a soldier turned baker and coffee maker, was always offering to help with my writing.

"I've no experience," he'd always say. "Just life experience. But that ain't nothin' to sneeze at."

"Of course," I said now. "If I find myself in a bind, you'll be my first call."

"I'll provide the sustenance," he said and then gave me a little salute and disappeared inside, the smell of fresh baked pastries and coffee wafting onto the sidewalk behind him.

I made my way home slowly, my best girl ambling quietly beside me as I kept an eye out for any accidental bathroom breaks. Thanks to the woman in the park, I was scarred for life. But also: to be a pet owner was to be aware at all times. I might've thanked her for reminding me, if she hadn't publicly ripped me a new one.

Still... those eyes.

"Stupid poo shoe lady," I said to Brontë, who looked back at me as if to say she agreed.

An alert sounded from my phone and I read the reminder I'd set for myself with an equal mix of happiness and dread.

LAUNCH PARTY. 7PM

My good friend, Jessa Reyne, was having a launch party for her new book tonight and, while I was excited to support her, I was not thrilled about having to dress up and be around some of the people who would likely be in attendance. There was always a handful that were overly eager to hear about how my current work in progress was going. The interest was lovely, but also oftentimes felt like pressure. Add in their curiosity about how I was doing personally post-divorce, all up in my business about women I might be seeing or friends they wanted to set me up with - or just outright flirting with me - and I immediately wanted to send a text saying I wouldn't be able to make it after all. "Sorry Jessa, can't make it. Turns out most writers *are* introverts. Who knew?" Or maybe, "I'd love to but my dog shat on a woman today and we're working through the trauma tonight with lots of behind-the-ear scritches (for me)."

But Jessa and I went way back, our debut books coming out the same year and in the same genre, leading us to doing a number of panels at conferences together. Our career trajectories had nearly mirrored one another's, and we'd kept in touch over the years, meeting up when we could – as she lived on the West Coast – and cheering one another on from afar on social media. There was no way I'd miss her event. She was worth the effort of changing out of sweatpants and throwing on some jeans.

"Gonna have to get out the good clothes tonight," I told Brontë as I unlocked the front door. She blinked at me and then heaved her old body over the threshold and headed straight for her bed in the kitchen.

A half hour later I left the present world for the fictional one on my laptop, a timer beside me counting down the minutes of an hour-long writing sprint that would hopefully get me through the current chapter I was in and into the next. My allotted time was nearly up when my phone rang.

I tried to ignore it but since it rarely rang these days – most normal people not being monsters and just sending a text – I worried it was an emergency. Either that or a telemarketer.

It was neither and I grinned as I answered the phone.

"Hey!" I said into the receiver.

"What up, G?"

I laughed at my kid sister's excited voice shouting through the earpiece. She'd recently read a book set in the 1990s and had taken on a little (too much) of the slang. I'd been subjected to "da bomb", "yo, home skillet", "as if", and too many "booyahs" to fathom in the past month. For her eighteenth birthday, which was right around the corner, I was planning to surprise her in person and gift her with a yellow Teletubby, a poster of Pearl Jam that had been signed by the band members circa nineteen ninety-two, and the rare and exotic banana clip for her hair – all found on eBay. She was also getting tickets to a concert she was dying to go to with her best friend, but I wouldn't give her that until after the other items.

Marley was my half-sister, born to my stepmother and father when I was sixteen. Having been an only child until then, I'd been enamored with her from the first moment I got to hold her, her big blue eyes staring up at me while her little pink mouth worked itself into shapes as if she were already preparing for all the crazy stories she'd tell me over the years.

"What up, M?" I said into the phone, turning off my timer and leaning back in my chair. I would pause the rotation of the Earth for Marley.

"It's not funny when you use *my* initial," she informed me. "And yours doesn't actually count because G is what people really said. Which... I don't understand. What's the G for?"

"Gangster," I said.

"Ahhhh..."

She was quiet for a moment and I could imagine her face staring off into the distance as she processed this new information.

"Yeah. I'm not going to call you that anymore," she said. "You definitely do *not* have gangster vibes."

"Yo! You offend me, girl."

"Please don't. You're embarrassing yourself. And me."

"*Fine*," I said, stifling a laugh. "So. What's the happs?"

"For real, Graham. We have talked about this. You're not allowed to try talking cool."

"Okay, okay. I apologize for lacking the rizz."

I could practically hear the face palm.

"I'll give you a pass this once since I know you're sad *and* I read your article about that crazy lady shouting at Brontë in the park," she said. "Is B okay? Has she recovered?"

"I'm fine. B is fine. Everyone is good. I actually think Brontë couldn't even hear the tirade. Lucky girl."

"I'd have kicked that chick's ass. Who even does that in public? I mean, I—"

Again an image of the woman's molten eyes filled my mind....

"Marley Bird," I said, using one of the roughly fifty-two nicknames I'd given her over the years to stop her own tirade. "Is everything okay over there? It worries me when you call instead of sending two hundred texts in rapid succession."

"Oh! Yeah! Sorry. I just wanted to call and tell you..." She paused for effect. "I got my dorm assignment and roommate's name!"

We chatted excitedly about her plans for the move from Colorado to Seattle in the next few months. She'd been accepted into her top three choices months ago and had gone for visits with the folks to see each campus. For several weeks afterwards we'd discussed the merits of each of the college's locations over facetime while eating our favorite snack: popcorn with chocolate chips sprinkled in.

"I mean, New York for obvious reasons," she'd said. But there was also California, "Sun!!! Beaches!!! Palm trees!!!" and Seattle, "Mountains!!! Lakes!!! Coffee!!!"

"What are the folks hoping for?" I'd asked.

"Well, obviously they're rooting for the West Coast," she'd said. "Since it's closest to home."

Home was Colorado where she lived with our dad and her mother, my stepmom.

"Obviously," I said.

"But of course New York would be good cuz I'd get to see you more."

"I mean... maybe once every couple of months.... I am *very* busy being a cool and famous author."

"Lies. I know all you do is lay around in that museum you live in and throw snacks to B cuz you can't be bothered to get up."

"Basically."

"Anyways..."

In the end, she'd chosen Seattle for its renowned medical research center. She wanted to be a general practitioner for children and women and open her own practice one day.

"Something cute and cozy," she'd told me. "Where people feel immediately comfortable as soon as they walk in."

I had no doubts she'd make it happen. Marley was a go-getter.

She went on another excited ramble then, telling me about all the things she and her mom were planning to buy for her dorm, and the activities she was planning on getting involved in. I grinned listening to her, remembering my own excitement when I'd left home for college, the world seeming to suddenly open up before me, my dreams that much closer.

After we got off the phone, following Marley making me promise for the hundredth time that I'd be there for her high school graduation – she didn't know I was going to surprise her on her birthday next week – we said goodbye and I got back to work.

The launch party for Jessa was set for seven o'clock, so at five I fed Brontë, shoved a piece of peanut butter toast in my mouth, and took the stairs two at a time to the third level to take a shower. A towel slung around my waist, I stood in the enormous walk-in closet that now sat mostly empty – save for what I referred to as my authorly wardrobe that had, for the most part, all been picked out by my ex. I was tempted to one day burn it all in exchange for clothing that didn't make me feel like a pompous asshole. But for now, and because I hated shopping, it would have to do.

I picked out a pair of jeans that hadn't cost a small fortune, a shirt that had, and a pair of shoes that said, "I like nice things, but I also care about comfort."

Satisfied I looked nice, I moved to the mirror to assess my hair and face. The person that greeted me was decidedly not the guy readers saw on the inside jacket of my novels. That guy was clean cut, clean shaven, and wore contacts. This guy, on the other hand, was a bit more unkempt. And while others probably thought I'd let myself go, I actually preferred this version of myself. The longer hair that had a slightly wild, likes-to-go-on-adventures look, the five o'clock shadow, and most importantly, the glasses. I hated wearing contacts. Hated putting stuff in my eyes. Really hated having to get them out at the end of the day when I was tired. As with everything else, they had been pushed on me by Nadia, my ex.

"The overall aesthetic is just so much more..." She'd peered at me. "Pleasing to the eye."

Pleasing to *her* eye, is what she'd meant. I preferred slipping on a pair of glasses at the start of the day, and then taking them off at the end and letting everything slightly blur as I drifted off to sleep. But I'd liked making her proud to be seen with me, and she'd enjoyed showing me off. Until it all became a bit much and every time I walked into a room she was scrutinizing me.

"Those sweats are too baggy," she'd say. "They don't show off your ass."

"I'm just hanging out at home working," I'd respond.

"But don't you want me to want you?"

I did. Until I started to not.

I arrived at the location of the event – a swanky bar with a large back room that had a small stage and a couple dozen chairs set up – at seven on the dot. It was standing room only and I stood just inside the door, smiling and laughing as my old friend expertly navigated questions before we all adjourned to the main area of the bar that had been rented out for the evening. There were two tables of appetizers, another with bite-sized desserts, and the wait-staff was walking around offering champagne for free – or one could go to the bar and purchase a cocktail if they pleased.

I grabbed a plate and surveyed the offerings, zoning in on cupcake liners in blue and black to match the cover of Jessa's new book, with fancy macaroni and cheese inside. I grabbed two and then, unable to resist, took a third.

Someone nearby chuckled and then I heard, "You gonna save any for the rest of us?"

The voice was decidedly female and definitely teasing.

I grinned, feeling slightly guilty, and looked up.

Golden-brown eyes... *Those* golden-brown eyes.

For a moment my heartbeat accelerated with excitement. And then I remembered the shit that had gone down.

Plus, you know, the literal shit.

And the smile on my face dissipated into the ether.

CHAPTER 6

Liar

The bespeckled guy from the park was standing on the other side of the appetizer table from me. Only I now realized with horror that he wasn't just any guy. He was Graham Forrester, author of my favorite novels... and *that* article in the Brooklyn Tribune. The one that painted me as a crazy person.

It's Mr. Meet-Poop himself.

The article had started off as sweet, lulling the reader in with descriptions of our little neighborhood, Prospect Park, his dog Brontë... before it quickly moved on, describing our encounter, with me taking a starring role as the childish woman who threw a tantrum over a little fecal matter before stomp/scuffing away. I mean, I was used to starring roles, but for Prada – not poop.

It had been embarrassing to read. And he'd absolutely blown my reaction out of proportion. Yes, I'd been mad. Yes, I'd yelled. But there were signs all over the park and the neighborhood about picking up after your pets. I'd noticed the dipshit hadn't said much about *his* part in the whole thing. Hadn't offered any explanation for letting his dog crap on the pavement and walking away. Mr. Author Man had turned all the attention on me, making himself out to be cute. Innocent. The victim. And as if he'd done no wrong.

And now here he was, standing on the other side of the table from me, looking annoyingly sexy with his glasses, whiskers, wavy, dark hair, and Armani t-shirt.

Dick.

He held my gaze as he exaggeratedly reached out and took a fourth mac-n-cheese bite.

"There are other people here, you know," I said, the amusement now gone from my voice. But if he was embarrassed by taking more than his fair share of food, he didn't show it.

"I didn't realize you policed other things besides poo," he said, moving to grab two caprese skewers and then pausing to make sure I was watching as he grabbed a third.

My chest rose as I inhaled, preparing to set this guy straight once and for all.

"Hey!"

I deflated a little as I turned to see the woman of the hour grinning from ear-to-ear behind me, her cheeks pink, eyes sparkling. I threw a smile on my face and gave her a giant hug.

"Congratulations!" I said. "You happy, tipsy, or a lot of both?"

"Both, of course!" she said. "I'm so glad you could make it. I wasn't sure. I know you're not often in town—" Her gaze strayed to the other side of the table. "Graham!" She let go of me and hurried to him, throwing her arms around him and nearly making him drop his plate of food, much to my annoyance. "You came!"

"Of course I came," he said. "I'd never hear the end of it if you came to Brooklyn and I didn't make your event."

She extricated herself and then looked from Graham to me.

"Do you two know each other?" she asked.

"Not exactly," Graham said.

"No," I said at the same time.

"Oh my gosh! How have two of my favorite people in the world never crossed paths?"

"We got lucky?" I muttered.

Jessa didn't hear me, but Graham certainly heard something, his pale eyes flashing towards me as he smiled and popped the entirety of a mac-and-cheese bite in his mouth.

"Graham Forrester," Jessa said. "New York Times bestselling author seven times over, meet Lior Flynn, world renowned fashion model and icon." She turned to me. "Graham and I met when our first books debuted and we've been rooting for each other ever since." She turned to Graham. "Lior and I met at the University of Washington when she and I and her best friend Addie shared a dorm room. Until Addie decided she wanted to be a veterinarian and Lior was discovered and moved to New York. She's actually an amazing wri—"

"Jessa," I interrupted, pointing behind her. "I believe they're looking for you."

She turned to see two women putting stacks of her new book on a table. "Shoot. I have to go sign. Are you guys going to stay a while? We should hang out. Get drinks afterwards?"

I looked to Graham. There was no way I was sitting and drinking with this man who one, clearly hated me, and two, had written a horrifyingly embarrassing article about me and poop. I couldn't imagine he had any interest in spending time with me either.

"I have an early shoot," I said, easily selling the oft told lie. "I should really get home soon. But only after you sign a book or two for me."

"Absolutely," she said. "Graham?"

"I wouldn't miss having drinks with you."

The way he said it made it sound like I obviously was the worse friend for not staying. I kept myself from rolling my eyes. *Suck up.*

As Jessa hurried away, I didn't even look at Graham when I said, "The gentlemanly thing to do would've been to bow out."

"The friendly thing to do would've been to not lie and go have a drink with your friend."

He looked pleased by his retort, giving me a smug little smile.

I turned and walked slowly around the table, stopping inches from him. He looked startled and started to back away but then held his ground, as if trying to prove he was undaunted.

I lowered my lashes and inhaled so that my breasts rose and fell, nearly touching him. I could feel the heat from his body and for a moment I forgot what I was doing. He smelled amazing and, fuck me, he was even hotter up close. But then I eyed his plate of food. Smiling softly, I looked up at him.

"You're probably right," I said. "But at least I know proper party etiquette."

With that, I took one of the mac-and-cheese bites from his plate, peeled the paper off, and took a slow bite, my eyes watching his as he stared at my mouth. I turned on my heel then and walked away, satisfied when I saw him staring after me in the reflection of the bar's window.

I stayed for another hour, buying three books and standing in line to have them signed for me, Addie, and one for Katya, who wouldn't read it, but would put it on her bookshelf and post it all over social media because she liked to look well-read.

While I mingled with some of the other guests I knew, I kept an eye on Graham, tracking his movements so we didn't accidentally run into each other again. I was curious about his friendship with Jessa, who was one of the most genuinely nice people I'd ever met, and had no idea how she could be friends with someone who was so full of himself. I couldn't believe I hadn't seen it before in some of the interviews I'd watched of him. But after his attack on me in a public newspaper, it was as clear as day – and I for one was going to do everything possible to make sure we never crossed paths again.

* * *

The following morning I woke early and ambled down the stairs to the kitchen, leaning on the counter as I waited for the espresso machine to work its magic. I then carefully carried my mug to the sofa where I sat and promptly spilled coffee on my new Calvin Klein pajama top that had arrived with a dozen other pieces from the designer two days before.

"Another one bites the dust," I muttered, pulling off the top and taking it straight to the laundry room where I sprayed it with stain fighter and dropped it into the washing machine. When I was back on the couch I picked up my laptop to start my usual coffee and word game routine.

But my eyes kept wandering to Jessa's new book perched on the corner of the coffee table, reminding me of my encounter with Graham Forrester the night before.

Graham. Forrester.

Graham-Let-My-Dog-Poo-All-Over-the-Park Forrester

What were the odds? And how had I never seen him as such a pompous ass that he couldn't be deigned to pick up after his sweet dog? I wonder if he even normally walked the dog like he sometimes claimed in his articles. Around the neighborhood my ass. Probably half the mentions in the column hadn't even happened.

I had been mildly horrified by my shouting in the park that morning while he'd just stood there staring at me with his old dog by his side, forlornly looking up at me with those big brown eyes. I didn't love making a spectacle of myself and, until I'd read his article, hadn't remembered a word I'd said. I'd barely been keeping it together in that moment, having just gotten the news about Addie's accident. The incident hadn't even registered in my brain seconds after it had happened. I'd just turned and – as appetizer-hog Graham had so kindly noted in his article – stomp/scuffed away. Until I'd found myself suddenly running, tears streaming down my face. I'd had to stop, breathless and blinded at the corner to wipe my eyes. Someone had asked if I was okay. It wasn't until I was on the plane to Seattle a few hours later that pieces of the morning came back to me. Words like, "irresponsible dolt" and "elitist canine snob". "You don't even deserve that beautiful dog!" I'd shouted.

To read how I'd behaved was humiliating. I felt ashamed. But also pissed. How convenient for him to take my misery and fear and splash it in the local paper for others to laugh at. I could imagine the responses he'd gotten. Probably even from some of my own neighbors, laughing and making fun of the "girl with the pearl colored..."

"Dammit," I said, realization dawning as I looked across the room to where my now easily recognizable headphones were lying on the kitchen island. "Now I have to get new headphones."

Goddamn his cleverness with words. It was why I'd always loved his writing. Had devoured each and every one of his books, dissecting phrases, reading the books he'd used for references. It was why I had savored his Sunday articles. He had a way of seeing things and stating them that made you think of them in a whole new way.

"It's like he can see into my soul," I'd said to Addie over the phone last year after waxing poetic about an intricate paragraph in his last book.

I stared up at my bookshelves and found the line-up of his novels where they sat beside other long-loved favorites, a framed picture of Addie and me, and a small metal Space Needle I'd bought and taken with me before moving to New York. Peering at his name lined up on my shelf, I gave him a one finger salute.

An hour later I was dressed in my usual baggy sweats ensemble, a baseball hat on my head, one of the numerous pairs of expensive headphones (in black) I'd been gifted from brands wanting me to be seen wearing their product. Unable to wear my favorite beat-up sneakers, the one still marred with poo and sitting on my front porch, I grimaced as I slid my feet into one of the many pairs Nike had sent me over the years. They were perfectly comfortable and incredibly cute with their seventy's orange and powder blue color scheme; they just weren't the beloved worn-in pair I'd had since leaving Seattle at nineteen.

I glared down at the pretty blue shoes, opened the door, and walked down the front steps. At the sidewalk I stopped, an image of Graham at the book launch party appearing in my mind. The way his blue eyes had flashed fire when he'd recognized me. The way the short sleeves of his shirt that had stretched over biceps that clearly had weekly sessions with weights. The slightly mussed hair... the Clark Kent glasses...

I clenched my fists, infuriated with my brain for having tracked anything attractive about the man. Taking in an angry breath, for the first time in the nine years I'd lived here, instead of taking a right and heading toward the park, I took a left.

CHAPTER 7

Graham

I woke as usual at six a.m. the morning after the book party and, as had become habit in the past month, peeked over the side of the bed to make sure Brontë hadn't tried going downstairs without me. Her gait on the descent had become precarious – her old legs wobbling under her weight – and I'd taken to going down backwards in front of her, in case she slipped and I could catch her.

But she was in her bed, as usual – one of the many I'd placed strategically around the house for whenever she was tired.

"Hey girl," I said, smiling sleepily.

She replied with two tail thwacks.

Together we walked blearily down to the kitchen and I turned on the espresso machine before heading to the back door and the garden where Brontë could relieve herself.

"Come on, B," I encouraged as we both stood in the doorway looking outside. The cool morning air caused me to shiver and she looked up at me, her big brown eyes asking, "Do I have to, Dad?"

"I know," I said. "I wouldn't want to go out there to do my business either, but since you wouldn't take me up on my offer to learn how to use the toilet when you were a puppy... here we are."

She exhaled, a small huff of disappointed acceptance, and made her way outside. When she returned a few minutes later, I received substantial side-eye before she laid heavily in her kitchen bed, the equivalent of a teenager throwing themself onto furniture in a petulant display of irritation.

I grinned. She was an old lady on the outside, but she still had the spirit of the puppy she'd been on the inside.

Espresso brewing, I went to the fridge for Brontë's fancy new dog food, my latest attempt to get calories in her. Fifteen minutes later I was sitting on the world's most uncomfortable couch, my laptop in front of me, along with a trusty dog – who had ignored her food and instead ate a handful of peanut butter flavored treats – at my feet in yet another bed.

I stared at the screen for a moment. The document for my new book was open and waiting for me to continue writing it. But rather than creating a new sentence, my finger accidentally slid to open a new tab.

The next thing I knew, I was typing Lior Flynn's name into the search bar.

Of course, I'd known who she was as soon as Jessa had introduced us. Her image was everywhere. Every newsstand, billboard, and side of bus. I'd seen her on the screens in Times Square, and she'd even had a tiny but memorable part in a movie I'd loved a couple years ago. I'd read articles in magazines she'd given, and had seen her interviewed on TV, where she came off as witty, intelligent, and a bit of a dork - which I'd found endearing.

But the woman I'd met at the book launch, with her ponytail, glasses, and unassuming jeans and sweater, looked so different from the glamorous images I'd seen of her over the years. And compare those two versions to the woman yelling at me in the park, her messy hair piled on top of her head, wearing a stained Chanel sweatshirt, an old pair of sneakers and staring at me with those eyes...

Damn those eyes. There was definitely something in them –

something that had captured me despite the rage in the park, despite the flash of anger at the book launch as I'd taken another appetizer just to rile her. There was an allure to them. A warmth. It was as if she was gravity and I was matter, unable to resist her pull. I wanted to get lost in them, and wondered what it would feel like to have her turn them on me with something else. With *want*.

I shook my head.

"What the hell is wrong with you, man?" I said aloud. "She's just like the rest of them. Probably worse."

To prove my point, I hit the return button on the keyboard and my screen filled with her digital persona. Articles from magazines and newspapers. Video clips from interviews on late-night talk shows. Images from paparazzi as she left a club, a restaurant, or sat in the stands at Wimbledon sandwiched between a rockstar and a famous female political news anchor.

The search results went on forever.

I clicked what looked like an aerial image of something and found myself staring at Lior's ass in a tiny red thong as she sunbathed topless on a yacht in the South of France.

"Fucking hell."

I quickly exited the screen.

I was wrong. She wasn't at all like the others. She was definitely worse. And yet that didn't stop me from opening another link, leading me straight to her personal social media page – which I scrolled with wary curiosity.

The photographs here were different. A mix of real life versus work life, many times within the same frame. Her in sweats and no makeup. Her in a backless, painted-on black dress, advertising perfume for a huge brand name. Her in a no-name track suit, hair piled messily on top of her head like it had been in the park. Her in a short, red dress with cutouts, her hair slicked back, and eyeliner that looked otherworldly while she held a small tube of the product in her hand.

In each picture she morphed into another version of herself, each more beautiful than the last.

I scrolled further. There were shots of Seattle, her and a pretty woman with light brown hair making faces at the camera in front of the Space Needle, a wall that looked like it was covered in gum, and a large troll. Two pairs of feet with painted toenails, two pairs of feet in snowshoes, two pairs of feet in cowboy boots.

And then there were the men. Chiseled, ripped, god-like specimens standing beside her, holding her, looking like they were about to kiss her or...

"Jesus," I said, staring at one of the pictures. "He looks like he's going to eat your face. Run, Lior, run!"

And then another one, the man looking completely uninterested in the beauty lying beside him.

"Yeah right, buddy," I said.

I looked down at Brontë who was staring up at me judgingly.

"Shut up. I am not jealous. I'm proving a point."

I scrolled further and found a photo of Lior and an older woman with similar facial features but different coloring.

"Happy Mother's Day, Mom," the caption read.

"Oh shit," I said aloud, recognizing the woman.

Liliana. One name. That's all one needed to say and a person knew exactly who you were talking about. She'd been *the* model a couple decades back. Beautiful in an inaccessible way with her pale blonde hair and ice-like blue eyes. I'd never have imagined she was Lior's mother. I could see the resemblance now, but while Liliana was undoubtedly stunning, there was something about Lior that was just... more. She was warmer, the light in her eyes was kinder. And her figure... She had curves her mother didn't.

I scrolled more and saw other images of the two women, stopping at a candid one of them in someone's living room, Lior sprawled on a tasteful pale blue sofa, sticking out her tongue, her mother, legs crossed at the ankles like a royal looking not amused at her daughter's antics. I grinned, then berated myself for being amused.

There was another of them that Lior had created in a side-by-side post, "Me and mom, both at 21 years old." The resemblance of the two women, despite their almost night-and-day coloring, was uncanny. But even at their young ages, there was still something softer about Lior's face. More peaceful. As if she was having a good time, whereas her mother's face looked tight, with no trace of humor. In fact, most of the pictures of her mom looked that way.

"She seems like a good time," I murmured. "And probably even more drama. It's like it's the family business."

I scrolled some more until I stopped, my breath catching as I clicked on an image to make it bigger.

It was a selfie, Lior's face free of makeup, her dark hair wild around her shoulders, and she looked like she wasn't wearing anything, her collarbones exposed, the rise of her breasts... and a smattering of the sexiest freckles I'd ever seen.

I shut the laptop and tossed it gently to the couch.

Giving Brontë a few pets, I got to my feet, and bounded up the stairs to the second-floor workout room to try and sweat thoughts of Lior Flynn's red thong out of my system. But at the sight of the white-on-white-on-taupe, too-bright gym Nadia had created, I found all I wanted to do was be anywhere else.

I threw on a sweatshirt and went to rouse Brontë from her slumber. Fifteen minutes later we ambled slowly down the front steps and, by habit, I started to head left down the sidewalk. But the thought of running into Lior stopped me.

"Sorry, girl," I said to Brontë as I pulled on her leash to get her to change directions. "We're taking a different route today."

While I was a creature of habit, it was nice to change up the morning routine and scenery for once. Different faces, different front stoops with different decor displayed, a new cluster of kids in their school uniforms, a coffee shop with a "Grand Opening" sign waving from the eaves (though I'd never cheat on Joe), and a sweet elderly couple holding hands as they crossed a street – the gentleman vigilant in his watching for cars.

And then it happened.

I saw her about a half a second before she saw me, her head turning my way until our eyes met and she too stopped in her tracks. For a moment the two of us just stood looking at one another.

Then Brontë's tail thwacked twice against my leg.

I glanced down at her, surprised. When I looked back up, Lior had turned and was walking briskly in the other direction.

CHAPTER 8

Lior

"Look up. Down... Can you move your right hip towards the camera just... there! Stop. Yes. Perfect, Lior."

I was bored, cold, and distracted. Though if anyone noticed, they thankfully hadn't said so.

The camera kept clicking as I shifted my body, head, and expression like the robot I'd become in the past few months. I'd enjoyed this once. The travel, the perks, the free clothes. But now? Now I wanted different.

I wanted more.

"Next look," someone called from behind the lights shining in my face.

Marion, the stylist, pulled a blue dress from the rack of clothes, looked it over, and handed it to me before shouting to one of the assistants, "Is Ty ready?"

My mood lifted. Ty was one of my favorite male models to work with. One, because he was hilarious and we inevitably ended up having a laugh attack over something. Two, he always had the best gossip. And three, he was gay and I didn't have to worry about getting hit on - which happened a lot with some of the straight male models.

I slipped into the blue dress and then stood while Marion zipped me, circled me, and made adjustments. Accessories were added and then taken away. Instructions were given to hair and makeup who moved in to smooth my hair into a new style and remove my lipstick to apply a different color. And then I was given five different pairs of heels to try on.

"Darling," Ty said, sweeping into the room and air kissing me on both cheeks.

He was a dark-skinned ray of sunshine with his sexy smile and shaved head – the Afro I'd last seen him sporting nowhere in sight.

"What is this?" I asked, reaching for his head.

He ran a hand over it and posed. "The boys like me shaved."

"I'll just bet they do, baby."

"Naughty," he said, wagging a finger at me and then sitting in a chair to get the shine on his skin powdered. "Now, tell me what's new with you. I heard you finally gave Oliver the boot, thank *god*. That man was the absolute worst and you had me a bit worried. You let him hang around longer than most. I thought perhaps you were actually going to try and be serious with the man." He wrinkled his perfect nose at the thought.

"You know me better than that."

"I do. And I know what you've been through. Oliver Manning is not the man you should be with after being with a user like your ex. If it went on much longer, I was gonna come pull you out. With a cane." He gave me an exaggerated wink and acted out what I assumed was his vision of caning a person. "Please tell me the rumors are true. Did you ever... you know...?"

I pressed my lips together, trying not to laugh while the makeup woman applied fake eyelashes to the outer corners of my eyes.

"I never had the pleasure of finding out," I said.

"Girl!" Ty shouted. "You had *one* job!"

"Sorry, Ty." I dropped my head in faux shame.

"You're forgiven. But do better next time. Now... are you ready for all the dirt?"

For the next four hours the crew and I were regaled with stories of who had been fired from what job, dropped from what designer, gotten a new ad campaign, had their boobs done ("tastefully, darling"), had their lips done ("he should've saved some of that filler for where he really needs it"), gained weight, lost weight, broke up with their significant other, was caught cheating, was cheated on, and the best Thai food restaurant he'd found last week.

"Their fresh salad rolls are on a whole other level," he said, tilting his head back, his full lips parted, eyes aimed seductively at the camera.

"You know how I love other-level fresh salad rolls," I said, arching my back and pressing into him, my own eyes half-closed.

We switched poses again, winding our bodies around one another's while we continued to change expressions for the camera and chat in-between looks.

"Oh my god," Ty said suddenly. "Have you been keeping up on Graham Forrester's Tribune articles? Why am I even asking. Of course you have. You're obsessed. And for good reason. That man is a dish. A yummy delicious dish I'd love to—"

My hand slipped from where it was propped on my knee and I nearly stumbled.

Ty caught me without losing his own balance and kept talking, much to my dismay.

"That meet-poop article from a couple weeks ago? Girl, I nearly died I laughed so hard. Seriously. I choked on an almond. Anyways, that poor, gorgeous man and his sweet pup. Can you even imagine? People are so crazy these days."

I smiled and nodded, pretending to concentrate on the directions we were being given by the photographer, my mind going to earlier this morning when I'd seen Graham on my walk after changing my usual route in an attempt at avoiding him. Unfortunately, he must've done the same thing.

For a moment we'd both just stood there staring at one another, neither of us seeming to know what to do next. When he'd looked down at his dog, I took the opportunity to get the hell out of there. I did not need people seeing us in close proximity on the street and putting two and two together.

I tuned back in to hear Ty recounting the article to the rest of the crew, cringing inside as he repeated some of the lines verbatim. I sounded like an ass and Graham, of course, the wounded hero of the story.

Jerk.

"Where do I find the article?" one of the assistants asked.

"The Brooklyn Tribune," Ty said. "Lior turned me onto it last year. She was raving about it. And him. Check out his photo, honey. Yum."

"He writes a great column," I said, my voice flat as we were given the go-ahead to rest for a minute while the lighting was changed.

"I'll bet that man *has* a great column," Ty said, raising his eyebrows suggestively. "I wouldn't mind him doing an article on me. He could do some *in-depth* reporting."

"Ty," I said, laughing despite myself.

"You've seen him. That man is delicious. I wonder if he's single..."

"Even if he is, I think he's straight."

"Lior. Why do you wish to wound me so?"

"Sorry, buddy."

"I get it. You want him for yourself. I mean, he would be a step-up from all those other guys I've seen you out with. Clearly he's smart. *And* funny. The two of you would look hot together. Not as hot as he and I would but, I'll throw you a bone."

"Ooh. Don't tease me, Ty."

"If only," he said wistfully. "You'd be my perfect mate. You're just missing an important piece of equipment."

"Alas."

Hours later, borrowed clothes returned and makeup scrubbed off, we said our goodbyes in the lobby of the hotel we'd been shooting in and I hurried home to get ready for a date I'd agreed to go on.

"Who is he?" Addie asked from the speaker on my phone, which I'd propped against the bathroom mirror while I did my makeup and hair.

She was recovering well, her mom, brother, and a few friends taking turns getting her groceries, cooking, and hanging out.

"Alex Clarke," I said. "Clarke with an E."

"Why do I know that name?"

"British author," I said, leaning forward to apply a coat of mascara. "He wrote "Bound" and "The Night We Died"."

"Oh! I loved both those books. He's super cute too. I'd forget my year of celibacy for that guy. How did you guys meet?"

I laughed. Whenever Addie was between boyfriends she claimed she was having a year of celibacy.

"We haven't met," I said. "It's a one-sided blind date."

"A what?"

"Jessa sent me a text the other day. She knows him. Apparently he's in town for a month doing a teaching gig at Columbia. She asked if I'd be interested in going out with him, but didn't tell him who I was. Just that I'm a good friend. You know, to keep expectations low and also discourage any possible paparazzi issues in case he's actually a douchebag and makes a few calls beforehand."

"But if he doesn't know who you are... how will he know who you are?"

"We're meeting at a place I know in Brooklyn. He's to tell the hostess to take him to table number eight."

"Smart."

"Not my first time, baby."

I flipped my head over and brushed my hair out, then flipped it back and watched it fall into place.

"So, I'm planning to fly out there in a few days," I said,

changing the subject. "If there's a carnival going on somewhere we should definitely go take a ride on the tilt-a-whirl."

"Ugh," she said. "Don't even joke about it. I still have a lingering headache and it hurts to breathe."

"Shit. Sorry, babe. But that's what happens when you go three rounds with a Lexus."

"I'll try and remember that."

I checked the clock, gave myself a once over, and said goodbye to Addie, promising to text her the next day to tell her how the date went. Thirty minutes later I was let in through the back door, seated at the table I'd reserved, and was sipping a glass of wine and waiting for my date to arrive, which he did right on time.

"Alex?" I said, standing to shake his hand. "I'm Lior. It's so nice to meet you."

"Oh," he said. "Wow. You're... Sorry, I just... wasn't expecting... you."

I was used to taking people by surprise and smiled, motioning for him to take a seat.

"I get the secrecy now," he said, looking around at our secluded spot away from the rest of the dinner crowd.

"Unfortunately, it's become a bit of a necessity if I want to go out and have any sort of privacy."

"Of course."

"Anyways." I leaned forward. "I loved your first two books," I said, trying to put him at ease by giving him something he knew well to talk about. "Are you writing a third or... Jessa said you're teaching a class at Columbia. Are you taking a break from writing while you do that?"

If he had been nervous, any sign of it evaporated as soon as he began talking about his work... and himself. I suddenly found myself on the other end of a litany of thoughts, opinions, and even advice I hadn't asked for. From his critical view of "uneducated" readers posting one-star reviews of his books, to other authors not deserving the success they'd had - and having the balls to name names. I was ready to go before dessert was offered, and inwardly groaned when my date ordered the cheesecake.

"And for you?" the waiter asked me. But I didn't want an excuse for this night to last longer than it already had.

"I'm good thank you," I said.

As he walked away, Alex leaned forward, his eyes moving down to my body.

"I think you can afford to eat a dessert or two."

I grinned tightly and took a large drink of my wine.

"How nice of you to say so," I said through clenched teeth.

"Now take Jessa," Alex said, returning to his thoughts about his contemporaries. "Nice girl, decent writer. Could do with a bit of finessing though."

"Her personality or her writing?" I asked.

He laughed. "You're funny! I never would've expected that from a model. Well done you."

I bit down on my tongue. I had no idea why Jessa had thought this guy would be a good match for me, but I was positive I was going to ask her as soon as I got out of here.

"Who else," he mused. "Sandra Lansing's work is a bit of a bore. John Chapman is full of himself. Graham Forrester—"

I perked up at the name.

"—is not nearly as good as he thinks he is."

The cheesecake came mercifully quick and I tapped my foot under the table while I waited for him to finish so I could go before he ruined British accents for me forever.

When the check came, he asked if we should split it.

"I've got it," I said.

"Really? I suppose you probably get a discount, or maybe even free meals whenever you go out."

"Only if I take a picture with the chef."

"Is that true? Because if that's the case, I'm dying to try this other place a few blocks down from here. Maybe we could go tomorrow night if you're free?"

I stared at him.

"No. It's not true. And I'm not free."

Jessa was going to get an earful.

"I'm just going to go take care of this," I said, holding up the bill and getting to my feet.

A few minutes later, the bill settled, I walked outside, not bothering to go back to the table to tell my date our evening was over.

"Hey!" Alex called from behind me. "I didn't realize you wanted me to meet you out here. Do you live nearby? I was thinking another drink is in order."

He stepped closer to me, his fingers grazing my arm. I stiffened just as the flash of a camera went off. Fuck. I'd been so distracted by anger, I'd forgotten to go out the back door.

Lowering my head, I turned toward the restaurant.

"I'll be going home alone tonight," I said. "I hope you enjoyed your meal."

"I have another date tomorrow, but if you're free the night after..."

"No thank you," I said, and hurried back inside.

Ten minutes later, with a piece of tiramisu in a to-go box, I was in the backseat of a cab headed for home. I pulled out my phone and opened up my text conversation with Jessa.

"I am rescinding your blind date privileges," I typed.

"Oh no!" she responded immediately. "Tell me."

We had moved to an actual phone call by the time the cab pulled up to my house, Jessa apologizing profusely for the bad match.

"He always seems so sweet and modest," she said. "And those looks with that accent..."

"He was sweet and modest. For about one minute. And then he didn't stop talking about himself, talking badly about other authors, crapping on his readers, and asking if we should split the bill. Oh, and he thought I could afford to eat a dessert or two. This was said after he looked me up and down."

"What the hell."

We talked for a while more and then I changed into my pajamas and climbed into bed with my well-deserved dessert, wanting nothing more than to put this night behind me. I was drifting off to sleep a half hour later when an alert sounded on my phone. I opened it to a picture of me and Alex Clarke outside the restaurant.

"New Couple Alert?" the headline said.

I pasted the link into a text to Jessa.

"You owe me," I typed.

"Sorry!!" she said. "If it's any consolation, he also texted me and said the date was 'brilliant. He thanked me for the connection."

"I hate you."

"I'll make it up to you. Any interest in Graham Forrester? He's single and I know for a fact he's not a jerk."

I stared at the message. Unable to find the words to respond, I turned off my phone, set it down, and went to sleep.

CHAPTER 9

Graham

"So, Francesca said you're a writer?"

Francesca was my agent. And Cara, the woman sitting across from me at the sunny little spot I'd picked for this blind-date lunch, was delicately picking at her salad as she asked about me. A salad that wasn't on the menu but one she'd explained in very specific detail to the waiter.

"I'd like the greens from the mixed green salad, as well as kale and spinach from these other two salads on the menu. And then, instead of chicken I'd like salmon. Three ounces, roasted. And no sauce or dressing."

When it had come, she'd finished off her third glass of water, signaled for more, and then removed a small container of pumpkin seeds from her purse and sprinkled them on top of the salad while launching into a speech about eating enough greens and protein. I'd responded by taking a large bite of the toast that came with my quiche, to which she'd said:

"Do you know what's in that bread?"

"Tiny flecks of heaven?" It was delicious.

My answer had apparently given her license to school me on additives. But the joke was on her – my ex-wife had already scolded me numerous times during our marriage for eating bread, so the information she was giving me was old news. Also, I didn't care. But I was smart enough not to say any of that and instead we ate in silence for a few minutes before she returned to asking what I did for a living.

"What kinds of things do you write?" Cara asked.

"Novels," I said. "And a weekly article for the Brooklyn Tribune. Francesca is actually my literary agent. Do you enjoy reading?"

"Ugh," she said, clearly not since she wasn't reading the room. "No. I'm not into sitting for hours reading made-up stories."

"Oh," I said, wondering exactly why Fran and her wife, who were known in their circle of friends as "the matchmakers", had thought this would be a good match. Unless the match in question was the kind you lit and then paired with a bin full of trash, doused in gasoline. "Well... there are always audiobooks."

But she wrinkled her nose and shook her head.

"I'm just not into this mass consumption of fiction that our society seems to be devouring. People are absolute slaves to it. They've become zombies. It's no way to live. I prefer to be outdoors, interacting with nature, seeing new places and learning new cultures. Do you like to hike? Do you travel much? What do you do for exercise? How do you keep the blood flowing and the brain alive?"

When Fran had told me Cara was a yoga instructor I'd thought, great! Yoga was a peaceful practice. She must be a gentle soul. But I'd never felt more stress around a person as I did with her. And after Nadia, that was saying something.

"I do like to hike," I said. "Though I don't go often. I do travel, though in the past few years it's been mostly for work, and I've basically bounced from one city to the next and haven't had much down time to explore much. As for exercise, I walk my dog Brontë every morning and lift weights."

Again with the nose wrinkle.

"I mean," she said. "Lifting weights is good and all, but truly, you should really consider yoga instead. It's gentler on the body and you become more in-tune with it the longer you practice."

"And the studies that say lifting weights is good for bone density and has numerous other health benefits?"

She waved a hand. "I'm not saying it's bad. Just overrated. Anyways... Brontë. Is that a family name?"

I nearly spit out my gulp of Bloody Mary.

"Ah... no. She's named after the Brontë sisters?" I posed it as a question, hoping she'd just forgotten the name of the dynamic literary sisters. But at her blank look, I knew I was mistaken.

"Mm," she said in response, her chest rising and falling in a long sigh.

I tried to move the conversation to other subjects, but things I was interested in held no value to her, so I moved back to travel.

"So, have you gone to many exotic locations?" I asked, taking the last bite of my quiche and noticing she had finished off her salmon. Please let this be over soon.

She perked up again.

"Yes! Costa Rica, Bali, Bora Bora, the south of France, Tahiti, Belize..."

"Lots of warm areas then," I said. "You must like a good tan."

Her hopeful expression turned disappointed and a buzzer went off in my head. Wrong again, Mr. Forrester. You lose one hundred billion points. Turn in your dating badge and go home.

I wished I could.

"I don't go for the tan lines, Graham," she said, her voice bitter. "I go for yoga retreats and the holistic experience. To connect with myself and the earth." She peered at me. "I really think you would benefit from the practice. You probably sit a lot for your job and your joints and tendons and muscles would thank you for it."

She wasn't wrong, but her holier than thou attitude, along with her disinterest in anything I liked or found fun had sealed the deal on any hope of this going any further. Now it was time to have a little fun. I mentally flexed my fingers and decided to put my storytelling skills to some use.

"The truth is," I said. "Yoga scares me."

"Scares you?" She gave me a confused smile.

"Yes." I turned my eyes downward and took a long breath in before meeting her gaze again. "Yoga is what killed my mom."

"What? Is that... that can't be true."

"It is. The doctor said she got so flexible that when she was walking down the stairs at her house, the muscles and tendons around her hip joint were too pliable and when the bone popped out, they couldn't hold it in and she fell."

The horror on her face was a delight.

"Oh my gosh. That's terrible. I can't— Is that really true?"

I nodded solemnly.

"I'm so sorry."

It was hard not to laugh and I almost felt bad for lying, but I was bored and irritated and I'd just wasted valuable writing time on this woman.

"Yeah. So you can see why I haven't wanted to practice it myself."

As she tried to wrap her mind around it all, I signaled for the bill, downed the rest of my Bloody Mary, paid, and led the way to the door.

"Cara," I said on the sidewalk. "It was lovely to meet you. Good luck with your practice. Maybe have your doctor check your hip flexors next time you see her or him."

"Oh. I don't see a medical doctor."

"Of course you don't," I said, and turned and walked away.

As I headed home, I called Francesca.

"Hey buddy," she said. "How was the date?"

"Fran, you are a brilliant agent. An incredible cook. Your taste in books and movies is impeccable."

"Yessss?" I could hear the smile in her voice as she waited for what she probably assumed was my gratitude at being set up with her friend.

"But I will quit writing before I let you set me up on a date again. *Ever*."

"What?" her wail of disbelief filled my ear. I pulled the phone away and grinned at a guy walking by with raised eyebrows.

I put the phone back to my ear. "Never again, Frannie."

"But Cara's lovely!"

"Fun fact, Cara is zero amounts of fun. She eats salad with no dressing, thinks fiction is a waste of time, and travels to beachy locations *not* to get tan lines, but to be one with the earth. Do you know me at all?"

"I mean, I knew about the salads, but I always thought she was just joking with me about not reading because of what I do."

"She was not. In fact, I don't even think Cara understands joking, so she couldn't have been joking with you."

"Damn. I owe you one. We do have this other friend—"

"Never again, Fran!"

"Fine. Next time I see you, I'll buy you a salad with *extra* dressing."

"Next time you see me, you'd better run in the opposite direction."

It was a relief to get home. I kicked off my shoes and found Brontë waiting for me on the uncomfortable couch she wasn't supposed to be on instead of one of her half dozen beds.

"Hey girl," I said, sitting beside the world's best dog. "I just had a date with someone who definitely could've used a little of your poo on her shoe..."

I stopped myself immediately, my mind going to where I'd been trying to keep it from going all morning.

Lior Flynn.

While the date with Cara had been awful on its own, it hadn't helped that I'd woken to Lior's face plastered all over social media due to her having her own date the night before. With Alex Clarke.

"Alex freaking Clarke?" I'd said to Brontë earlier, practically slamming my cup of coffee down on the table.

I'd closed the tab on my laptop in disgust and opened the document for my book. There was no reason for me to feel any sort of way about who Lior Flynn went out with. But Alex Clarke was a pompous prick. We'd met three years ago at a conference when his first book had come out. Being the friendly sort of guy I was, and knowing how daunting it could be to go from writing in seclusion to being put on a stage of sorts and expected to be charming, I'd introduced myself - and regretted it immediately. I'd never had a man look me up-and-down before, but Alex Clarke had done just that before smirking, giving me a limp handshake, and then turning and walking away.

Later, while on a panel, when he was asked what he thought about his books being compared to mine, he'd said, "Who? I don't know his work."

We were not friends, and seeing him with his hand on Lior's arm made me angry for reasons I couldn't comprehend. Why should I care who she went out with? Maybe I didn't. Maybe it was just seeing two people together who'd been rude to me. It was infuriating. They deserved each other.

In an effort to clean the slate of the day, I boiled water for a cup of tea, ate a cookie while the tea steeped, and then sat down to work. I was so near the end of the first draft of this book I could practically taste the victory. Victory being a celebratory drink with Fran, as was our tradition. And apparently now a salad with extra dressing.

After an hour my alarm went off, signaling I either set it again and keep going, or take a break. Knowing there was little in the fridge and if I didn't shop now I never would – thus either eating cookies for dinner or getting takeout... again – I decided a break was in order.

I made a quick list, grabbed my reusable grocery bags, gave

Brontë a kiss on her head, and hurried out the door, walking the few blocks to the local grocery store.

A few minutes later I was walking through the produce section when I saw her.

At first I wasn't sure it was her – with her hair pulled back into a low ponytail, and a baseball cap pulled low over her face. It was the pale-yellow overalls that gave her away. I'd seen her wearing them in a couple of her photos on her social media page. They'd stood out to me because it wasn't something I would expect a famous fashion model to wear.

And she'd looked adorable in them.

"What are the fucking odds," I murmured, wondering if I should duck and cover, turn and run, or act like an adult. I was still deciding when she saw me.

She stood staring at me for a moment, as if she too were determining her next move, and then grabbed a small bunch of bananas, put them in her cart, and walked the other way, disappearing around the corner.

A few minutes later I was perusing the pasta options when she turned her cart down the same aisle. She turned her head, her chest rising and falling in a sigh. I had that effect on women it seemed. Grabbing what she'd come down the aisle for, she tossed it in her cart and turned back the way she'd come and disappeared again.

I was suddenly angry. First my horrible blind date today and now this. I hadn't done anything to warrant the kind of treatment I was getting. I was a nice guy! I was thoughtful and empathetic and some people even found me charming. I'd done nothing wrong and had no reason to cower and hide in a damn grocery store. *She* should be hiding.

I turned down the next aisle with a newfound smugness. She wasn't there. Distracted, I forgot to grab the cereal I wanted. I turned down the next aisle. Again no Lior to see how unbothered I was that she was at the same store. I quickened my step, hurrying past the peanut butter on my list. Two more aisles and I'd now basically forgotten I was there to buy food and was angry at myself for wondering if she'd left.

One more aisle with no sign of her and I assumed she'd gone. Irritated with myself for having to now backtrack to grab all the things I'd passed, I spun my cart around and nearly collided with her's.

"Shit," I said.

"Again?" she asked, lifting her foot and looking at the bottom of her shoe. When those eyes of hers met mine again, she was pursing her lips as if trying to stop from smiling.

She was quick, I'd give her that.

"Well," I said. "So much for my valiant efforts to avoid you."

And so much for showing her how unbothered I was.

"I thought if I waited it out in the bakery department long enough, you'd surely be gone by now." She glanced down at her cart. "Instead, you're still here and I apparently have no self-control."

I looked into her cart now too and couldn't help myself. I grinned at the three packages of different flavored donut holes sitting in the basket of her cart alongside one small bunch of bananas and a bag of pasta. Seems she too might have been a little distracted. I wanted to say something funny, but the image I'd seen of her and Alex Clarke this morning flashed in my mind and I was instantly no longer amused. My smile disappeared.

"Can we call a ceasefire while we're here?" I asked, all business now. "I've missed half the things on my list and I'm starving."

"Same," she said, and then lifted her hand, made a finger-gun, and holstered it. With a little grin she turned and walked away while I tried and failed not to check out her ass, remembering that red thong from the picture online.

"Get it together, man," I whispered to myself, and then headed down the aisle in search of cereal.

CHAPTER 10

Lior

"I'm getting too old for this," I said to my friend Lane, as we sipped glasses of Prosecco at the bar and watched her girlfriend Greta try to twerk on the dance floor surrounded by a dozen of her closest friends.

"Dear god," Lane said, covering her eyes as she laughed. Greta had zero rhythm. "Make it stop."

Lane worked in the upper echelons of Dior. We'd met years ago and became instant friends due to her naughty humor and infectious laugh. When I'd gotten the invitation in the mail for Greta's birthday, to be held at a popular nightclub they were renting out, I'd immediately texted, "Whyyyyyy?"

Followed, of course, by a yes.

"She's turning thirty," Lane had explained when she'd called rather than texted back. "And thought it would be fun to see her twenties out in the same way she saw them in. At least, I hope that's all this is, and not a cry for help or an early mid-life crisis."

There were at least a hundred people in attendance. They included a handful of Lane's friends from the industry, and then ninety of Greta's closest pals.

I recognized several people from gatherings at Lane and Greta's house over the years, but most were strangers who were trying and failing not to stare at me, and so I'd found a safe spot at the far end of the bar and wasn't surprised at all when Lane joined me. While she was happy to do whatever Greta wanted, clubs had never been her scene.

"Is it over yet?" she asked. "I swear I've already lost ten percent of my hearing and three brain cells just by being here."

"I mean, one might argue you lost those brain cells when you agreed to this party."

"How could I deny her? Look how happy she is!"

I looked to the dance floor again where Greta was now bouncing up-and-down, her bobbed black hair swinging just slightly off-beat, a huge smile on her face.

"Is she drunk or high?" I asked.

"A little of both," Lane said. "Maybe that's what I need to get through this."

"Stick to the alcohol," I said. "Or you won't want to get out of bed tomorrow."

"You'd think it would get easier with age. Like we've trained for it or something. Why does it get harder?"

"That is the cruel twist of fate, my friend. At least you look amazing."

Her platinum hair was braided and wrapped around her head, her makeup was pure 1950s pinup, and her clothes screamed punk rock. High end punk rock. She was in head-to-toe Dior after all.

Greta spotted us and yelled, waving us over.

"Shit," we both said, before downing our drinks and making our way through the crowd, Lane dragging me by the hand.

I danced until I was sweaty, forgetting the onlookers with their phones pointed in our direction – or at least ignoring them as best I could. My hair stuck to my neck and back as the alcohol and pulsating music pulled me in and relaxed me. It had been a while since I'd let myself go on a dance floor and it felt freeing. Joyful. A release of pent-up emotions. All my worry for Addie. Stress about work. Irritation towards stupid Graham Forrester.

As he appeared in my mind, he also somehow appeared across the room.

I stopped moving, my breath catching in my throat as I met his gaze through the crowd. And then Lane grabbed my arm and spun me around.

"I need another drink!" she shouted over the music before taking my hand and pulling me through the sea of bodies to the bar.

While she ordered us two more glasses of sparkling wine, I searched the faces for Graham, wondering if he'd been illusion and I was now just seeing him everywhere. But a moment later I spotted him leaning against the partition separating the dance floor from a bunch of tables and chairs, talking to another man.

"Do you know Graham Forrester?" I asked Lane as she handed me a wine glass.

"Who?"

"Graham Forrester. The author."

"Doesn't sound familiar. Is he here or something?"

"Yes."

"He must be a client of Greta and Jessica's then." Jessica was the editor Greta worked with. "Why? Do you want to meet him? I can tell Greta to introduce you."

"No!" I said, shaking my head. "No, no. Not necessary. I was just curious."

"Curious about what?" We turned to see Greta standing behind us, her cheeks pink from dancing, her adorable micro-bangs plastered to her forehead.

"Lior was asking about Graham..." She looked to me. "What's his last name again?"

"Nothing," I said just as Greta said, "Forrester!"

"That's him," Lane said.

"Oh! Is he here?" Greta asked, getting on her tiptoes and

looking around. "That man is gorgeous. If I were into men, I'd climb him like a jungle gym and swing from his di—"

"Ack!" I said, pressing my hands to my ears.

"I would actually pay to see that," Lane said, laughing.

"Do you want to meet him?" Greta asked me.

"No," I said, firmly. "We've met. I was just surprised to see him here."

"He's been a client of Jessica's forever. I worked on his last book, and I get to work on this next one too. He's really lovely. Sucks what he's been through. He doesn't deserve any of it."

I frowned. Was she talking about what he'd described in that damn article? I mean, it wasn't that bad. I only yelled at him. He could take it. He was a grown man after all.

"What do you mean?" I asked.

"Oh," she said and then sat down on one of the bar stools and fanned herself with a stack of cocktail napkins. "Well, for starters there was his mom's death a few years ago. They were really close apparently. And then his wife, now ex-wife, cheated on him with one of her clients. And then he had a run-in with some psycho lady in the park and..."

I tuned her out. I did not need to hear one more person rehash my bad behavior. Instead, I sipped my wine and thought about the other things she'd said. About his mom and the ex-wife. Nadia. I'd met her a couple of times before she got into public relations and was still a hard-partying socialite and influencer. I'd never found her very pleasant to be around. She'd been catty and liked to wrangle secrets out of people and then they'd mysteriously end up in the gossip magazines. When I'd heard she'd changed her tune and got into public relations, I'd been skeptical. At one point she'd reached out to my agent in the hope of doing some work for me. When I ran into her at an event where she was representing another model I knew, she asked if I'd reconsider working with her. I'd acted like I had no idea what she was talking about and told her I left all those decisions up to my business manager who I knew really liked the person we'd been working with.

Truth be told, when I'd found out she'd inquired, I'd said hell no.

And then, when I'd heard she'd married none other than one of my favorite authors of all time, Graham Forrester, I hadn't known what to believe anymore. Surely someone like him wouldn't be with someone like her unless she really had changed her ways. When they'd divorced, I'd wondered what happened. There had been surprisingly little in the papers. Hearing now that she'd cheated on him made me sad. Even if he had dragged me in an article, no one deserved that.

I glanced across the room again but he and the man he'd been talking to were gone.

"Hey," Greta said, snapping her fingers in front of my face, her glittery nails flashing under the strobe lights. "We're gonna go dance some more. You coming?"

I smiled and gave her a sticky hug. "I'm going to finish this glass of wine and then crawl back to my little corner of the bar and hang for a bit longer before heading home. I have an early flight to Seattle tomorrow to see Addie. But happiest birthday wishes to you. Let's have lunch when I'm back in town."

I hugged Lane next and then waved as they disappeared into the crowd, Greta's head bouncing to the beat.

Turning to face the bar again, I took a long, slow sip of my wine, watching the party-goers in the long mirror that faced the room.

"Hey there," a male voice said, a warm hand sliding across my back. "Buy you another drink?"

I froze, my teeth clenching as I turned my head to take in a man I'd never seen before, his eyes staring south of my eyes.

"Please take your hand off of me," I said, my voice measured as I tried to keep from making a scene at my friend's party.

"Come on, love," he said, leaning closer, hand tightening, his thumb rubbing against my ribcage. "You look lonely. I could keep you company."

I just didn't understand it. How did one see a person and just decide it was okay to put their hands on them?

Holding tight to my glass, I raised my foot and put it down on his, the sharp edge of my Jimmy Choo's digging into the top of his shoe. His eyes widened and he tried to move away. But now I had him.

"I said," I repeated. "Take your hand off me."

This time he did as I said. I removed my foot, turned, and weaved through the crowd, heading to the end of the bar and furious that tears were welling in my eyes.

I stopped as two women blocked my path, then wound my way around them and stopped again when I saw the space I'd staked as my own for the night was occupied.

By Graham Forrester.

He looked up from his phone and stared back at me, his expression turning from a friendly smile, to one of resignment, to concern.

"Hey. Are you okay?" he asked, getting to his feet.

I nodded quickly, gave him a tight grin, and turned away. I had to get out of here. But as I took a step in the other direction, his hand caught my arm.

I spun around, glaring.

"Don't," I said

He raised his hands, as if in surrender.

"I'm sorry," he said. "I just... Are you sure you're okay? Do you want to sit here? I can move."

"I'm fine." But as I said it, my eyes betrayed me, a tear falling to my cheek. I swiped it away angrily.

"Lior—"

I was tired and upset and I wanted to go home. But if anyone saw me in this state, there would inevitably be pictures online tomorrow. I exhaled, my shoulders sagging.

"I'm too old for this bullshit," I said.

"This bullshit?" He motioned to us. "Or that bullshit." He gestured to the rest of the club.

"Both."

"You seemed to be having a good time a little while ago."

"I was. But now I just want to go home, put on my pajamas and—"

"Eat some donut holes?"

Despite being upset, I grinned. "You say that with the confidence of thinking there are any left."

He chuckled. "I have a feeling, in your line of business, you have more self-control than most."

I shrugged a shoulder. "I do. And good genes. Although three packages of donut holes would probably put both to the test."

He smiled and nodded, then gestured to the stool again.

"Thank you," I said. "But I think I'm just going to go. I'm officially partied out." I took a last sip of my wine and squeezed past him to put it on the bar.

"What do you see in Alex Clarke?" he asked suddenly and I frowned, stepping back and standing up to my full height.

"Excuse me?"

"I just... I saw it online this morning and—"

"And thought it was any of your business? Why? Do you want to put that in your article too?" I blinked back more tears. What the hell was wrong with me tonight? Normally I could shrug this shit off.

Furious that I was getting so emotional and annoyed at the gall of the man, I lost the filter I usually kept on a tight reign.

"Jesus, what is with men anyways?" I asked. "You know, you had no idea what I was going through that morning. Not that I owe you any explanation, but I had just gotten some terrifying news. And then I stepped in your dog's shit that you hadn't bothered to pick up and... I was scared and then embarrassed about making a scene. And you took my moment of vulnerability and made a joke out of it. Are you planning on doing that about my love life now too? Well, have at it. It won't be the first time and certainly won't be the last either."

I gulped back a sob and turned on my heel, bumping into people as I headed for the hallway that led to the back door.

"Oh!" I said as I stepped outside and was hit with a deluge of rain, the door slamming shut behind me. "Shit!"

I turned around and reached for the handle but at that moment the door swung open again and I stepped back to avoid it, the heel of my shoe catching on a crack in the pavement and breaking off, sending me careening backwards toward the pavement. Two hands caught me by my forearms and hauled me upright again.

I looked up to see Graham's face inches from mine, his hair plastered to his head by the rain.

"Are you okay?" he asked.

I nodded and then shivered, rain soaking through my black satin tank top and jeans.

He turned and grabbed the handle of the door.

"Fuck. It's locked."

He pounded on it but the music was so loud there was no way anyone inside could hear it.

I shivered and he immediately held out the jacket that was hanging from his arm.

"Take it," he said.

I wanted to tell him no, I didn't want his jacket. Didn't want his help. But I was cold and angry and didn't have the energy to fight him.

I slid my arms in and he reached forward and zipped me up, his head bent toward me as water dripped from his hair to his glasses, sending little rivulets down the inside of the lenses. Without thinking, I reached up and pushed his hair back and our eyes met.

I inhaled as his gaze moved to my lips, the heat from his body making me shiver in a different kind of way, and then a deep rumble thundered overhead, startling both of us. I took a step back, forgetting the broken heel and nearly fell again.

"Shit," I said, grabbing onto his arm, which was warm and more muscular than I would've imagined a writer's arm would be. Guess all that typing had some benefits.

"Come on," he said, reaching out like he was going to take my hand and then pulling back, thinking better of it. "We'll go around to the front."

But when we rounded the front of the building, the doorman that had been there to greet Greta's guests was nowhere to be found, and the front door was locked too.

I closed an eye and looked up at the thunderous black cloud above us. "Well, here we are," I said. "In yet another mess."

Graham gave me a wet smile and then pointed.

"We can stand under there."

I turned to see a small awning over the door of a delicatessen that was closed for the night. He took my arm and I limped quickly beside him until we were underneath it and he was pulling out his phone.

"Cab?" he asked and I nodded. "Do you mind sharing?" I shook my head.

We were quiet while we waited, the sound of the rain thudding against the awning loud as we huddled beneath it, not wanting to get dripped on by the water streaming off it but also trying not to touch one another.

I tried to think of something to say and peeked up at him, wondering if he was doing the same, but his face was turned away from me, giving me a nice view of his strong, stubble covered jawline.

It was interesting to me how different he looked from the picture on his book jackets. I wondered if he'd seen any of my work, if he'd thought the same about me. The woman he'd seen in the park was certainly not the one plastered on billboards or in magazines. And this guy standing here now with the glasses and gruff but sexy appearance, was definitely not the slick, clean-shaven, hair perfectly in place man I'd seen in photos. He had serious Clark Kent/Superman vibes.

I wondered what magic he could make in a phone booth.

The thought made me snort softly and I pretended I was covering my mouth from a yawn when he glanced over.

The taxi arrived and Graham held the door for me as we hurried inside and gave the driver our addresses.

"Thanks for agreeing to share," Graham said as we settled in, the windows momentarily steaming from the combination of heat and wet. "Seemed silly to get two cabs when we're headed to the same area."

"It was the least I could do for taking your coat in this downpour." I glanced over at him. "And for yelling at you."

"This time? Or last time." He grinned.

I bit my lip to keep from smiling.

"Last time," I said. "I stand by my right for yelling at you this time."

"That's valid. It was none of my business."

"It wasn't."

"Still..."

"Really?" I asked, turning in my seat to face him. "What do you have against Alex Clarke? Is it a competition thing? Did his last book outsell yours?"

"It did not," he said and smiled proudly. "But *he* is a pompous ass."

I wasn't about to tell him I agreed with him, even though I did. He had no right to ask me about who I was dating, nor give an opinion on him. I was so tired of men feeling like they had a right to push their thoughts and insecurities on me.

"Maybe he is to you," I said.

He was about to say more but then I shivered and he leaned forward and tapped on the glass separating us from the driver instead.

"Hey, can you turn up the heat please?"

"Sure thing," the driver said.

"Thank you," I said to Graham.

"Have to get my jacket back somehow," he said, trying to fight off a grin and failing.

I started to unzip it but he held up a hand.

"Wear it until we get there. I insist."

We drove in silence for a while and then—

"Is everything okay now?" he asked.

I frowned, turning to meet his gaze across the dim light of the backseat.

"What do you mean?"

"You said you got terrifying news that day."

I took in a long breath and blew it out, not sure I wanted to let him in on my personal life but then deciding I didn't care. If he wrote about Addie, I'd know what kind of person he truly was.

"My best friend got in a horrific car accident. I literally got the news seconds before stepping in shit."

"Is she okay?"

I nodded.

"She is. Mostly. Still pretty banged up though. She broke her cheekbone, her arm, some ribs... I'm actually flying to Seattle tomorrow to see her again. She's home now."

"Damn." He reached out and this time didn't pull back before giving my arm a gentle squeeze. "Well, that would certainly make me lose my shit over some shit too."

I couldn't help it. I laughed.

"I am sorry," I said. "I actually barely remember it. I was in such a state. Absolutely blinded with fear. I couldn't even recall most of what I said.... until I read it in your article. And then I was horribly ashamed and embarrassed. But, you know. Still self-righteous because..."

"I didn't pick up the poo?"

I nodded.

"She's dying," he said, his voice soft.

I frowned, not understanding, and then my body filled with sadness.

"Brontë?" I whispered.

"Yeah."

"Oh. Graham. I'm so sorry."

"I didn't even realize she'd... apparently it can happen when dogs get older. They lose their ability to hold it and they just go."

"And then I lost *my* shit."

Despite himself, Graham laughed.

"Shit happens," he said, making me laugh now too.

"Apparently," I said and then glanced out the window as the cab slowed and pulled over. "This is me."

I grabbed my purse to pay but Graham stopped me.

"I've got it," he said.

"No. I owe you."

"You can get it next time we find ourselves stuck outside in a rainstorm together."

I smiled. "Deal."

I unzipped his jacket and handed it across the seat to him and then got out of the car, glad the rain had calmed to a sensible drizzle.

"Hey," he said and I ducked my head back in.

"Do you know who Brontë is named after?"

"I'm assuming Charlotte, Anne, or Emily. Or perhaps all three?"

He nodded. "Just checking."

I gave him a confused smile and then started to shut the door but stopped to duck my head in once more.

"Oh, and Alex Clarke *is* a pompous ass."

I grinned at the sound of his laughter as I hurried up the front steps to my house.

CHAPTER 11

Graham

I t was hard to call my third time walking by Lior's brownstone accidental when I was carrying a note for her in my pocket.

It wasn't anything scandalous. Just a little, "Hope your friend is feeling better" message. But I felt like I was in middle school every time I slowed down near her stoop, and then inevitably kept walking, afraid she'd think I was uncool, like most girls in middle school had when I was there.

Also, why was I trying to make contact with the woman I'd sworn, childishly I admit, to hate forever? As our initial meeting had shown, she was clearly the type I often fell for and regretted later. I was a magnet for women who could only be described as brats.

Except, that wasn't exactly true in Lior's case. Or at least, I'd perhaps jumped the gun on my opinion of her. Granted, that first impression hadn't been great on her end, but now I knew why.

Still. There was that age-old saying, wasn't there?

If someone shows you who they are, believe them.

"Does that still count in this case?" I asked Brontë.

A soft breeze kicked up and she lifted her face, sniffing at the air.

"Was that a yes or no? I could really use more clarity, please."

Suddenly my slow-moving old girl was pulling on her leash and stepping onto the first step of Lior's front porch.

"Whoa," I said, panicking. "What are you doing?"

But she was on a mission, ignoring my gentle tugs on the leash as she pushed onwards and upwards towards the front door.

"I guess this is your way of saying I should leave the damn note already?"

Fine. She had a point. But still, my heart was pounding in my chest. What if Lior opened the door and wasn't exactly thrilled to see me standing there?

"Fuck it," I murmured, sliding my hand into my pocket and grasping the folded paper with my fingertips.

When we got to the top, Brontë beelined for an item in the corner near the doormat.

The shoe.

"Ah," I said. "You smell *you*! I'm not sure if I'm impressed or disgusted, my friend."

She sniffed at it, her tail thwacking twice against my leg, and then nosed the sneaker, knocking it over so that I could see the bottom and that it was indeed *the* shoe, the underside still marred by poo. I let go of the note in my pocket and leaned down, grabbing it by the laces and lifting it above Brontë's head.

"I suppose the least we could do is clean it and give it back, right? What do you think. We might even make a new friend as a result. At the very least, she might stop glaring at me when she sees me." I stared down at Brontë and she looked up, her soulful brown eyes meeting mine. "I'll take that as a yes."

Her tail thumped against the doorframe twice and then she headed back towards the steps and led the way down to the sidewalk, me following with a leash in one hand, a smelly shoe in the other.

At home I made quick work of cleaning the dirtied treads, then put the sneaker outside on the back patio to dry. I'd return it tomorrow morning when B and I were out for our next walk. I wasn't worried Lior would miss it since she'd told me when we'd shared a cab that she was going to Seattle. I assumed since she was visiting her friend that she'd probably be gone at least a few days. And, thanks to some light stalking the past couple of nights, I knew she was definitely there – she'd posted a few pictures from the trip of her and her friend, and their freshly painted toenails.

Checking the time, I sat at the kitchen table – Brontë beside me in her bed – and set my timer, preparing to get back to work on my novel. Right now I was at that delicate emotional stage between "Okay, maybe this isn't as awful as I thought it was" and "I'm a hack and I will probably never get a deal again."

The author life was nothing if not a roller coaster ride filled with climbs, swerves, loopty-loops, and heart-stopping drops. It was a mix of constant delusions, visions of grandeur, and douses of crippling self-doubt. Throw in the inevitable bouts of imposter syndrome and weeee! Welcome to the what I liked to call the Carnival of Hell.

Wouldn't trade it for anything. Being a writer was fun. Capital F.U.N.

When the timer dinged, I sat back, stretching my arms above my head and debating whether to do another hour of work or take a short break to eat and scroll social media for a bit. Thoughts of seeing Lior helped make the case for a break and I rose to make a snack.

A few minutes later – a plate of tortilla chips liberally layered with shredded cheese and microwaved into a gooey delicious mess beside me – I began what had become my new secret obsession in the past couple of days: finding out what famous fashion model Lior Flynn had been up to.

She had uploaded a dozen or so photos already this morning, and I paused on each one, reading the witty captions beneath.

A haughty-looking white cat with a black beauty mark glared at the camera.

"What say you, Morticia? Is this love?" the first line read.

"Die, mortal fool," read the second line.

Next was a gorgeous looking pan containing what looked to be a rice dish, complete with pistachios, tofu, cilantro, and bell peppers. "Don't tell me I don't know how to cook!" the caption read. In the background was a bag advertising a well-known food delivery service company.

There was a picture of another cat, this one black and looking like he'd be right at home smoking a cigar; an image of seashells; one of a to-go cup of coffee with the word *Ampersand* on the side of it; and images of Lior and her friend, whom I now knew was named Addie, smiling and laughing, despite Addie's face being heavily bruised and bandaged on the left side.

They looked like two overgrown kids having way too much fun together. A dangerous combination, as noted on another image showcasing a pile of boxes and bags from what was apparently a drunken online shopping spree.

"Oops, we did it again," Lior had written.

Reaching the last of the images, I glanced at the section where people had commented, then how long ago she'd posted the photos. In less than eight hours she'd garnered over five hundred thousand likes and had over one hundred thousand comments.

"Fucking hell," I said.

I had a decent following myself, but nothing like the millions she had. I imagined how many more books I'd sell if I had comparable numbers and glanced down at Brontë.

"We could *give* this place away. Or burn it to the ground and start from scratch." She blinked at me and went back to sleep.

I returned my gaze to the screen and scrolled down past images I'd already seen. My text alert sounded, startling me and I jumped, my finger unintentionally pressing a button.

"Shit!" I said, staring at my laptop screen. I'd just accidentally liked the red bikini photo. "What do I do?" I asked the blonde dog at my feet. But B was no help. She merely sighed in her sleep and stretched out a leg. "Shit, shit, *shit*."

To unlike or not to unlike? What was the move? What if she was online and had seen me like the image? And *that* one in particular? Fucking hell. I would come off like a total creeper. She'd obviously tell her friend and then there would be discussions about what a slimeball I was liking only *that* photo. And since we weren't friends on the site, she'd know I had come to her page specifically and—

I hit unlike and then sat like a statue staring at the screen, waiting for something to happen. But what? A DM from her saying, "Saw ya, loser. Stop stalking me."

But nothing happened. There was no message. No social media police pointing their virtual fingers at me and laughing. Maybe no one had noticed and I was... in the clear?

I waited another minute and was about to close my laptop, feeling a little relieved, when a wave of curiosity I hadn't felt in a long while swept over me.

"Don't do it, man," I murmured to myself as I opened the search bar and typed in a name I hadn't in a while. "You are just a glutton for punishment today."

Instantly my eyes were assaulted with flashy images of my ex-wife Nadia at a number of fancy events, her bright white smile and blonde highlighted hair practically blinding me at every turn. Every item of clothing she wore was vibrant in color. Every pose perfectly executed to show off some part of her toned body. Every piece of jewelry was oversized and sparking dramatically at the camera lens. She'd gotten a dog, a tiny thing she'd over-accessorized to the point of it looking more toy than real. And then there was the boyfriend. I'd never been particularly fond of Brett Harrison's music, and as far as I knew neither had Nadia. Until she was. Or at least until she saw an opportunity and jumped, quite literally, on top of it. I stared in disgust at an image of her in a too-tight t-shirt with his name emblazoned across it, her breasts looking like they were fighting for air.

I made a strange sound in my throat and then clicked in the search engine again, a sick sort of curiosity now piquing my brain. Typing in the name of the woman I had dated before meeting Nadia, I held my breath as her feed filled my screen with similar images to the ones Nadia had posted. I closed my eyes for a moment and then returned to the search box, this time typing in the name of my high school girlfriend, Elizabeth Bristol. The first to break my heart. The one I'd thought for a long time had gotten away.

Once again the images were eerily similar to the other two women's. Bright. Flashy. Obnoxious. And gave me an acute feeling of chaos.

I was an unstoppable moron so I typed in Lior's name again.

While the content was more high-end, and the aesthetic classier, sweeter, and more authentic, to me it sort of read the same as the other two women. Drama. It was all drama. Lior's life was filled with it by the very nature of her job. Travel, celebrity, money... Drama was the name of that game, and no matter how many pictures she posted doing "normal people" things, she would never be "normal". She would never not be followed and photographed. Her stained scarf would always have a tag that read Burberry or Dior. And her broken heel would always come from a Jimmy Choo or a Manolo.

My mind went to the decades-old, worn-in sneaker I'd taken from her porch this morning. That certainly hadn't felt contrived in any way. Maybe she did have a little bit of "normal" in her life after all?

"Oh, fuck off," I told myself, shutting my laptop in disgust. "Don't give her another thought. The last thing you need is any sort of drama, created or otherwise. Or a woman to be obsessing over. We are all about work now, right girl?"

I reached down to give Brontë some scratches behind the ears, then went upstairs to my home gym to work out the frustrations I was clearly in denial about.

The following morning, Brontë's leash in one hand, Lior's now-clean sneaker in the other, we exited the house and began what was now becoming our new familiar walk. At the corner we paused to let a group of school kids dressed in uniforms go by, and a few blocks later we stood aside to allow two harried-looking women leading a dozen or so preschoolers across the street to a small playground. I grinned as one of the kids shot me a slobbery smile and then continued on my way, ignoring the confused looks I got when people noticed the shoe in my hand.

As we approached Lior's home, I paused, causing Brontë to look back at me with a question in her big brown eyes as the leash tightened.

"Sorry, girl," I said, nervous suddenly as I realized I had no idea when Lior was returning. She could've flown in last night and was in her house now. What if she saw me? What if she was irritated I'd been there and taken her shoe?

"Jesus, grow up, Graham," I told myself.

Taking a breath, I resumed walking, Brontë shuffling along beside me until she seemed to realize where she was and picked up speed, her head directed towards the stoop leading to Lior's door.

We climbed the steps and I set the shoe back in the corner where Brontë had found it, putting a new note inside and then heading back home.

CHAPTER 12

Liar

I woke to the sound of a crash and sprinted out of the guest room bed wearing nothing but a tank top and the underwear Addie had gotten me for Christmas with beavers all over them.

"Addie?" I shouted as I hurried down the hall, looking in doorways as I went, my bare feet slapping against the hardwoods.

"I'm fine!" she yelled.

I entered the kitchen to a cloud of flour and my best friend smiling with the one side of her face that wasn't broken, stitched, and bruised.

"What happened?" I asked, standing just outside the doorway in hopes of avoiding looking like she did. "Are you trying to impersonate a powdered donut? Cuz you know I get all hot and bothered for a donut."

"This is me surprising with you pancakes." She reached her arms out to her sides and waved her hands, kicking up another cloud. "Surprise!"

"Fool. You can't cook. You must've hit your head harder than we thought."

She glanced down at the frying pan on the floor and the spilled bag of flour.

"Wanna go out to eat?" she asked.

"Like we've done every morning? Yes. Obviously."

She opened the French doors to the back deck then and walked out to the yard, giving her hair a gentle shake and dusting off her t-shirt and shorts as best she could before coming back inside.

"Go shower," I said, pointing in the direction of her room. "I'll..." I looked around at the flour covered surfaces. "Figure this out."

I was still wiping down appliances and countertops when she emerged twenty minutes later, her light brown hair pulled back in a ponytail that accentuated her long neck and bruised face – which was now an interesting rainbow of colors. She was dressed in a pair of white jean shorts and a strappy black tank top that did little to conceal more bruised skin on her shoulder, clavicle, and arm.

"Lookin' to turn heads today, eh?" I said.

"I have to find some way to get men to notice me over you."

"Next time maybe opt for a boob job."

"That still wouldn't do it."

"What if you got double Gs?"

"How would I tend to the animals though?" She mimed trying to reach around larger boobs.

"Fine. Get in car accidents. See if I care."

"A girl's gotta do what a girl's gotta do. I keep telling you!"

"Always trying to steal my limelight."

"I just want a sliver of the lime," she said. "Preferably with an ice-cold Corona."

"Believe me," I said. "You don't." I looked around the mostly clean kitchen. "Soooo... Alki Café for breakfast then?"

"Absofuckinglutely."

I hurried to my own room to change and run a brush through my hair before twisting it into a long braid that hung down my back. After throwing on my favorite worn-in baseball cap and a pair of flip-flops, we were out the door.

We walked the few blocks to our favorite breakfast spot while chatting about her clinic. She was annoyed that her partner, a lovely woman called Alexandra, who was two decades older than us, had called on another local vet to help with Addie's patients.

"I mean," Addie said. "Obviously she had to call *someone*. She can't handle my patients and hers all on her own, but why did she have to call *him*."

The him in question was Addie's sworn enemy. At least, that's what she'd made him out to be, despite not having met him once. Her opinion was based solely off his fancy clinic, state of the art equipment, and good looks that were "too good to take seriously".

"He's a cad," she said now.

"How do you know?"

"I just do. I've known men like him all my life. He's good looking and he knows it and he uses it."

I raised my eyebrows. "You mean like me?"

She elbowed me. "You know what I mean."

I did, but it didn't mean I didn't get to give her shit.

"Maybe he's nice," I said. "Animals wouldn't like him if he wasn't."

"Animals can be dumb."

"Addie!" I said, laughing.

She smirked.

"Don't tell my clients I said that," she said. "Except Wilbur the greyhound. He's well aware of his mental shortcomings."

We ordered a carafe of passionfruit mimosas as soon as we were seated and then perused the menu, landing as always on our favorites: French toast, a veggie omelet, roasted potatoes, and vegan sausage. Like we'd been doing since we were girls, we would share it all.

"So," Addie said, sipping her mimosa. "Spill."

"Spill what?" I said, eyes wide. But she wasn't buying it.

"I know you've been avoiding telling me anything of importance. And while I appreciate you not wanting to bother me with anything more serious than a bad date with a cute Brit while I've got all this going on..." She waved a hand towards her body. "I'm bored of your bullshit. You leave tomorrow. So spill it. What's happening with that designer Daniela? Is a photo shoot happening soon? Have you made any decisions about next career moves? What about Avery's offer to write for the Post? Have you given that any more thought?"

Avery was an old classmate from high school and then college, until both Addie and I left. After graduating from the University of Washington with a writing degree, she'd left the country in search of adventure and newsworthy stories, which gained her a slew of injuries acquired while reporting on events all over the map, the last of which – a conflict – was serious enough to send her back stateside to reconsider her life's choices. She returned to Seattle at twenty eight and found herself taking a lead desk job at the Seattle Post. I'd run into her during one of my visits to see Addie last year and she said she'd been meaning to call me about an idea she'd had which would involve me writing for the paper.

"Fine," I said to Addie, making a face and stabbing a slice of strawberry. "Yes, to the photo shoot. No, to making any career decisions. Yes, I've thought a lot about her offer."

"And?"

"And..." I shrugged. "It's enticing for sure. To maybe move back here and be near you. To be doing something I've always loved and wanted to pursue. I just..."

"You just what?"

"It would be a big change. I'm scared. And what if it doesn't pan out?"

"One, it's not like you have to completely give up modeling. You could still book jobs, and even incorporate them into your new job if it's an interesting angle, shoot, or location. And two, if it doesn't pan out how you and Avery envisage, you just look for something else to do. Or maybe take a break. It's not like you can't afford to take a minute to figure out something else."

"I suppose," I said. "And what about the scared part?"

"Fuck scared. I got mowed down by a Lexus and am lucky to be sitting here. Life's short, baby. Grab your opportunities by the balls. And if the balls shrivel up, let go and find a new pair."

I pursed my lips as the man at the table next to us turned bright red and choked on his bite of pancake.

Addie grinned. "That's what he gets for eavesdropping."

When we got back to Addie's house, she called her clinic to check in while I took another turn in the kitchen, marveling at the number of crevices there were for flour to settle into.

"Stop cleaning," Addie said from the doorway, a large floppy hat on her head and hands on hips. "Let's go to the beach."

I took a last swipe at the handle of the refrigerator and tossed the sponge in the sink.

"Deal."

After a quick stop for iced coffees, we flip-flopped our way across the street to the beach, dodging a rollerblader, a foursome on a surrey, and a small group of preschoolers being led and followed by their smiling and singing teachers.

Making ourselves a little nest of sunbathing bliss, a rarity for late spring in Seattle, we stripped off our shorts and tanks and slathered on the SPF before trying to get comfortable on the queen size sheet Addie had brought.

"What else?" Addie said from beneath the brim of her large sunhat.

"What else what?" I murmured, breathing in the warm air and luxuriating over being back in one of my favorite places on Earth, beside my absolute favorite person on Earth.

"Tell me more," she said. "My life has been doctors' appointments and binge watching every show available to man. Tell me something real. How's Katya? I saw her on a billboard for the new

Calvin Klein perfume a few weeks ago. She looked amazing. Is she dating anyone?"

"Kat's good. Same old Kat. I think she's in Milan right now doing a shoot for Elle magazine. No men, or women for that matter, for her these days. She said she's had it with the dating scene. Of course, she says that and the next thing I'll hear is that she's in love."

She always loved hearing about Katya's many exploits. The two women had met a handful of times and each thought the other was hilarious. Plus, they had one major thing in common – they both loved to tease me.

"Anything newsworthy about your mother and Cal?" Addie continued. "Do they know you're in town again? Have any men who aren't assholes or idiots or narcissists made it onto your radar?"

"Damn," I said. "You're on a roll today. No, I didn't tell my mother I'm here because they're in Paris. Nothing noteworthy in their lives that I've heard about. And no. No men to speak of." An image of Graham flashed in my mind. "I did have an unpleasant run-in the morning of your accident that will make you laugh though."

"Ooh." She lifted the brim of her hat. "Tell me."

"I was out for my morning walk when your mom called, which of course sent me into a total state of panic, I'll have you know. Next thing I knew I'd stepped in dog poo and totally went off on the dog's owner, who couldn't have looked more bewildered. I'm sure I looked like an absolute lunatic but I—"

"Oh my god," Addie said, sitting up and almost losing the bikini top she'd untied, her eyes wide, her open mouth turning into an almost evil grin. "You're the Meet-Poop Girl!"

I felt my face turn red and covered it with my hands.

"You read it?" I asked, my voice muffled and full of agony and regrets.

Addie howled with laughter and I reached over and pulled her hat down over her eyes.

"Shut up!" I said.

"Ohmygod, ohmygod, ohmygod. Lior!" She laughed some more, pushing her hat up and then grabbing onto her injured ribs and swearing, but still laughing.

"You deserve any pain you cause yourself," I said, crossing my arms over my chest.

"Holy shit," she said and then laughed at her accidental pun. "How have you not told me this before now?"

"It's a giant turd of a story?" I offered and took great joy when she groaned, her body shaking with more laughter. "Sorry," I said. "Stop laughing before you hurt yourself worse."

"Seriously, Lior. Why did you keep this from me? It's just cruel."

"Because I didn't know you still read his column and… it was terrible. And embarrassing. And I didn't know it was him!"

"How? You've seen him in person before."

"He doesn't look the same. He's all undercover journalist Clark Kent with some seriously sexy scruff and glasses. And his hair is longer. Plus he was in sweats, not fancy author clothes like in his pictures or when we went to his book signings."

"Oh my god." She grinned gleefully.

"Stop saying that and smiling like that, jerk."

"Have you seen him since?"

"Ugh. Yes. I ran into him at Jessa's launch party where he was a total asshat. And then again at a birthday party where we ended up sharing a cab afterwards which was… kind of nice."

"Shut. Up."

"I didn't know his dog is dying." I covered my face with my hands again.

"Brontë is dying?" Her eyes filled with empathy.

"Yeah. And he didn't realize she'd been… using the bathroom while walking."

Addie nodded. "That can happen. Poor thing. Both of them. I wish I were there to help."

I smiled. She had always been so good with animals and people alike. Ever since we were little and she'd convinced her parents to allow what seemed like a constant parade of animals and creatures into their house. Cats, dogs, rabbits, an iguana, fish, turtles, gerbils, garter snakes... It's why her clinic had flourished since she'd opened it four years ago. Creatures flocked to her. I often joked she was like a Disney princess. All she had to do was open a window and give a little whistle and they all came clamoring.

"Anyways," she said. "Let's get back to the fact that he wrote an article about you."

"Can we not?" I asked. "It's humiliating. I saw it when I was sitting in the airport on my way back home from seeing you after the accident and spilled my matcha all over the floor."

Addie snickered. "Meet-poop," she whispered. "So clever."

"Shut up."

"I'll bet he's even cuter all scruffy."

I pictured him once more, my stomach giving a little happy cartwheel at the image.

"Shut up," I said again, this time more to myself than to my friend, and then turned over onto my stomach and closed my eyes.

* * *

"I'll be back next month," I said, rolling my suitcase to the front door and parking it there to give my friend a hug.

"You're making me feel like a charity case," Addie said.

"We'll beach by day and order in food by night."

"Fine. Woo me. See if I care."

"Don't do anything stupid while I'm gone."

"I will absolutely wait until you get back."

"And be nice to Dr. Doolittle," I said. "I think you should give him a chance. Let him settle those ruffled feathers of yours with those big strong hands."

I'd looked up her 'nemesis' and was shocked at how good looking the guy was. She hadn't been joking.

She opened the door. "And now it is time for you to go," she said.

"Seriously, Addie-roo." I grabbed my suitcase and rolled it out onto the front porch. "I'll bet he could make you purr."

The door slammed shut and I laughed all the way to my rental car.

Many hours later a cab delivered me to the sidewalk outside my house. I waited patiently for the driver to unload my bags from the trunk and then I carried them up the front steps, sleepy from the flight and happy to be home, despite being sad to have left Seattle and my friend.

I unlocked the front door and glanced over at the corner of my stoop, as had become habit, to the marred shoe I'd left there in disgust weeks ago. Except it looked as if someone had moved it. And there was something inside.

Hauling my bags into the house, I turned on the foyer light and stepped back outside, crouching to get a better look at the shoe and what looked like a tiny scroll inside, tied with a blue ribbon.

"What the hell?" I murmured, grabbing the rolled paper and pulling off the ribbon.

With a bemused look, I unrolled the thick piece of parchment paper and read the poem written inside.

Roses are red
Violets are blue
I have cleaned the poo
From your favorite shoe

. . .

~Graham Forrester

I laughed and picked up the shoe, turning it over to find that was in fact now clean. And then my heart gave a little thump of delight knowing he'd been here and had touched my sneaker.

"Worst Cinderella retelling ever," I said and chuckled.

Going inside, I set my now clean shoe next to its mate, then padded into the kitchen to make a cup of cocoa before bed. I was reaching for a mug when I realized I was still holding the poem, clasping it to my heart like a lovelorn character from a Regency era novel.

"Well shit," I said, and then tossed it to the countertop as if it had suddenly caught fire.

CHAPTER 13

Graham

"Graham!"

I could hear my kid sister's squeal from a hundred feet away and watched as students' heads turned to follow Marley tearing across the school lawn. Bracing myself for impact, I laughed, pleased that despite being one of the "popular" girls in school, it had never deterred her from unabashedly showing her love for her big brother. Especially today, seeing as I'd flown from New York to Colorado to surprise her on her eighteenth birthday.

"Happy birthday, kiddo," I said as she leapt on me in a tackle hug.

"Hey," she said, quickly letting me go and standing back, hands on hips. "I'm officially an adult now. No more of this kiddo stuff!"

"You paying for your phone and car insurance?"

She glared.

"Kiddo it is," I said.

"Your reasoning is stupid. I don't have a job to pay for that stuff."

"Fine. Let's go with degenerate."

Her bubblegum pink lips formed a shocked "O" and she took a swipe at me, which I easily ducked.

"Miss Forrester," a stern female voice called. "We don't hit others."

"But he's my brother," Marley whined while I laughed, put her in a headlock, waved good-naturedly at the teacher standing by, and pulled my little sister along with me to where I'd parked my rental car as she punched me repeatedly in the thigh until I let her go.

"Are you here until my graduation?" she asked, throwing her backpack into the back seat and smoothing her hair as she got into the passenger seat.

"No. Just for a couple days," I said, sliding behind the steering wheel. "But I'll be back."

"You'd better be."

"Oh yeah?"

"Yeah!"

She reached forward and paired her phone with the car and then turned up the volume to a decibel level that threatened to shatter our eardrums.

I turned the volume down again and she pouted for a good half second before launching into her plans for her birthday party, which was happening on Saturday, two days from now. I wouldn't be here for that though. I'd be leaving that morning, escaping before I could be put to work on decorations or made to sit through a fashion show while Marley pretended to need my opinion and then ignored every single one I gave.

"Smart man," my stepmother, Lisa, had said when I'd told her and my dad about my early flight out.

My father had leaned into me quietly. "Take me with you," he'd begged.

"So then," Marley said now. "We'll have cake and all that boring stuff to please the folks of course, and presents—"

"To please you," I broke in.

"Obviously. And then movies and music and snacks..."

She went on and on, and I grinned, letting her words and excitement wash over me. For the first sixteen years of my life I'd felt I'd missed out on having a younger sibling, but had made my peace with it. So when Marley came along, I'd not known at first what to think of her. But one look at that impish face, which had only grown lovelier with each year, and I was hooked. The doting big brother, reporting for duty.

I tried not to spoil her, but it was hard. She was intelligent, funny, and had more style in a single discerning raised eyebrow than I did in my entire body. Not only that, but she saw people. Really saw them. Not in the same way I did, which she said was through some romanticized hazy lens, walking across misty moors.

She could tell a person's character within seconds of meeting them. Which was why I'd never live down marrying Nadia. Marley had warned me, but I'd blown off her concerns with a "you're too young to understand" naïveté that had bitten me, quite hard, in the ass when I'd learned my now ex had been cheating on me for the better part of a year.

Or, to put it another way, for most of our marriage.

There had been no "I told you so" from my little sister, which had been kind of her, since I'd been shell-shocked, demoralized, and heartbroken. But anytime she got even a whiff of a woman in my life, she became a bloodhound keen on the scent of female pheromones. Because she didn't just read other people. She could read me as well.

I pulled up to a stoplight and felt her eyes on me.

"Are you seeing someone?" she asked, turning down the volume so that it was still loud, but with only minimal bleeding from the ears.

"No," I said, keeping my eyes on the intersection. It wasn't a lie, but for some reason I still felt I'd been caught out.

"Interested in someone?"

I took a long breath in, held it, and exhaled before turning to her scrutinizing glare.

"No. Why?"

"Because I've been blasting sappy love songs for the past ten minutes and you haven't said a word. Normally you'd threaten to embarrass me with one of your butt rock songs from prehistoric times if I didn't turn it off."

"I'm evolving as a man," I said and turned back to stare imploringly at the traffic light.

"Bout time."

"I'm offended."

"Sorry. You're right. You're the most evolved man I know. Wanna talk about my menstrual cycle?"

The light mercifully turned green and I simultaneously hit the gas and turned the volume back up.

We pulled into the illustrious cul de sac my father and Lisa had moved into when I'd left for college. Marley was a whirlwind of movement as she grabbed her things and bounded towards the front door, shouting over her shoulder, "Don't think you've knocked me off the scent. Something is up with you and I'm going to find out!"

I groaned and slid from the car, shutting the door and locking it before following along, meeting my dad's grinning face as he waited for me on the threshold of the house.

"Already got her hooks in you?"

"She's relentless."

"She on to something?"

"Is she ever not?"

He laughed and wrapped an arm around my shoulder as we walked to the kitchen together, the smell of something baking filling the air and making my mouth water.

"Marley's birthday cake," my dad explained. "As well as two different kinds of cookies."

"How are you still so fit?" I asked, eyeing my dad's physique admirably.

"See that pool outside?" my dad asked with a laugh. "And the home gym? And the bikes and kayaks?"

Lisa, a successful attorney-turned-baker, owned a high-end bakery in Boulder. When she wasn't there, she was often trying out new recipes at home. I'd received overnighted boxes of treats at least twice a month for years, which I'd had to stop when I'd married Nadia because, "I cannot have that homemade, country-bumpkin, sugar-filled junk in my home".

As soon as she moved out, the boxes had resumed.

Marley's birthday cakes had never been made by anyone but her mom. Beautiful creations that you almost felt bad about digging into. Until you got a taste of them. And then all the guilt would quietly slip away as you began unabashedly shoving them into your face.

A timer rang out and Lisa appeared, flour in her dark hair, waving a yellow, ladybug-decorated potholder at us, before turning off the timer and opening the oven.

The scent of chocolate wafted over.

"Help yourself," she said, nodding toward a plate of peanut butter sandwich cookies. "There's strawberry frosting inside."

"How have you done all this in the time I was gone?" I asked, snagging a cookie and taking a bite.

I'd only left two hours ago, after flying in this morning and then going to peruse a couple of bookstores before surprising my sister at school. In that time, Lisa had somehow baked two layers of cake, two different kinds of cookies, and there was a bowl of frosting sitting in wait on the end of the counter.

She shrugged, her freckled nose crinkling as she smiled.

It was interesting to me that my father ended up with Lisa after being with my mother, who'd had a similar look, temperament and style, although she couldn't bake to save her life. Somehow, whenever she'd tried to make cookies, they'd spread so thin we'd always joked she'd made pancakes instead.

Why does one pick someone so similar when it clearly didn't work out the first time?

Or the second... or the third...?

It was this very thing that scared me about getting into a relationship again. I had chosen, or had been chosen, by women who found me charming and interesting in the beginning, and then tried to change me, got angry when I didn't adhere to some strange set of rules they thought I should have, and wound up deciding I was actually boring. Which they had no problem telling me. Often quite brutally.

What did that say about me, that I ended up with people like this? And could I break the cycle? How could I know if the next woman I ended up with would be any different?

I didn't. And that's why I'd determined I was going to most likely end up alone, writing increasingly depressing stories about humans trying to escape their lives in one way or another.

"So," my dad said. "I was thinking, since the big party is Saturday, the four of us would go out to dinner tonight to celebrate Marley? Somewhere nicer than the usual burger joint?"

"Sounds good," I said.

Lisa finished covering the cakes in cling wrap and put them in the freezer.

"I'm in," she said, untying her apron. "Just let me shower first."

"As you wish," Dad said as she grabbed a cookie, took a bite, and gave him a crumby kiss as she passed by on her way to the staircase.

"Wanna beer?" Dad asked me.

"Yes, please."

We sat out on the back patio, staring at the view and sipping our beers while chatting about work, his as an architect, and mine as a writer. Since I was little, I'd been fascinated by the drawings I used to find in my dad's home office, each one telling its own complicated story. Mazes of math, systems, and structures. For a time, he and my mother thought I'd follow in his footsteps. They didn't realize until much later that all of the perusing I was doing was setting the stage for my own career. I wasn't trying to decipher what he was building, I was using his creations as settings for stories. Down his carefully drawn passageways lived families, lovers torn apart and coming together, best friends plotting escapes from any number of villains. When he finally figured it out, he began giving me his cast-off drawings, which I then used to draw all those characters into.

"How's the latest novel going?" he asked. "Hit the midpoint yet?"

I grinned and took a long pull from my bottle. My parents had always been good listeners, taking in what I told them intently. Being invested in who I was and what I was interested in. When I began to take storytelling seriously, they learned the terms, asked questions, and bought me books on the subject. They understood it was important to me and encouraged me to keep experimenting and learning. And when they divorced, an event the three of us had dubbed the world's most amicable divorce in history, both continued to keep asking and spurring me on. Despite their split, we somehow remained a threesome of sorts. The Three Musketeers – even when we each lived in a different state.

"Midpoint done and dusted," I said. "The end is in sight."

"Itching to get back to it?"

I laughed. He knew me well. Being so close to the end made it hard to stop, even for a couple nights away to celebrate my little sister's big birthday.

"It's killing me," I said. "But it's good to feel this anticipation. It means I'm on to something. If it were easy to set aside, then I'd be worried."

He lifted his bottle toward me and I clinked it.

"What else?" he asked. "How's B getting along?"

I showed him a picture the dog sitter had sent just this morning and then sighed. "Not gonna lie. The end is nearing and it's not easy to watch."

"She's a good girl. Been there for you through a lot."

I nodded, thinking back to how she'd climbed into my lap the day I'd returned home after my mother had died. She hadn't left my side for days, her big brown eyes constantly seeking me out, silently asking if I was okay. And then later, when Nadia left, she had nudged me every day, asking me to take her for a walk, as if it were her who needed to get out of the house, not me. Losing her was not going to go well for me.

"She has. I'm heartbroken thinking about her not being around anymore."

"Have you considered getting a puppy? To help maybe ease the blow? And the emptiness?"

"I did, once," I said, finishing off my beer and setting it on the small glass table between us. "But it almost felt..."

"Traitorous?"

"Yeah."

"I get it. Well... loss is a part of life. Part of having a pet. Part of being human."

"And it sucks."

"Damn right it does." He finished his beer and set it beside mine. "What about women? Have you met anyone new of note?"

An image of Lior, wet from the rain and sitting beside me in the back of a cab flashed in my mind.

"Not really, no."

"No?"

He peered at me and I shrugged, turning my face away, but Marley had gotten her keen sense of seeing people from him, and I'd walked right into his casual beer on the patio chat-trap.

"No," I said a little more vehemently than I'd meant to.

"Since when do we lie to each other?"

Most people I knew would do anything – years of therapy,

exorcism – to not end up like their parents. Me? I'd always asked why I couldn't be more like mine. They always seemed to make healthy choices for themselves, and didn't regret much in life.

Whereas I...

"How have you managed to not find one, but two amazing women who didn't set out to change you, use you, make your life miserable, and then leave you in a pile of ashes?" I asked.

Dad's eyes widened and he sat up, leaning his elbows on his knees as he considered me.

"Well," he said, chuckling and then immediately looking guilty. "Sorry. I'm not laughing at you. I know you've had a bad go of things with the women in your life. The truth is, as wonderful as your mom was and Lisa is, it's not always easy. We're separate human beings coming together to form a life and bringing with us our own ideas and ways of doing things. And even if those things align, we're still human. And humans are messy. There is no instruction manual on how to get through life. One person can live one way and be successful, and another can try mimicking it and fail miserably. We all have our own paths and you just hope you can find a partner with whom your paths can co-exist in a peaceful, if not fun, way."

"But how did you end up with women that were innately kind and decent? And I've..." I let the sentence trail off, knowing I didn't need to elaborate. He'd met them all.

"I have a theory," he said. "And it's only that."

"Go ahead," I said, leaning forward on my knees now, intently listening as always to the wisdom imparted by my father.

"You live a lot in your head. In worlds of your own creation. And when you come out, I think you realize that beyond your career, you haven't built much of a life for yourself. It's a great career, but when you aren't writing or doing things related to writing, you aren't doing much except visiting us and walking Brontë. I rarely hear you talk about any of your friends from school anymore. Whatever happened to Cooper? And I think you feel that 'lack of' more. So then you meet one of these women and they are full of life and laughter, and they sparkle and offer excitement and fun and parties and a social group. You get sucked in. You're now part of something. It's all good, son. But also not. Because the women who you end up with have a honing device, seeking a partner who's seeking what they offer. Which is all very surface level. And you're deeper than that. But you let them take over. For some reason you think you're wrong and they must be right because they've curated a life that looks good. At least in pictures. Next thing you know, your home isn't home anymore and your clothes cost four times what they used to. Ruining a t-shirt is no longer no big deal, it's an investment down the toilet."

"How do I stop it?" I asked, throwing myself back into my chair in frustration. "How do I identify these women before they get their hooks in me?"

He laughed. "One, don't blame them. They know what they want and they go for it. It's your fault if you fall for it." He shrugged in response to my glare. "Two, get a life outside that house, Graham. Seriously, where's Coop? You guys used to talk all the time and now you never even mention him. And also, for fuck's sake, redecorate that house or sell the damn thing. Nadia ruined it. Someone will want it, but it's definitely not you. And three, trust yourself. Trust what someone shows you about them the first time."

"But what if the first thing she shows me is an emotional tirade because she's going through something I know nothing about... yet."

He peered at me, as if working something out and then—

"Is this about the Meet-Poop Girl?"

"Jesus," I said, running a hand over my face. "Did everyone read that article? Can we not call her that?"

"I read all your articles, you know that! Do you know her name then? Have you two run into one another again?"

"I do. And yes we have. A few times."

"And?"

"And... I don't know. There's something about her. I assumed she was a brat after our first meeting."

"Understandable."

"And she didn't dispel my idea of her after our next couple of run-ins. But after the last one..." I shook my head. "I think she might not be what I thought she was. I may have misjudged her. And yet there's still the matter of her being famous."

"She's famous?"

I dropped my head into my hands.

"Yeah. Really famous. Millions of followers famous. Thousands of comments on a simple post on social media famous. Billboards and sides of buses and Times Square famous." I dragged my hands down my face. "People prying into her life, the scrutiny of the press, paparazzi famous."

"Ah."

After my experience with Nadia, who had been hungry for that kind of rabid attention, my father knew well what my tolerance levels were for that kind of crap.

"Sounds like a no-go then," he said.

"Yeah. Except..."

"Except what?"

I shook my head. "I don't know. Something."

"Well, Graham. Sometimes that's all you get. A little something that could turn into a big everything."

His words followed me around for the rest of my visit. From my friend Cooper, who I'd ghosted at the constant badgering of Nadia because she just didn't like him and I'd wanted the relationship with her to work, to his assessment of relationships and taking chances.

I ruminated over it all during Marley's birthday dinner, then at Flagstaff as I hiked and got inspired by the views, and then when picking my sister up from school again and treating her to a small shopping spree at the mall for some extra birthday gifts.

I was still turning my father's words over in my head on the plane ride home Saturday morning, and directed the cab driver to a route that would take us past Lior's house. As we drove by, I wondered if my poem had made her laugh. I realized then that I never would've written something that included the word "poo" to any of the women I'd been with in the past. They'd have found it "icky" and in poor taste. But Lior, despite being one of the world's most famous models, seemed like she might appreciate the terrible poem. And that right there was another little something to take note of.

CHAPTER 14

Lior

I slid into my favorite pair of worn-in sneakers – once again restored to their pre-poo glory thanks to Graham – and stepped out onto the stoop, breathing in the warm summer air. It was going to be a hot one today, which was why I'd hurried through my morning word games and cappuccino. I wanted to get my walk in before the heat turned from tolerable to melting-the-clothes-to-my-body hot. That way I'd have enough time to shower and cool down before my meeting with Daniela, the newest rising star designer in the fashion world. She'd touched base the evening before to let me know we'd be doing a fitting for several pieces she hoped would be used in the shoot that would be happening for Vogue.

It was a coup for her. Old hat for me at this point. I'd posed for Vogue more than my mother had now, which was a point of pride for me that didn't come without a little jealousy from her, as evidenced by the way she always changed the subject when any mention of the magazine or its famed president was mentioned.

Since arriving back home, I'd been admittedly, if not begrudgingly, bummed not to run into Graham. Not even a glimpse of him and his trusty sidekick had been spotted. I knew he still existed thanks to the clean shoe, the poem he'd left in it – which I'd framed and set in the bookcase of my living room, because a Graham Forrester original wasn't something to be hidden away – and of course his column in the Sunday paper this morning. But we hadn't bumped into each other again and I wondered if he was out of town? Or, worse, maybe something had happened to Brontë?

I'd practically ripped the paper apart this morning getting to his weekly article in hopes of some sort of clue about his whereabouts... but it was a charming piece on one of the local bakery owners. No word about Brontë. No hint at where he'd been the past few days. No suggestions to why I hadn't seen the two of them walking in the neighborhood.

At the bottom of the steps I took a left, as had become my new habit. I found it curious that Graham must have changed his route as well. I assumed to avoid me just like I'd done to avoid him. And yet, having both done the same – probably with the same intention – we had seen each other more often, if only from a distance. Well, except for the past few days.

Maybe he'd decided to go back to his old route.

Also, I found it unfair that he knew where I lived, but I had no idea where he resided. I wondered if I did, would I have the guts to walk by? And what would be my excuse to do so? I supposed I could always leave some form of 'Thank you' on his doorstep. But then he'd know I'd tracked him down, and maybe he didn't want to be found. At least not by me.

* * *

"Thank you for coming on a Sunday," Daniela said, letting me in through the back door of her workshop, which was conveniently located only a few blocks away from my house.

"Of course," I said, leaning in to hug the diminutive designer. "I'm excited to work with you. And see what you've got in store for the shoot."

"Lior!" a woman's voice said as I entered Daniela's sewing room.

I grinned at the familiar face of Risa Collins, the creative director for Vogue, and hurried over to give her a hug as well.

"I didn't know you'd be here too," I said.

Risa had the kind of instincts and intelligence that both awed and frightened me. Pair those things with an innate sense of style and the effortless way she conducted herself and she was a lethal combination several times over. Along with her boss, she could make or break a career. But despite her professional prowess, I always found myself at ease in her company.

Unlike Katya, who I knew was terrified of her.

"She's like a predator," she'd said to me once. "She makes you feel falsely at ease, and then goes for the carotid."

"Please stop watching the National Geographic channel," I'd responded. It was actually listed as her favorite channel on her bio and it wasn't a joke. I'd lost count of the number of times I'd had to ask her to stop telling me creepy creature facts while we were on a shoot. It was hard giving fuck-me eyes when she was going on and on about the sex lives of bean beetles.

"Daniela and I had lunch the other day," Risa said to me, smoothing a hand over her thick auburn hair, which was twisted into its signature sleek bun at the nape of her neck. "She mentioned you were doing a fitting today so I thought I'd drop in to see some of the designs – and you of course." Her voice lowered. "In case you have good Oliver Manning dirt to share."

I laughed. "I hate to disappoint but, other than him being exactly how the media has portrayed him over the years, I've got nothing. No dirt... no injuries by cane."

Her deep-throated chuckle filled the room.

"Dammit," she said, and then we both turned to survey the scene around us.

Daniela's workshop was a large space filled with gorgeous pastel fabrics, set against white-painted walls.

"I feel like I'm in a painting," I said, wandering carefully and running a hand over satins and silks and a crisp lavender cotton. "It's like walking through one of Monet's garden scenes."

The designer smiled and shrugged, looking around the room herself.

"I've always loved soft things," Daniela said. "Colors like these are calming. They bring me a sense of peace when the world around me feels like chaos."

"And then she adds something like this," Risa said, holding up a matte black shackle.

"I mean..." Daniela said, a glint in her eyes. "Who doesn't like a little calm with a hefty side of S&M?"

Risa nodded with a level of sincerity I wasn't prepared for.

"I am *into* it," she said.

I kept my mouth shut. To say anything would most likely bring us back to the subject of Oliver Manning, and that mediocre worm needed to be shoved back into his can, sealed, and tossed in a river. I'd never forgive myself for being so stupid.

"Okay," Daniela said, getting down to business and turning to me. "I have your measurements, but I'd like to do my own while I have you here, and then I'll have you try on the finished pieces so we can see how those fit. After that, I'll drape a few things on you and pin them. There are a couple designs I wanted to wait to sew until I saw how the fabric fell across your body, and I also just wanted to see the material hanging off you to see what it inspires. I have my mannequins but they don't move and sometimes what I thought was a good idea becomes an even better one when I see movement. Sound good?"

"Let's go," I said and pulled off my sweatshirt.

We spent the next several hours talking, laughing, and watching Daniela work her magic as she pulled straight pins from a pin cushion attached to a piece of elastic on her wrist and twisted fabrics, pinned them, re-pinned them, considered, and re-pinned again. All this while grabbing pieces of faux leather, latex, chains and more, and placing them carefully at my neck, waist, and wrists.

Risa ordered in food, as well as champagne, and what began as a fitting became an impromptu party. The usually buttoned-up, top-tier Vogue employee soon let her hair down – both literally and figuratively – her auburn waves now flowing down her back, blazer thrown haphazardly on the head of a mannequin, lipstick rubbed off. And while Daniela and I took minimalist sips from our glasses, Risa was on her second glass and barely picking at her plate of food. She'd become louder and more talkative as the day went on.

"Turn this way," Daniela said to me.

I was standing on a round, white riser in the corner of the room in front of a three-way mirror, a swath of iridescent white fabric folded and tucked around me, held in place at my neck by the large shackle Risa had found earlier, and at my wrists by two smaller versions.

"I'll take two of those," Risa said, taking a large gulp of champagne and then popping a bit of cheese in her mouth.

I caught Daniela's eye in the mirror, a move that wasn't missed by Vogue's creative director.

"I'm getting a divorce," she said. "He doesn't know it yet."

"Oh." My mouth formed a small circle as my brain raced to find something appropriate to say, Daniela furiously pinning, her lips pressed together as she worked. I prayed I didn't get poked in the midst of her frenzied avoidance tactic.

"I found out last night he's cheating on me," Risa continued.

"Oh Risa," I said. "I'm so sorry."

Daniela quit pinning, a look of defeat on her face. I assumed not because the gown didn't look divine – it was stunning – but because she now had to participate in this uncomfortable conversation.

"So if you could make me a shackle dress too," Risa said to Daniela. "Preferably with less material... maybe just a couple of strips here and here?" She gestured across her breasts and then her crotch.

Daniela's eyes again met mine in the mirror. This time we all laughed.

"What a dick," Daniela said, reaching for her glass. She downed the liquid and speared a ball of mozzarella. "Just tell me when your first date with someone good is and I'll make you something amazing."

I wasn't sure if Risa would remember our conversation that day and regret it, or be glad for it. We weren't her people, but sometimes those kinds of people were the best kind to have around when you needed to let loose. Maybe new friendships would form because of it. Maybe she'd get home later and bury her head in a pillow and scream, and then send Daniela and I gift baskets tomorrow with cards thanking us for being so discreet. To which we would read between the not-written lines "Say a fucking word and I'll end your career". Who knew? But for now, she was in a safe place and seemed to know it, and maybe that was good enough.

"My ex-husband and I had one of those rooms like in Fifty Shades," Daniela said, helping me out of the dress.

The room went still as both Risa and I stared at the petite blonde with her wide-set green eyes and faintly freckled nose.

"Well," Risa said. "That explains a lot."

She and I stared around the room at the designer's work.

"I suppose an outfit just doesn't feel complete to me without a touch of a bondage element," Daniela said.

"How come he's your ex?" Risa asked. "Sounds like a match made in heaven."

"Or in the Pleasure Chest," I said, naming the well-known Manhattan adult store.

"He said he grew a conscience." Daniela sighed. "And didn't want to spank his wife anymore."

I grabbed my own drink now and took a swig, trying to get the image of this spritely woman being spanked out of my head.

"Should we..." I pointed to a piece of material hanging on a rack.

"Oh! Yes," Daniela said, sliding her little pin cushion bracelet back on. "So what I'm thinking for this one is..."

Two hours later we were done, five new gowns pinned into shape ready for her sewing needle, me back in my clothes, Risa's hair pulled back into a loose ponytail.

"Thanks for letting me crash your party today, ladies," Risa said.

"It wouldn't have been a party without you," I said.

She turned to Daniela. "I'm really excited for what we have in mind for this shoot. We're doing something a little different and seeing the clothes today has confirmed that it's a brilliant idea."

"Can you tell us more?" I asked.

"We're going with a storytelling theme. Daniela's designs bring to mind fairytales. They're lightness and darkness. Good versus evil. The innocent and the villain. The seductress and her prey." She paused and gave us a wink. "Her pieces tell stories, and there's a juxtaposition within each one. We're going to do a play on that by pairing each piece with actual literature. A line of poetry. A quote from a famous novel. A lyric from a song... And all by female artists. The words will scroll across the page while the models..." she looked to me, "...show off the clothing."

"That sounds amazing," Daniela said, her eyes lighting up.

"I love it," I said.

"The best part is," Risa said. "We're trying to get an actual writer to play against you as your sexy adversary."

A pit opened in my stomach.

"Oh really?" I asked, my voice faint.

"Yes!" Her excitement echoed off the small lobby of Daniela's workshop. "We have a few names in mind but one definite favorite."

"And who is that?" I asked.

But I knew before the name passed through her lips.

"Graham Forrester!"

CHAPTER 15

Graham

"Come on, B," I said, coaxing my sweet girl from her bed. "You can do it."

For the past four days it had taken a monumental effort to get her up and out of the house for our morning walks. Part of me thought maybe I was being cruel. Maybe she just didn't want to. Maybe she couldn't. But once she was up, she'd give that two-thump wag against my leg and look up at me with those big brown eyes, a spark of the younger gal I'd known still inside.

It had been hard being patient. By leaving later, I knew we were missing our opportunity to cross paths with Lior, whom I assumed was back in town because her social media page hadn't been updated with new photos of her and her friend Addie in days. Either that or she was on a job somewhere. I imagined her on a beach in Ibiza. Maybe Costa Rica... in that red thong.

"Seriously, dude," I said to myself. "Knock it off."

But since our shared cab ride the previous week, I couldn't stop picturing her wet hair, water streaming from the dark strands down her arms and collar bones. Her black satin tank pressed against her breasts, leaving little to the imagination.

"Fuck," I whispered, running a hand through my hair and staring down at Brontë who was now looking up at me with concern. "Sorry girl. My brain is having untoward thoughts. Let's go."

It was an hour later than we usually left, and as had happened the past few days, I was tempted to walk by Lior's house. But it felt a little stalker-ish, and so instead we loped along at a leisurely pace and stopped at Mornin' Joe's for a visit with the man himself, a cappuccino and cardamom bun for me, and homemade doggie treats for B.

"How are my two favorite customers today?" Joe asked, pulling out the metal bistro chair across from me and taking a seat.

"It's taking us a while to get going this morning," I said.

He reached down to pet Brontë. "Nothing wrong with that, right girl?"

She gave a thwack of her tail and closed her eyes.

Joe smiled, gave her a last pat, and turned to me. "How's the book? Making it shine?"

I grinned. He forgot nothing of our previous conversations.

"Not yet," I said. "Still have to finish it. Then I'll at least try to make it sound not quite so rudimentary, so my editor won't think I'm completely daft."

"I'll never believe you don't write anything but glorious first drafts, my friend."

"You are very generous, Joe."

"You tip well."

I laughed.

"Want a hot tip for your next article?" he asked.

"Always."

He pointed. "A couple blocks down that way, take a right, and a few houses down there's a gorgeous hollowed-out tree trunk the owner had made into a free little library. I even glimpsed one of your books in there."

I pressed a hand to my chest. "Only one?"

"Shameful, I know. But maybe they treasure the others."

"Well now I need to know which one they didn't like enough to keep."

Joe laughed. "And there's your story. The One They Didn't Keep."

Brontë and I made sure to pass by the woodland creation on our way home. It was a perfect way to make use of the old tree, and felt very storybook-like with its strand of tiny fairy lights and small selection of books tucked within. I noted with a grin that my book was no longer there, took a few pictures with my phone, memorized the location, and decided the free little libraries in the area definitely needed to be recognized. I couldn't wait to hear how I was going to owe Joe for this particular tip.

An hour later I was at my laptop, deep into a new chapter. When the timer went off, I saved my file, shut the laptop, gave Brontë a treat, refilled her water bowl, and took the stairs two at a time, hurrying upstairs for a quick workout followed by a shower.

Having hit my word count for the day, I spent the rest of the afternoon doing chores, paying bills, and perusing the internet for homes for sale in the area, as well as homes for sale in Seattle where Marley would be attending college. I then checked to see if Lior had posted anything new.

"Where is she?" I whined aloud. Brontë's ears perked and she glanced up at me. "Do you know?" I leaned down and petted her head, staring into her age-fogged eyes.

If she did know, she wasn't saying.

Bored, I opened my work in progress again, but my heart wasn't in it. I was distracted, thoughts of Lior and that damn slinky black tank from our moment in the rain filling my mind again. The way the raindrops clung to her eyelashes and lips. I felt myself going hard and exhaled.

"Well, at least I know I'm not completely dead inside," I muttered and pushed back from the table.

Nothing could wilt a promising erection like walking through the stark, cold home you'd shared with your now ex-wife. So that's what I did for the next half hour.

I meandered from room to room, staring at the empty walls, angular, uncomfortable furniture, and the mostly empty side of her closet – save for a box of stuff she'd left behind and had never come back for. I lifted off the lid now and reeled at the image that greeted me. I'd forgotten I'd thrown a framed wedding photo of us inside. I picked it up and looked at what was beneath it. Trinkets that had sat on top of her dresser, makeup, a hairbrush, a pair of slippers, and some other odds and ends.

"Screw it," I said, heaving the box into my arms. "To the trash you go."

I had just dropped these last remnants of my marriage into the outside bin when my phone began to ring.

Francesca, my agent. My spirits lifted. She only ever called if it was good news.

"Hey, Fran. What's up?" I said, walking back into the house feeling a little bit lighter.

"You have dinner plans this evening?" she asked.

"Just hanging with Brontë. Might crack open a can of chili."

"That is the most depressing thing I've ever heard."

"And it's a lie. I only have cans of tuna and dog food."

She made a sound like she was vomiting.

"Think Brontë can manage without you for a few hours?" she asked when she was done heaving. "I've had an interesting call and want to discuss it with you."

"That's it?" I asked, laughing. "That's all you're gonna give me?"

"You know I like to be mysterious."

"I do. Fine. Yeah, I'm free," I said. "Where and what time?"

"Nobu? Seven o'clock?"

"I'll be there."

I was, in fact, three minutes early. Francesca though, was

known for arriving at least fifteen minutes early for anything, so I found her at a table by the window, doing something on her phone while sipping a cocktail, a plate of edamame in front of her.

"Hey!" she said, her face brightening as I approached the table. She set her phone down and looked guiltily at her drink and food. "Sorry. Was in meetings all day and missed lunch. Couldn't wait."

"You always miss lunch," I said, kissing her cheek before taking a seat and stealing a piece of her appetizer. "And I don't mind."

"How's the book coming along?"

"Nearly done."

"And?"

I grinned. "I'm loving it."

"That means it's going to be a bestseller."

"You always say that."

"Have I ever been wrong?" She raised a perfectly arched eyebrow and I laughed.

There was something about Francesca that had intrigued me from our first meeting at a writer's conference over a decade ago. She had an air of mystery about her. A hint of the diabolical. And a fashion style not many could pull off. Case in point, she was wearing a bright red blouse with the largest collar I'd ever seen, but on her it somehow looked natural. Maybe it was because the rest of her was dramatic as well, from her raven black hair pulled back into a high ponytail, wide blue eyes behind cat-eye, purple-framed glasses, and full lips that were always painted so dark I often wondered if she was actually a vampire.

"So?" I said, smiling and resting my elbows on the table. "What was this interesting call you had?"

"Hang on," she said and signaled to the waiter. "What are you having?" She pointed to her cocktail.

"I'll have the amber ale," I told the waiter, who nodded and hurried away. I turned back to Fran who was now grinning like the Cheshire Cat. "Uh oh."

"No uh-oh," she said. "This is... unprecedented." She tilted her head and narrowed her eyes. "Except, maybe not."

I leaned back in my seat and crossed my arms over my chest, peering at her... waiting.

"What do you think about doing a photo shoot for Vogue," she said.

The noise in the restaurant turned into white noise as I processed what I thought I'd just heard her say.

"I'm sorry?"

"Risa Collins, the creative director at Vogue, called me and asked what you might say to being part of a campaign."

"For Vogue?"

"Yes."

"Magazine?"

"Yes."

"I... what?"

She laughed and leaned forward, popping a piece of edamame in her mouth and then offering the plate to me, but I shook my head, still trying to work out what was happening.

"They're featuring a new designer," she said. "And apparently the clothing has a fairytale-like quality to it. They thought it would be a cool idea to do a literary themed shoot and, instead of using one of their usual models, they'd bring in an actual author. Specifically you."

"Why me?"

She cleared her throat and gave me a look.

"I'm sorry Graham, but have you seen you? You're not exactly hard to look at."

I felt my face warm and shrugged. I had never been comfortable with compliments unless it was about my work.

"You're adorable," she said, grinning even wider than before now. "They also want you to write a piece for the magazine. Subject matter to be discussed." Her phone buzzed with a text message and she shot me an apologetic smile as she picked it up, her eyes scanning quickly, and then began texting back.

I took in a breath, held it, and let it out slowly, still trying to wrap my head around the whole thing. My beer was delivered and I took a long sip, my eyes raising to the window behind Fran. It was dark outside, making the window more of a mirror, which was why I was able to perfectly see the hostess leading a couple past us to another table.

I recognized the man as the guitar player for one of the hottest bands in the world right now.

His date was Lior.

"Graham?" Fran said, putting her phone back down on the table. I blinked and set my glass down a little too hard, the liquid sloshing over the side.

"Shit," I said, mopping it up with my napkin. "Sorry. Um..." I glanced in the window again and could see Lior and her date had been seated several tables away from us. "Uh..." I ran a hand through my hair, trying to remember what we were talking about. "How did this come about?"

"I don't know. Does it matter? It's Vogue. Think of the exposure!"

I was, and it wasn't exactly that thrilling to be honest. Being married to Nadia had subjected me to the media in ways I'd never fathomed and hadn't enjoyed. Our divorce had lessened all that exponentially – after the initial circus – and I'd been happy to return to the normal-sized and oh-so-temporary attention I got when a new novel came out.

But this was Vogue. And exposure could mean a few things.

"I'm not going to actually *be* exposed, am I?" I asked, trying not to show any panic.

Fran laughed at the idea and I didn't know whether to be offended or relieved.

"Look, I'm sure they won't have you show anything you're not comfortable with. Or will at least place a book in front of...it."

I glared at her.

"Definitely trade sized, not mass market. Hard cover, if needed."

"Fran!?"

"I'm kidding," she said, laughing. "Maybe. Truly though. It's an amazing opportunity."

"It is but... I don't know. I don't want to be standing there posing all by myself. That seems weird and uncomfortable. I'm not a model."

"Oh, you won't be alone. The designer they're featuring makes women's clothing, so you'll be paired with a female model. You'll be the antagonist to her protagonist. And vice versa."

"Huh," I said, picking up my glass again, the wheels in my brain starting to spin. "Well that's not so bad I guess. I like the idea of it, at least. Any idea who the female model is?"

"No idea," she said, glancing at her phone again and beginning to type. "But it's going to be a huge spread, from what I've been told, so probably someone famous. Ooh! Maybe it will be Lior Flynn! Can you imagine? Get me an autograph if it is."

I nearly dropped my entire glass in my lap. Clearly Fran hadn't noticed Lior was actually in the restaurant right now.

I glanced in the window, looking for her reflection in the glass. I wondered if she'd heard anything about this Vogue idea and, if so, if she knew they were asking me to be involved.

Fran and I ordered food and our conversation moved to other topics. We chatted about my next book ideas, her upcoming vacation to Italy, and my trip to Colorado for my sister's graduation, all while passing plates of sushi back and forth and me trying to get glimpses of Lior in the window again. She and her date were seated four tables away from us and I managed twice to see her face in the reflection, noting with some sort of strange satisfaction that she didn't look particularly enthralled by her date.

Satisfied because I didn't want her to be happy? Or satisfied because I didn't want her to be having a good time with him? I wasn't sure, but when she discreetly yawned behind her napkin I nearly laughed with relief.

Fran paid the bill and we sat for a while more, finishing our drinks as she brought the conversation back around to the reason we were here in the first place.

"So what do you think?" she asked.

"I don't know. It feels... weird? I'm used to sitting in front of a laptop in my underwear writing fictional characters who do way more interesting things than me. This photo shoot... it's something I'd write about, not something I'd do. Truly, Fran, I'm an author, not a model."

"So? Why can't you be both for a day? There are people in the world that do more than one job."

"You know what I mean. I have no aspirations to be featured in photos in a fancy magazine. That kind of attention feels weird. And after Nadia..."

Fran made a face. She'd never been a fan of my ex-wife and hadn't disguised it well when we were together.

"I know you're scarred from all that," she said. "But Nadia was... something else. She was The National Enquirer. This is Vogue."

I snorted laughter.

"Also... the opportunity for even more sales would thrill your publisher."

"Obviously," I said. "But... what will people say?"

"Out of jealousy, they'll say you want attention. You're banking on your looks. Selling out, using..."

I held up a hand. "Thanks. I think I've got the picture."

"Look. Who cares what people say? It's fucking Vogue, Graham."

She wasn't wrong. Vogue was huge. And they wanted me to write an article for them as well, something I'd never had the opportunity to do. It would be another notch in my wood-framed glasses.

"Okay," I said.

"Okay?" Fran asked. "As in yes?"

"Fine. Yes."

She gave a quiet little whoop and then ordered another round of drinks.

A half hour later, after a last look toward Lior's table, I exited the restaurant with Fran. We said goodbye on the sidewalk and, as her cab drove away, I turned and headed a few blocks up to The Bar Room for another beer before going home.

It was just after nine and the place was relatively quiet. I took a seat at the far end of the dark wood bar and smiled at the bartender pouring a beer.

"Graham," he said with a nod, setting the drink on a tray. Wiping his hands on a towel, he headed toward me. "How are things? You want your usual?"

"Heya Cole. Yes, please."

"You got it." He grabbed a glass from the shelf behind him and headed back to pour my drink. "I haven't seen you in a while. You deep in another book?"

He strode back, tossed a coaster on the bar in front of me, and set the lager down.

"I am," I said, taking a sip. "How have things been here?"

Whenever I was in-between books, I found myself frequenting Manhattan more often, wandering the parks and shops, cafes and bars. Looking for inspiration in the sounds and sights and smells. This was how I'd found The Bar Room and Cole one rainy Tuesday evening. Only three other people had been here at the time. I'd sat in the same place I was now, and we'd ended up talking about everything from beer to books to Brontë.

After a brief conversation about his trip to the Bahamas – and me updating him on B – he left me to take a drink order from a couple that had just come in.

I took my phone out of my pocket and saw I'd missed twelve messages, all from Marley, who was once again asking if I'd be coming to her graduation. Followed by threats if I didn't. Followed by pleading eyes emojis. Followed by, "Peace out, bro."

I chuckled and shook my head as someone walked past me, stopped, and then moved to stand beside me.

"Well," a woman's voice said. "Fancy meeting you here."

I looked up and found myself staring into a pair of familiar golden-brown eyes.

CHAPTER 16

Lior

Graham Forrester stared back at me and I held his gaze a moment too long, distracted by the flecks of gray I'd never before noticed in his blue eyes.

He was wearing a fitted charcoal tee and black jeans that looked soft to the touch and molded to his thighs in such a way that it took a concerted effort not to reach out and run my hand down one of them. He broke eye contact, glanced around in confusion, and then met my gaze again, a cautious smile on his face.

"Where's your date?" he asked.

"What date?" I asked.

"I was at Nobu."

I scrunched my nose, caught, but not wanting to discuss my date.

"I didn't think you saw me," I admitted, leaning on the bar.

"You walked behind me on your way to your table. I saw you in the reflection of the window."

"Well then."

We stared at one another, the seconds ticking by as the air between us grew warm with tension, something deep inside me tightening with anticipation. Of what though? A little more verbal sparring? Or something else. It didn't feel contentious. It felt more—

Shit. I was staring at his mouth.

I cleared my throat. "What happened to *your* date?" I asked, tearing my eyes from his lips and glancing toward the hallway that led to the bathroom, as if she might walk out at any moment. But there was no drink waiting for her on the bar. No jacket on the seat beside him.

"I believe I asked you first," he said, one side of his mouth lifting charmingly.

What the hell was happening and why had my heartbeat just quickened? Traitor.

"I bailed."

"You bailed on Caleb Malone? World-famous rock god, sex god, guitar player?"

"Do you think it says that in his bio?" I asked and he laughed.

"I think I'll be disappointed if it doesn't."

I grinned and turned my attention to the approaching bartender.

"Hey Cole," I said.

"Miss Flynn," he said. "Your usual?"

"Yes, please."

He gave me a nod and began pulling bottles from different shelves while I looked back at Graham.

"Yes. I bailed on Caleb Malone. Somehow he managed to be boring and obnoxious all at once."

"Damn. And here I was thinking we authors had cornered the market on boring and obnoxious."

"Hate to break it to you, but it might be an all-artist trait."

He shook his head in faux disappointment and asked, "Tell me more?"

I laughed and shrugged. Why not. Addie was having dinner with her folks tonight, and Katya was in Australia for a job. It would be nice to rehash the evening. Even if it was with Graham Forrester.

"Well," I said. "He went on and on about the band's upcoming tour, his killer riffs, the diet and workouts he'd been doing to prepare..." I rolled my eyes. "He picked me up, cut off my hello, and never stopped talking the entire time. He even interrupted my dinner order to comment on my choice of protein and why he hasn't consumed it for the past three months."

"Maybe he was nervous and trying to impress you."

"Pretty sure that wasn't it."

"How do you know?"

I peered at him, wondering if he was friend or foe. We'd had a nice moment in the cab the week before. And then there was the shoe and the poem...

"Well," I said. "In between bites of his salad he told me we'd have to fuck slow later because he was trying to conserve energy."

Graham's mouth hung slack for a moment. I tried not to laugh as I turned toward Cole, who was delivering a shimmering white cocktail with a swirl of lemon peel. It matched my white dress and bright yellow, faux leather obi belt.

"It's gorgeous," I said and took a sip. "You've outdone yourself, my friend."

He tipped an imaginary hat and moved back down the bar.

"What is it?" Graham asked, pointing to the drink.

"I've no idea."

"I thought it was your usual."

"My usual is whatever Cole feels like making me. I don't think he's ever served me the same drink twice." I took another sip and looked back to Graham. "So? No response to Caleb Malone's version of romantic first date banter?"

"I think I'm speechless."

"I was too. And then I excused myself and went out the back door."

"I can't say I blame you." He paused, a frown creasing his brow as though trying to make a decision, and then gestured to the stool beside him. "Do you want to sit."

I glanced over my shoulder. The bar was still empty, but I knew it wouldn't be for long.

"For a minute," I said, sliding onto the stool. I took another sip of my drink and then turned toward him so that my back was to the rest of the room. "And now it's your turn to tell me why you're here alone and not with your date." I said, looking at him expectantly.

"That wasn't a date. That was a meeting with my agent, Francesca."

"That's your agent? Damn. She's gorgeous."

"She is."

"No... extracurricular activities happening there?"

"She's a lesbian."

"Welp. Bummer for you."

"Not really, since she's my agent. It's in my contract that I'm obligated to give her 15% and *nothing else.*" He took a sip of his drink.

"But 15% of *what?*" I asked and he snorted, covering his mouth.

"That was close," he said.

I laughed. "Sorry. Anyways, yeah. I suppose a relationship between agent and author could get messy."

"Very. Though I do know one couple it worked out for."

"There's always one and they always make it look easy."

An easy silence fell between us as we sipped our drinks and watched the room through the reflection of the mirror across from us.

I wanted to ask about the Vogue shoot. If he'd been asked. If he'd said yes. But part of me didn't want to know. What if he had been asked, told he'd been working with me, and had said no? Or, what if they'd decided not to go with him after all? My asking would probably just make him feel bad.

"So," I said.

"So."

"I owe you a thank you."

"Oh yeah? For what?"

"My shoe."

He grinned and my stomach did a jazzy little dance.

"It was the least I could do."

"And yet, you wrote me a poem as well."

"That was all Brontë."

I smiled. "She's a talent. You'll thank her for me?"

"Of course."

A burst of voices filled the bar and I sucked in a breath, glancing in the mirror to see a group of at least a dozen people filtering in.

"Shit," I said, starting to slide from my stool. "I should probably go."

"They haven't seen you."

I chewed the inside of my lip, watching him. Was that his way of saying he wanted me to stay?

"Maybe just one more drink," I said, catching Cole's eye and tapping the rim of my nearly empty glass. He nodded and pulled down a glass exactly like the one he'd served me in the first time.

"I'll give you a head's up if anyone comes this way," Graham said.

"Thank you. I'm really not in the mood to deal with people. They can be so disrespectful of my personal life." I held up a hand. "And I know – it comes with the territory. But that doesn't mean it's fun."

He stared at me for a long moment and I figured he must think I was full of shit. I really wasn't in the mood for that either. Sighing, I slid from the stool and reached for my purse.

"What are you doing?" he asked, frowning.

"I really should just go."

"Lior."

My name on his lips did something to me and I paused.

"Stay?" he asked.

I stared at him for a long moment, and then settled back onto my stool.

Making good on his word, he warned me every time someone headed in our direction so I could lower my head, letting my hair fall like a curtain in front of my face. Meanwhile, we drank, our wariness toward one another wavering as we batted silly questions back-and-forth.

"All-time favorite movie?" I asked.

"Ooh. That's hard. Can it be in a certain genre?"

"Nope."

He propped his elbows on the bar and put his face in his hands. A moment later he popped back up.

"The correct answer is Aliens."

"Good call," I said. "Too bad they ruined that storyline with the third film."

"Absolute travesty. Now you. What's yours?"

I swirled the lemon peel around the edge of my drink.

"You know, I've answered this question so many times over the years for interviews, but every time I'm asked, I still have to think for a minute, just in case another movie has knocked it from its spot."

He tapped his watch. "You're stalling."

"I didn't know it was a timed answer! Pride and Prejudice? No. The Matrix! No. Pride and Prejudice!"

"Which is it, Flynn?"

I snort-laughed and then hiccuped, covering my mouth with my hand, my head light from the two and a half drinks I'd had. So much for moderation.

"Pride and Prejudice."

"The hand flex?"

"It's sooo dreamy..." I leaned my head on my hand and stared blurrily off into the distance. "Though Keanu Reeves saying 'I know Kung Fu' is fun as fuck."

"Cheers to that." Graham clinked his beer glass to my coupe. "Hey. Heads up."

I tilted my head forward, letting my hair fall forward again while he pretended to be very interested in the drink menu Cole had left for us to use as a shield.

"She's gone," Graham whispered.

I tucked a lock of hair behind my ear and set my glass down, watching the shimmer Cole had added swirl around the bottom.

"This was... fun," I said.

"You look confused," he said and I laughed.

"I guess I am."

"Or maybe just drunk."

"There is a high probability of that too." And before I knew what I was saying (thanks, alcohol) I started talking about my morning. "This is actually the second time I had drinks today."

"I know."

"You know?"

"I saw your glass of wine at dinner."

"Oh damn. Make that three times then."

"Life of a world-famous fashion model, huh?"

I rolled my eyes. "Hardly. No. I had a fitting this morning and champagne was brought in."

"Brought in." He made air quotes. "That's fancy world-famous fashion model talk if I've ever heard it. Which... I haven't actually. Continue, please."

I smacked him lightly on the arm, thrilling in the warmth of his skin on my fingertips (Jesus, I was drunk) and continued.

"As I was saying," I said, slurring a little. "We had champagne. Ordered by..." I paused for effect. "The *creative director* of *Vogue Magazine.*"

His cheeks colored and I pointed gleefully at him.

"It's you, isn't it?"

"And, assuming we're talking about the same thing... it's you?"

For a long moment his eyes stayed locked on mine, my chest rising and falling, a delicious tightening happening deep within my center.

"Hey, Miss?" I heard Cole say loudly, interrupting the moment. "Respect people's privacy, yeah?"

"Sorry," a woman said, scampering away, her phone in her hand.

"And that's my cue," I said, reaching for my purse.

"I've got it," Graham said, taking out his wallet and handing Cole his card.

"I think I got her before she took a picture," Cole said. "Sorry she got past me though. Slipped by while I was serving someone else."

"Not your fault, Cole," Graham said. "I was supposed to be on watch."

"It's fine," I said. "But I need to get out of here now. Can I use the back door?"

"You know you don't even need to ask," Cole said.

"Share a cab?" Graham asked.

"Deal," I said, and led the way to the back door.

"Well, here we are again," I said as the cab he'd hailed sped toward Brooklyn.

"We seem to be forming a habit."

But I didn't respond, my mind somewhere else.

"You okay?" Graham asked.

I felt my eyes well and looked out the window, embarrassed.

"Lior?"

"I'm fine. I'm just so tired of it," I said, my voice soft. "Imagine if she'd gotten the shot. The media would've had a field day."

"Why?"

I turned to look at him in the dark, the little screen on the back of the seat in front of him flashing strange shapes across his chin and throat.

"Two guys in one night. That's what they'd print. First Caleb. Then you." I closed my eyes and leaned my head back. "I'm sorry in advance, in case anyone else figured out who we were and got a picture from afar."

"You don't have to apologize to me because other people suck. Besides, I'm the one that failed you. So, I'm the one that's sorry."

"It's not your job to protect me. I know better. I just..."

"You just what?"

"I was having a nice time."

"Me too." His expression turned serious then and he seemed to shrink away from me just the slightest bit, but enough for me to notice.

"So," I said brightly, changing the subject. "Vogue. Are you really going to do it?"

"Despite myself, I have agreed to do it. When did you find out?"

"I didn't really. Risa, the creative director, mentioned this morning that there were a few contenders, but you were the top get. I assumed you'd been asked and when you blushed well..."

"Damn my modesty," he said and we both laughed. "Is it going to be awful?"

"The shoot?"

"Yeah."

"They'll treat you like royalty."

"I won't have to be naked at any point, will I?"

The cab pulled up to my house and I opened the door and started to get out, a sly grin on my face.

"Lior." He caught my wrist, his tone pleading.

"Probably only a little naked," I said, slipping my arm from his grip and shutting the door behind me.

"Hey!"

I turned to see he'd rolled down the window.

"Yes?"

"Any chance you'll be in Seattle again soon?"

I gave him a quizzical look. "I'll be there next weekend, why?"

"Me too."

I walked back to the car. "Oh yeah?"

"My younger sister got into the University of Washington. I promised to help her move in."

"U Dub."

"What?"

"We call it U Dub."

"U Dub," he repeated with a nod. "Noted. Do you think… Would you maybe want to meet us for lunch Saturday or Sunday?"

I stared at him, chewing my lower lip as I considered the idea.

"I think I would," I said, nodding slowly.

"Yeah?"

"Sure," I said. "Addie's working Saturday so I'll have that day free."

"Perfect. I'm helping Marley move in that morning. We could meet after?"

"Sounds good."

There was only the streetlight several feet away for light so I couldn't be sure, but I was pretty sure he blushed when he asked if he could have my phone number.

I bounded up the stairs to my room a few minutes later, dialing Addie as I went.

"I just had drinks with GRAHAM FREAKING FORRESTER!" I shouted into the receiver as soon as she answered.

"Wait," she said. "Didn't you call me four hours ago telling me you had a date with Caleb freaking Malone?"

"I did."

"And… what happened to that?"

"He's a tool and I bailed. Hang on."

I put her on speaker, unzipped my dress, and grabbed hold of the hem, pulling upwards. But instead of slipping off over my head, it got stuck at my shoulders and I was trapped.

"Oh my god," I said, my voice muffled in the fabric as I twisted back and forth, trying to get the frock to move.

"Li?" I heard Addie say.

"I'm stuck in my dress!" Panic filled my voice. "Addie! I can't get it off! It's—"

"It is not trying to strangle you." Her own voice had taken on the soothing tone she used on her animal patients. "You are not going to be stuck in the dress forever. You will not die there."

"Stop talking to me like I'm a feral cat!"

I was thrashing around now, twisting and pulling, my nude-thonged ass exposed, my arms pinned to the side of my head, hands getting tired from pulling.

"Lior..." I could barely hear Addie now thanks to my arms pressing against my ears. "What is happening?"

"I can't get out of my dress and I can't remember if my curtains are open!"

"Okay. We've been here before. It wouldn't be the first time you've flashed your neighbors. Stop panicking and take a breath."

I did as she said, arms raised above my head, shoulders wedged sufficiently against fabric that had little to no give.

"What if I die like this?" I asked, my lips brushing the white fabric covering my face. "What if I'm found dead with my ass hanging out."

"Nothing to be embarrassed about. You happen to have a nice ass. I've always been jealous."

"Addie!"

"Right. Ready to try again?" she asked.

I took in a deep breath and let it out.

"Yes," I said my voice small.

"Nice and easy," Addie said. "Relax your shoulders and—"

I grabbed two fistfuls of fabric and tugged, bending at the waist as I did. There was a ferocious sounding rip and suddenly I was free.

"I'm out!" I shouted gleefully, dropping the dress unceremoniously onto the bed.

"What was that sound, Lior."

"Um…" I glanced at the pile of fabric and wrinkled my nose. "I might've ripped the dress."

"Please tell me it wasn't a nice dress."

"I mean… it wasn't a *not* nice dress."

"And the label on that dress?"

I winced and stared down at the pretty label staring back at me.

"It may or may not start with a C."

"Jesus. Did you just tear a Chanel?"

"It was from Costco."

She snorted and I grinned and collapsed on my bed.

"You're an abomination to the fashion world, Lior Flynn. Now, are the curtains open and tell me about your date with Graham Forrester."

I spun around, having forgot about the curtains, and was relieved to see they were closed.

"Curtains are closed and it wasn't a date," I reported. "We found ourselves at the same bar and sat together."

"And?"

"And… it was fun."

"And?"

"He's nice."

Addie was quiet.

"Ads?" I said, checking to make sure the connection was still good.

"Did you just call me to simply tell me that Graham Forrester is fun and nice?"

"I did."

"Not that you made out or touched his red rocket or fell in love?"

"Addie!"

"What?"

I could hear her trying to muffle her laughter.

"I really hope you don't call it that to the men you date," I said.

"I absolutely do."

"Oh yeah?" Now I was laughing. "Tell me. Tell me how you say it."

But she was laughing too hard now to get out any words.

"Veterinarians are twisted little souls," I said. "I always knew it."

"We have to have some comic relief," she said. 'You have no idea the things we have to deal with."

"I do know. Because unfortunately you tell me."

"I like to share my life with you."

"Share less."

"Okay but seriously," she said. "Did anything happen?"

"No. It was just a nice time, until someone tried to get a drive-by photo."

"Jerks."

I yawned then and hauled myself up to a sitting position.

"I should get to bed," I said. "I drank more than I do in a month today and I'm gonna be hurting tomorrow. Also, Graham invited me to lunch when I'm in Seattle next weekend because he's going to be there too."

I hung up while she was still shouting "WHAT?"

CHAPTER 17

Graham

"Tell me," Marley said, blue eyes glaring at me over the heart art in the foam of her caramel latte.

We were sipping iced coffees in the front window of the Ugly Mug Café, a cute little place with butter-yellow walls, exposed brick, and mismatched tables and chairs. It had been recommended by Lior when I'd texted her the day before to set up a meeting place, though I hadn't told Marley that. She was going to flip when she realized what I had in store for her this afternoon. All I'd told her and the folks, who had driven across four states with my younger sister to move her into her new dorm room, was that she and I were going to have lunch and explore the area around the college a little.

"Without the old folks," I'd added, making Marley giggle while my stepmom Lisa punched me in the arm and our dad chuckled.

When we'd arrived at the coffee shop, I'd told her I had a bit of a surprise – a friend would be joining us.

"I thought you liked surprises," I said now, glancing out the window.

"I do. Unless it's some horrible woman you think you're in

love with because, let me tell you big brother, you are fired from making your own love matches. From now on, I'm in charge."

I rolled my eyes, though I was tempted to tell her that was fine with me because I clearly had no idea what I was doing, But I didn't want to encourage her. And while I found Lior intriguing with her combination of wit and beauty, I was wary of the fact that she was both very likeable... and very famous.

"I promise I'm not in love."

"But it is a woman?"

"We're just friends. Sort of."

Her eyes widened and I held up a hand.

"We are barely friends. More like acquaintances. She just happens to be in town this weekend and she's from Seattle and went to U Dub so I asked if she could show us around a little bit."

The eyes went back to glaring. She'd be scary if she wasn't so short, so pretty, and wasn't dressed in a cropped purple t-shirt with a shimmering gold W.

A flash of yellow out the window caught my eye and there was Lior, hurrying across the street in a yellow t-shirt, baggy jeans, a white ball cap covering her chestnut hair, sunglasses, and white sneakers on her feet. She was the epitome of an easy summer's day. And my fucking heart sped up.

For fuck's sake, traitor. Control yourself.

But as the bell on the door to the cafe jingled, I had a strong wave of regret. What had I been thinking? She was Lior Flynn. Had I just invited chaos into my sister's life? Was her picture going to be everywhere tomorrow?

To my relief though, the few other people in the coffee shop looked up when she walked in and then went back to what they were doing. Maybe out of context, in a place not expected, wearing clothes that practically mirrored Marley's, she was as invisible as the rest of us.

A smile spread across my face and Marley caught me, rolling

her eyes before turning to take in the vision that was heading toward us.

"Holy f—"

"Watch it," I said quickly. I usually let her swear when the parents weren't around to hear, but I tried to keep it to a minimum.

"—frankincense," she finished in a loud whisper. "That looks like...*oh my god she's coming over here!*"

She turned back to look at me, her eyes now so wide I wondered if they might fall out of her head.

"I know," I whispered. "Be cool."

"Hey," Lior said, smiling first at me, then at Marley.

"Hey," I said, standing to... what? Was I going to hug her? Kiss her cheek? Shake her hand? Where were we in this sort of friendship?

She answered the question for me by leaning in and giving me a one-armed hug before turning back to my sister who was frozen in her seat. Which, I didn't mind saying, was pretty gratifying. She never thought I was cool and now she knew that I knew a famous fashion model. That I, in fact, knew *the* famous fashion model.

"You're..." Marley said but didn't finish her sentence.

"You must be Marley," Lior held out a hand. "I'm Lior. It's really nice to meet you and I *love* your outfit. Thanks for letting me hang out with you guys today."

Marley's mouth finally shut and a hand moved as if in slow motion toward Lior's. The two women shook hands and then Lior pointed to the seat I'd been sitting in and I nodded, sliding over on the bench and laughing at Marley's hand that was still outstretched.

"It's going to be so fun reminding you how uncool you were in this moment," I said.

"Graham!" Lior said, elbowing me as Marley sank onto the bench across from us. "Be nice. Marley, ignore him. I've had this exact moment a few times myself. And truly, it's very flattering that you know who I am, and seem kind of... I don't know. Excited to meet me too?"

My sister took a breath, her hand now tucked under her thigh, and gave an embarrassed smile.

"Can we pretend that didn't happen and start again?" Marley asked.

"Absolutely," Lior said. "How would you like it to go?"

They ran through a couple of scenarios and then Lior went outside and came back in, pretending to see us for the first time, giving me another hug (she smelled like heaven, the scent so subtle it almost wasn't there), and turning to Marley who shook her hand this time as if she wasn't completely and ridiculously overwhelmed by the moment and the woman.

"Forevermore, that's the version I'll tell of our first meeting," Lior said.

Marley blushed with happiness and took a sip of her coffee. If Lior saw that her hand was trembling, she was kind enough not to say.

"What can I get you?" I asked her.

"No, let me," Marley said, getting to her feet. I had to fight hard not to laugh. She was having a moment but I would not risk Lior's wrath.

Lior leaned forward, her voice lowered. "Wouldn't it be so much cooler to tell your friends that Lior Flynn bought *you* something?"

This seemed to stump Marley.

"Here," Lior said, pulling a credit card from her wallet. "If you don't mind grabbing me whatever you're having, and anything else you might want, I'm going to sit here for a minute and talk to your brother about the job we have coming up."

"You have a job with him?"

Lior looked to me and I shrugged.

"You didn't tell her?" she asked.

"I thought it might be more fun if you did," I said. "Plus, she probably wouldn't believe me."

Lior turned back to Marley. "How about you get the coffee and then we'll tell you all about it while we explore. And then I want to hear about your dorm, your roommate, what classes you're taking, and what professors you have."

"Deal!" Marley said and hurried off, Lior's credit card clutched in her hand.

"She's like eighteen going on eight right now," I said, watching my sister stare down at Lior's card like it was the most precious thing she'd ever touched.

"She's sweet."

"And smart," I said. "And a smart ass."

"I like her even more now."

"Yeah, she's pretty great." I ran my hand over my jaw, wondering how to approach the subject of her fame and what that might look like today as we wandered.

"What's on your mind?" she asked. "I can see your wheels turning."

"Paparazzi."

"Oh. Of course." She gave me a smile that somehow immediately calmed me. "I don't normally get a lot of attention around here. One, I try not to." She pointed to the hat and the sunglasses she was still wearing. "And two, people don't expect to see me here so there aren't photographers sent out en masse to hound me. We should be okay. If I'd thought it would be a problem, I wouldn't have come. And if it does become an issue, I'll make myself scarce. Deal?"

"Thank you. I should have thought ahead and mentioned it. I just don't want Marley's face plastered all over the place."

"Of course. And me neither. It's really not a way to live."

She turned then with a bright smile aimed at my sister who looked like at any moment she might float off into the sky on a cloud of pure happiness. She handed the drink in her hand to Lior and then held up a small white paper bag.

"Donut holes," she said, her cheeks turning pink. "I read in an article once that you love them." She looked so unsure that I wanted to hug her.

"They're my favorite!" Lior said. "Thank you." She took the bag, opened it, and popped one of the round confections into her mouth, the tiniest bit of powdered sugar dotting her lower lip. She then held out the bag to Marley and me, both of us helping ourselves to a donut as she asked, "Shall we get going?"

At Marley's nod, she got to her feet, linked her arm through my sister's, and led her out the front door while I followed behind.

I couldn't have planned a better day if I'd tried. I loved listening and watching the two women talk animatedly about school, friends, clothes, and food. As soon as Marley professed her love of Mexican food, Lior claimed she had just the place to take us.

We ate fish tacos piled high with mango salsa on the deck of the bright green Agua Verde Cafe that overlooked Lake Union while watching the people below climb into their rented kayaks.

"Ten bucks says that guy falls off before he gets twenty feet from the dock," Lior said, nodding her head toward a beefy looking blond guy. The dude seemed pretty confident to me as he waited for the slender young female employee to put his paddleboard in the water.

"He looks like he knows what he's doing," I said.

Lior met Marley's gaze across the table and the two women gave each other a knowing grin.

"You gonna take the bet then?" Lior asked, goading me.

Marley looked smugly my way. Never in the history of any of the women I'd been with had Marley sided against me in a bet. But none of those women had been Lior Flynn.

"Twenty bucks," I said.

"Done," Lior said, reaching across the table to shake my hand.

The three of us turned to watch, the two women laughing a few minutes later when the guy fell in the water as soon as he pushed off.

"We win!" Marley shouted and she and Lior did a triumphant fist bump over the table. "Men are so predictable."

We walked around the U District a little more after lunch, popping in shops and laughing more than I had in a long time.

We debated terrible tattoos outside a tattoo parlor, drank the bubble tea Marley swore we'd love, Lior and I making faces every time we got a "bubble" in our mouth, and then stood outside Lior's rented SUV, chatting about what we had planned for the rest of our stay.

She pointed suddenly and Marley and I turned to see a stunning view of a mountain peeking from between the buildings around us.

"Mountain's out," she said and then grinned when we looked at her questioningly. "It's something you say when you live here. That's Mt. Rainier. She doesn't show herself all the time because of the cloud cover. But when she does... it's glorious. We're very proud of our pretty lady."

I looked past her at the mountain and nodded. One certainly didn't get views like this in Brooklyn.

"Well, you two," Lior said, smiling first at Marley, then at me. "Today was a blast. Thanks for letting me tag along." She turned to Marley. "It was an absolute pleasure to meet you, Marley. You have my number. Text me anytime with questions, fashion or otherwise."

"I will!" Marley said, and then threw her arms around Lior, who laughed and hugged her back.

Once she was free of my sister, she turned to me.

"Graham, this was really fun. Thank you. See you back in Brooklyn?"

"See you there," I said.

We engaged in an awkward hug in front of my sister and then

hurriedly pulled apart. I could feel the heat in my face and was happy to see two pale pink splotches on her cheeks.

She climbed into the SUV then, and Marley and I stood on the sidewalk and waved goodbye until she drove out of sight.

"Now there's a woman I approve of," Marley said, elbowing me.

"Not happening, kiddo," I said.

"For a smart guy you really are clueless, aren't you?" she said and led the way to my rental car.

CHAPTER 18

Liar

"How was it?" Addie asked.

She had worked a half day at her clinic and come home and immediately showered. By four pm she was dressed in mismatched pajamas – iguanas on top, cats on the bottom. One of the apparent perks of working with animals was their owners gifting her animal-themed presents for Christmas or as thank yous. She had an impressive collection of pajamas, socks, and mugs, although right now I was more intrigued by the strange flower arrangement perched on her kitchen island.

"What *is* it?" I asked, leaning forward to inspect what was definitely flowers but in some weird configuration.

"A mermaid poodle," she said, as if I should've known. "One of its eyes fell off on my walk home though so it's a little winky."

"Right."

"So?" she said, looking at me expectantly. "How *was* it?"

Her bruises had faded and there were only a few yellow and pale green areas left along her cheekbone, jaw, and collarbone. The stitches had come out two days before I arrived, and most of the swelling had gone down. But I could tell by the careful way she moved that she was still in pain, and I made a mental note to keep our activities for the next few days low-key.

In the meantime, I apparently needed to keep her spirits up by spilling the details of my meeting with Graham.

"It's imperative to my physical healing," she said whilst looking very solemn.

"It was fun," I said, and then recounted my afternoon with the author and his sister.

"You like him," she said.

"He's nice."

"No... You *like* him like him."

I rolled my eyes and laughed. "Are you going to give me a little note with boxes to check?"

Her blue eyes widened and she opened a drawer and pulled out a notepad and pen and started writing. A moment later a folded piece of paper came skidding across the kitchen island toward me. It read:

Do you:
   1) like Graham Forrester?
   2) like like Graham Forrester?
   3) want to bone Graham Forrester?

I cracked up, marked one of the squares, then refolded the note and tucked it deep inside my bra.

"As if I wouldn't go get that," Addie said, turning to pull a premade salad from the fridge.

"You sure you don't want to come with me for dinner at Lilian and Cal's house?" I asked. "It's sure to be delicious."

"But will it have..." She peered at the label on her salad container. "Crispy onion wisps?"

"I cannot confirm or deny."

"As much as I'd love to see your mother..." She vehemently shook her head. "I'm going to have to pass. I have a date with my couch and the TV."

"I didn't know you were into threesomes."

"I've gotten kinky in my old age."

I grinned and turned to head to the guest room to change my clothes.

"You gonna date him?" Addie asked.

I turned back around and gave her a sad smile, shaking my head. "Even if he was interested, which I'm sure he is not, I can't. I only have the bandwidth for flings these days and, actually, I don't even think I have that anymore. Avoiding being used and hurt again takes a lot of energy. I'm tired. Of the effort, and the men."

"There is a lot of life left to live, my friend," Addie said, walking around the kitchen island and giving me a hug. "Don't let the assholes from your past ruin it for you"

"Funny. I told Ty the same thing once," I said, referring to my famous gay model pal.

Addie wheezed a laugh, shaking her head as she held her ribcage.

"Dammit," I said. "Sorry! Stop laughing!"

It took her several minutes and some slow and steady breathing to be able to speak again.

"You deserve nice things and hot sex, Lilu. Preferably all wrapped up in one delicious, dark-haired authorly type."

"I could probably set *you* up with him," I said.

"Nah. You know I like my men on the stupid side, that way they don't notice when I steal their cool band t-shirts."

It was true, she did have an impressive collection thanks to her dating history.

"Enjoy your couch and salad date," I said, kissing the top of her head and then hurrying to my room to change.

Thirty minutes later I was crossing the threshold of my mother and stepdad's beautiful home tucked in the hills overlooking the Puget Sound.

"Lior, darling," my mother said in her thick Swedish accent that was somehow unaffected by her decades living in the States.

She kissed me on both cheeks and then held me at arm's length while I stood, waiting for the scrutiny, the flick of her ice-blue eyes darting over my face, hair, and body, looking for flaws to comment on.

"You look lovely," she said, but I could hear the disappointment in her voice and I nearly laughed out loud. Was it the messy ponytail I'd pulled my hair into as I'd walked out the door? Or perhaps it was my choice of footwear – my old pair of worn-out sneakers. Or maybe it was the Blondie t-shirt and cut-off white shorts that weren't to her liking. (Probably. She hated graphic tees. According to her they were "classless".)

"Thanks," I said. "You too."

She actually did though. It was annoying and inspirational at the same time. Her white-blonde hair was tucked into a bun low on her nape, makeup minimal and on point, beige linen dress classic and somehow with nary a wrinkle in it. I didn't know how she always managed to look so effortlessly chic. Even when dressed for a black-tie event she somehow looked natural and at ease in a gown that cost as much as my rental car.

"Where's Cal?" I asked, gazing around the spotless living room that looked out over the water.

"He was tinkering in the garage," she said, heading toward the kitchen. Liliana Flynn didn't roll her eyes, but one could hear the roll in her tone of voice. "He'll be up shortly. Tea?"

We drank tea and then dinner was served. A salad made from vegetables in the garden my stepfather lovingly tended to, grilled chicken, and freshly baked bread (for me and Cal). For dessert we had a small scoop of lemon sorbet garnished with a mint leaf and a single raspberry, served in crystal parfait glasses with small silver spoons.

Life with my mother had always been like this. Perfect. Clean. Quiet. And masking a dozen or more issues one didn't talk about because to do so was unsavory. I'd always hated it. It wasn't me. It was a falsehood just asking to be stripped away to reveal the messy underbelly. How many times as a kid had I fought back? How many times had my pushing and arguing failed? Lillian Flynn didn't and wouldn't react. Her life was a façade and she was perfectly happy living with her mask firmly in place. Which had made her the perfect model. She lived the notion of being someone she wasn't... until that's exactly who she was. And while I had tried it myself, it turns out it wasn't for me. And that realization was what had led me to where I was now: wanting out.

While we ate, I could feel my mother's eyes on me. Her restraint was impressive, but I could feel the pull of her desire to comment. Cal must've said something before my arrival to stop her. Perhaps he mentioned I might visit more if she weren't so critical.

I hadn't known if they'd been aware I'd been in town twice recently. Not until she called the day before I was heading back to Seattle to see Addie and asked when I'd be returning. I figured she'd either lowered her usual standards and checked out my Instagram page, or someone in her circle had casually mentioned seeing my pictures. Lying was futile. So I'd promised to stop by.

"What's next on the docket?" she asked me as our dishes were cleared and a pitcher of white wine sangria was brought out. I raised an eyebrow at Cal and he suppressed a grin, turning his head so as not to let his wife see him trying not to laugh. A simple glass of wine was her standard. Anything more fun was a telltale sign she was trying to keep from being her usual too-uptight self. Unfortunately, her use of the word 'docket' indicated the alcohol had arrived a moment too late.

"A Vogue shoot," I said.

"For?" The tension in her voice could've been cut with one of her fancy rose gold-handled steak knives. I wanted to ask, does it matter? It was Vogue. But to her it did. She was modeling royalty. And she wanted her only child, who was part of her legacy, to be dressed only in the best.

"Daniela Rossi," I said, taking a large sip of my sangria. "You probably haven't heard of her. She's new to the—"

"Of course I've heard of her." She sniffed delicately as if I'd offended her knowledge. "I actually quite like her work. Delicate, but with an edge."

I almost laughed out loud. I could feel what she wasn't saying. She was imagining herself as a good fit for Daniela's clothes. I would not be the one to inform her that, for once, I was the better fit, because I understood and exuded delicacy, and she was always all edges.

"Cover?" she asked.

I quietly sighed. "Yes, and a ten-page spread."

At that she looked up, her icy blue gaze meeting my eyes straight on. Was that... was she impressed?

"Ten pages?" she asked. "Well, she's certainly proved something with Anna."

Of course. She wasn't impressed with me landing such a coveted number of Vogue pages... she was impressed with Daniela. As she should be, but still.

"Congratulations," Cal said, leaning forward and patting my hand.

"Thanks," I said. I could always count on him to give me credit. My mother waved a hand though, dismissing my accomplishment.

"Of course she got it. Look who her mother is."

I downed my drink and pushed back from the table.

"Hate to cut this short." I didn't. "But I have to get back."

"How is Addie?" my mother asked. "Did she get the flowers we sent? I don't recall seeing a thank you card."

"Probably because she could've died and was concentrating on not being dead," I said, leaning over to air kiss her cheek.

Cal stood and gave me one of his warm, bear-like hugs. As always, it soothed the sharp edges of the visit. I hugged him back, letting my shoulders drop and eyes close for a moment. If not for him, I'd no longer have parents at all. I'd have cut off communication long ago. It was an unspoken understanding we both acknowledged through this simple form of affection.

"Walk you out?" he asked, letting me go and taking the only warmth to grace this house with him.

"Yes, please," I said. "See ya, ma."

She blinked at my casual use of words, clearly trying to decide if she should acknowledge them or not, then waved a limp hand my way and topped off her glass.

"Sangria, eh?" I said as soon as we were out of earshot.

"She's coming to terms with some things about life. It's helping soften the blows."

"Should I ask?"

"Seventy is on the horizon. She's not taking it well."

"That's six years away," I said, trying to keep my laughter quiet and choking on it as a result.

"Oh Lior," he said, giving me an exasperated smile. "I am so very aware."

"She's still getting offers for work though, right?"

"Always. Skincare, makeup, fashion, vacation destinations... god I wish she'd take them up on those. I've always wanted to go on a cruise."

"They offered her a cruise?" I asked, eyes wide. "Oh dear. Kiss of death. What were they thinking?"

"She nearly blocked her agent's number when that offer came through."

My mother thought cruises were filled with sweaty Americans, too-warm buffet food, and subpar entertainment. "Why don't they just spend the money and treat themselves to the culture of Milan or Paris?" she'd said several times whenever the subject of cruises came up – which was surprisingly often. The comment always made me and Addie laugh.

"What does your mother know about the culture in those areas?" Addie had said once. "The only things she sees there are the insides of her penthouse suites, the car driving her places, and designer shops."

It was the truth. My mother, an international phenomenon in her heyday, had traveled the world extensively and only stepped foot on a beach or historic landmark if paid. And then was whisked back to the safety of her opulent hotel room immediately to shower. It was also true that she never got sick – so maybe there was something to her methods. But I'd take a little sickness to experience the world. What was the point otherwise?

"How much longer are you in town for?" Cal asked.

"A couple days."

"And how's Addie?"

"Much better."

"And you?"

I smiled. I never understood how my mother, the beautiful monster that she was, had ended up with two incredible husbands, but here we were. They were saints, clearly. Gluttons for punishment, maybe. I'd stopped questioning the sanity behind their reasons and just considered myself lucky to have them in my life, caring about me.

"I'm okay," I said, staring out at the view, the water of the Sound sparking under the sunlight. Seattle was beautiful in the summer, a well-kept secret from the rest of the world that thought we were being constantly showered with rain.

"How's Brooklyn looking?"

I turned and met his eyes. He was Scandinavian like my mother, but somehow his pale blue eyes always exuded warmth, unlike her icy stare.

"She's pretty," I said. "Lively. Entertaining." I looked out at the water again. "But somehow she's losing her allure."

"And the job?"

I loved how sometimes he was a man of interesting and lengthy conversations, but could also make an impact with hardly any words at all.

"Ditto," I said.

"You'll figure it out kiddo." He gave me a hug then, mussed my hair, and sent me on my way.

I returned to the colorful comfort of Addie's house and found her sprawled on the sofa with a huge bowl of popcorn, an open Ben and Jerry's pint, and a bottle of beer on the coffee table.

"Ummm..." I said, tilting my head as I took in the scene.

"You look like a doggy when you tilt your head like that," she said.

"I'll let that slide because I know it's your highest compliment. But uh..." I waved a hand at her outfit. "What's happening here?"

"The salad wasn't enough. How was dinner at Madame Flynn's."

"Delightful, darling," I said, impersonating my mother's accent.

"Did she like your outfit?"

"She said I looked lovely."

Addie snorted.

"She mentioned she hasn't received a thank you note for the flowers she had her assistant send. I told her you were planning to bring one by in person."

"You did not," she said, glaring at me.

"I did not."

She sat up carefully then and patted the cushion beside her.

"I was looking at something after you left that you might be interested in."

"I know we're close, Ads, but I don't want to watch porn with you."

She flipped me off and waited for me to sit before grabbing her laptop and opening it. On it was a real estate website.

"I made a favorites folder," she said proudly, resting her head on my shoulder. "Move here. Just do it. Take the job Avery offered. We can take walks on the beach every morning, watch movies and eat pizza at night, and go to therapy together to work out why we pick awful men."

"That sounds almost exactly how we spent our high school years."

"I know! It'll be so fun!"

I laughed and leaned forward, grabbing her beer and taking a drink before settling back on the sofa.

"Show me what you found," I said, pointing to the screen of her laptop.

CHAPTER 19

Graham

"Brontë told me to ask if you wanted to meet us for a walk sometime," I texted Lior the evening I got back from Seattle.

I then immediately wondered if I could unsend it. Was she even home yet? Would she even want to? But I realized if she'd seen it, and was thinking about it, it would be embarrassing to then unsend. And I didn't want to be embarrassing.

"I suppose I could tell her I meant to send it to someone else," I said to Brontë, who stared up at me from her bed next to mine and gave two thumps of her tail. "It's a bad idea, right? I should not engage. We could be friends though. Who doesn't want a supermodel for a bestie? All that free fashion advice and birthday gifts from Prada?"

My text alert went off.

"Please tell her I'd be honored," Lior said. "Tomorrow too soon?"

We agreed on a time and then I sent her a landmark for a meeting spot, set my phone face down on my bedside table, and turned out the light.

"Fuck," I whispered in the dark. "What am I doing?"

Brontë's tail thumped twice on her bed beside mine.

I woke in the morning after spending half the night going over everything I knew about Lior from the internet, and that which I knew from our in-person encounters. Every word, every look, every joke, every smile. Every on purpose and accidental touch. Every sweet moment with my sister this past weekend in Seattle.

Maybe the drama of her life didn't actually matter? Maybe I could handle it after all?

"And the constant barrage of strangers feeling they have the right to do whatever they want because she's in the public eye?" I'd thought. "No thanks."

While I definitely felt empathy for her, having been faced with that kind of attention myself when I was on book tours and having been married to Nadia, that part of her life repelled me. I was glad to see she was not enamored by it, and that she actually seemed to hate it, but it didn't change the fact that it existed. And probably always would.

"So why did I ask her to walk with us?" I moaned loudly as I lay in bed this morning, the sun peeking through the blinds.

I rolled over and gazed at Brontë.

"I even used to you to lure her in," I said. "What a cad! Forgive me?"

She stared up at me with her big brown eyes and I reached out to give her a pet before rolling onto my back again and resuming my emotional self-flagellation.

I was sure it wasn't a big deal. Positive she wouldn't think it wasn't anything more than what it was – a walk. But even I wasn't buying that. There had been something between us the other night at the bar. An electricity. A tension.

Of course, we'd also been drinking. But then there had been our little tour of the U District in Seattle, our eyes meeting time and time again over Marley's head.

Fucking hell. I just needed to get laid. That's all this was.

Except... *was* it all this was? Was I making something out of nothing? It had certainly been a while. Maybe I needed to let Fran set me up again.

"For fuck's sake," I said to the ceiling. "I am a glutton for punishment, aren't I."

I knew this wasn't just about sex though. True, it had been months since I'd had any, but the women I'd been set up with or had met on my own in the park, in bookstores, and at bars, had done nothing for me. There was no spark. No visceral or romantic need.

But with Lior...

I pulled the pillow from behind my head and pressed it to my face, letting out a groan of frustration before tossing it to the foot of the bed and getting up and heading to the bathroom for a shower. I had two hours before I was to meet her at our agreed upon meeting place and I was in desperate need of three things: coffee, a shower, and some self-gratification.

Fresh from the shower, I stood at the espresso machine watching Brontë nose at her food while I foamed the milk for my cappuccino. We had an hour now before we had to leave to meet Lior. A little tremor of anticipation eked up my spine. I shook it off, poured the milk in my cup, and was about to take a seat at the kitchen table when someone knocked on the front door.

I glanced down at Brontë, but she had moved to her bed and hadn't seemed to notice.

Running a hand through my damp hair, I loped down the hall to the entryway, wondering if I'd forgotten I'd ordered something, and opened the door with an expectant smile.

"Grammy!" exclaimed a voice, as two spindly tan arms wrapped around my neck.

I tried not to choke on the tsunami of perfume that overtook me, nor at the panic of realizing it was the familiar 'Dirty Violet', a lovely scent when worn as intended, rather having been bathed in.

Nadia.

"What are you doing here?" I asked, untangling myself and not even pretending a little bit to be happy to see her.

She brushed past me into the house, a whirlwind of movement and noise. Somehow I'd forgotten how heavily she walked for such a small human. How she picked things up, studied them, and then slammed them back down. She'd set my nerves alight a dozen time a day when she'd lived here – slamming doors, toilet seats, plates. For such a diminutive person, she was chaos personified.

She stopped and stared at the living room, wrinkling her nose when she caught sight of Brontë's new blue bed in front of the tacky white patent leather sofa she'd picked out.

"I'm in town for a bit and my hotel has the worst lighting. I knew you'd be home. You never leave. I need to do a promo spot for a new lipstick." She spun and gave me her signature pout. "What do you think?"

"I don't."

She rolled her eyes and took a step toward the stairs.

"Where are you going?" I asked.

"To my office. It has the best natural lighting. It'll be perfect."

"It's not your office anymore."

She gave me one of her overdramatic sighs, her entire body lifting and falling.

"Don't be a baby, Graham. Just because we broke up doesn't mean we can't be friends."

"We didn't just break up. We got divorced. And I don't want to be friends with the woman who cheated on me."

She started to slink toward me but when I took a step back she stopped.

"Fine," she said. "Whatever. I just need the room for a few minutes."

"Your new boyfriend can't get you a better hotel room to shoot in?"

Her bright demeanor faltered for a moment before she righted the ship and slid her smile back in place.

"We're having a few issues at the moment. Nothing that can't be worked out as soon as he stops pouting," she said, smoothing the skirt of what looked to be some sort of outlandish tennis outfit. She was always repurposing clothing. It was part of what had made her so popular on social media. "He's back in L.A. I had to come out here for another client." She took a step in my direction again. "Actually, if you want, we could go get dinner tonight. It's my only night free."

I stared at her, wondering what was wrong with her that she would actually think I'd be interested in sharing a meal with her after I'd just told her point blank that I didn't want to be friends.

"Nah, I'm good. Me and B have a hot date tonight," I said, stepping around her as I headed for the kitchen. "You know where your office used to be. Please be quick. I need to leave soon."

I heard her stomp up the staircase and then the clatter of her moving furniture around, the walls and ceiling shuddering.

"Christ," I said to Brontë. "She's a goddamn cyclone."

I had hoped to get in a few minutes of work before I left, but I was on edge now, the appearance of Nadia putting a pall over the atmosphere of the house, my anxiety level somewhere around my ears. I reached under the table and gave Brontë a pet, taking deep breaths and checking the time. I'd give her three more minutes and then I was going up.

I found Nadia sitting in her old office chair, which she'd unearthed from the pile of taupe throw blankets and set in front of the window. Leaning in the doorway, I watched as she didn't even pause her video at my appearance in the background. She just kept talking, preening, selling.

When she was done, she clicked the stop button with one of her cream-painted talons and spun to face me.

"You gonna reshoot that?" I asked.

"Nah. It was a perfect take. I'll just edit you out."

"Great. I have to go so... you have to go."

She hopped out of the chair and strode toward me. Slowing as she passed me, she reached up and put a hand on my arm.

"You look good," she said, her voice lowered. "Sure you have to go? I have a few minutes. We could..." Her eyes moved to the staircase leading to the master bedroom.

"Jesus. What?" I said, backing away from her. "I definitely have to go." I gestured to the staircase leading to the downstairs. "After you."

Her laugh echoed off the walls as she headed to the lower floor. "You were always such a prude, Graham. Have a little fun once in a while!"

"Don't you have a serious boyfriend?"

"Yep," she said, turning to face me in the bright entryway of my home that she'd ruined. "And having a little extracurricular action on the side is what makes our relationship more fun."

"Does he know that?"

But she didn't answer. At that moment both of our phones chirped with alerts. I pulled mine from my pocket a second after she swiped a manicured finger across the face of hers. I was still trying to make sense of what I was reading when she exclaimed and held up her phone toward me.

"You're dating Lior Flynn?" she asked, her baby blues wide with shock.

I was actually more surprised by her shock than by the picture of me, Lior, and Marley none of us had noticed being taken when we were at lunch. But little shocked Nadia. One of her best traits (her only one?) was that she took everything in stride, always able to spin something bad into something less bad and even great.

As I was about to answer her, more or less, three things happened in quick succession. First my text alert went off. Lior.

"I'm here!" she said, including a picture of the flower shop on the corner we'd agreed to meet at.

Then Nadia screamed because Brontë, who'd entered the foyer

without me seeing, had peed on the floor... and also Nadia's shoe. Which caused the beautiful chaos demon to jump into me, loosening my grip on my phone, which then landed in the puddle of urine.

Fuck.

Ignoring Nadia's shrieks of outrage and disgust, I calmly led Brontë to the back door and let her outside.

"I know you just went," I told her. "I'm just trying to spare you from that." I pointed in the direction of my ex. "I'll be back soon."

I shut the door, took a breath, and headed back to where Nadia had left her one soiled shoe in the puddle, the other kicked toward the corner of the entryway.

"I'm taking a shower," she shouted from the second story.

"What? No! Goddammit, I have to go!" But the water was already running. And by the sound of it, she was in *my* bathroom rather than the second-floor guest bathroom. Because of course.

Fuming, I stared down at my phone resting in a puddle of Brontë's pee. She had never gone in the house before and I wondered if she'd done it out of fear of Nadia, or on purpose because she hated her. I wanted to believe it was the latter.

The issue now was that I couldn't text Lior back. Because, much as I loved my dog, her pee was not so precious that I was willing to put my hands in it just to save a phone. I'd have to run out and get a new one as soon as Nadia got out of my damn shower.

The phone went off again with another text alert. I leaned over and looked at the screen.

"You still coming?"

Lior.

Shit.

With a long sigh, I picked my phone up out of the puddle just as the screen blurred and then went blank. Awesome. Suddenly very tired, I set the phone on the side of the sink, washed my hands, and sat down at the kitchen table.

Nadia appeared in my kitchen nearly an hour later with damp hair and wearing the same jeans she'd had on, but with one of my t-shirts, which she was practically drowning in.

"I don't recall B peeing on your shirt," I said.

"It got wet when I turned on the shower."

"How?"

She shrugged and I exhaled slowly, silently counting to ten.

"Are you leaving now?" I asked.

"I am."

I got to my feet.

"So are you going to tell me about you and Lior Flynn?" she asked as we headed to the front door.

"I am not."

"I've met her before, you know."

"That's great."

"I can't believe you're not having a fit about Marley being photographed."

She was leaning against the wall, still as pretty as ever on the outside. But I'd seen her for who she was, and all the outward beauty in the world couldn't make up for the ugly that was inside her.

"I really have to get going," I said, ushering her toward the front door. "I'll have your shoe cleaned and sent to you."

She stopped and waited for me to open the door for her. She was holding the clean shoe in her hand.

"Don't worry about it. I'll just buy a new pair."

"Super. I'm assuming you have a ride?" I asked.

She pointed to the black sedan waiting by the curb.

"Cool. See ya."

But rather than hurry off, she lingered on the front porch and then seemingly accidentally dropped the shoe. Being the gentleman I'd been trained to be, I stepped outside, picked it up, and held it out to her. She smiled coyly and moved in close, her fingers overlapping mine as she took it and looked up at me. Before I had a chance to move away, I heard the click of a camera nearby.

CHAPTER 20

Lior

"He stood me up," I texted Addie after I'd returned home from the corner where I'd agreed to meet Graham. "He asked me if I wanted to go for a walk. He even used Brontë as the reason why. And then he fucking stood me up!"

"Do you think something happened to Brontë?" she texted back.

"Shit. Well now I do!"

I threw myself on my sofa and closed my eyes. Something must've happened to his dog. He had no reason to ignore me otherwise. Especially after he was the one to ask me if I wanted to go for a walk. Now I felt terrible for all the rude things I'd thought about him on my way home.

"Should I text him and ask?" I asked Addie.

"No. If something has happened, he might be in a state. He'll already see that you texted so just wait for him to text you."

"Okay. Good call. Thanks."

"What else is new since I saw you two days ago?" she texted.

We went back and forth for a few minutes and then I got a text from my agent Jen.

"Have you seen this?" she asked.

I clicked the link she'd attached and there it was. A picture of Graham, Marley and me at lunch at Agua Verde last Saturday.

Crap.

"Welp," I texted Addie. "I think I know why he stood me up. I'm surprised you didn't text this to me."

"I turned off the alerts for you. There were too many. Send it to me."

I took a screenshot and sent it.

"Crap," she texted a moment later. "But also, that's not your fault and he should know that."

"I know. But it's his kid sister and he's protective. Rightly so. I feel terr—"

Just then Jen texted again with another link attached. It was the story I'd feared when Graham and I had been spotted at The Bar Room.

"Lior Flynn, From One to the Next. Get it, Girl!" was the headline on the online magazine, followed by side-by-side pictures of me and Caleb at Nobu and Graham and me later that night. The second one was a faraway grainy picture taken from the other end of the bar. You wouldn't even have known it was me if not for the dress.

I sent the link to Addie.

"You're on a roll," she said. "You okay?"

"No," I said, my voice soft.

She was quiet for a minute and then made a small noise and swore under her breath.

"What's going on?" I asked.

"Shit, Li. I actually don't think either of those are the reason... but this might be."

A moment later my phone pinged and I clicked the link she'd sent. I didn't say a word as the article popped up, "Love 2.0?" the headline read. There was a short paragraph about Graham being seen with me and his sister in Seattle, followed by something about his ex, Nadia, that I skimmed over before clicking yet another link that led me to one of her social media pages. The post tagged showed her promoting a lipstick. I nearly exited, confused what one thing had to do with the other, and then I saw him, standing behind her in the doorway.

I went back to the article and scrolled down further to find an image of the two of them standing on a front porch, her hair was wet and she was wearing a too-big t-shirt, her shoes dangling from her fingertips. It was dated and timed stamped. Today, eight forty-nine am.

Asshole.

"Lior?" Addie said. I'd forgotten she was on the line.

"I'm here. I guess that mystery is solved then."

"You okay?"

"Of course. It was just a walk. It's not like we had an actual date planned."

"Still."

"He should've texted, but it looks like he was distracted. It happens. I will say though... yuck."

"She's the literal worst," Addie said.

"Hey," I said. "I'm gonna go. I promised Avery I'd send over all the articles I've written in the past ten years. She wants to read through them and come back to me with some ideas for the column."

"Really? Yay!"

I grinned. Despite the disappointment of being stood up by Graham for what looked like a tryst with his ex, I was excited about this possible new direction for my life. Maybe being stood up was just a sign that I was on the right track. If I'd started to like Graham, I'd probably hold off on any major life changes, and when our relationship inevitably went south, I'd have wasted precious time.

"I also left a message with a realtor in Seattle," I said. "I might be back sooner than I planned to look at some houses."

I was sure Addie's scream of happiness could be heard all the way down the block.

Rather than email Avery back like I'd told Addie I was going to do, I went back to the link she'd sent me, then Nadia's social media post, then the picture of her and Graham on the porch. It looked intimate. Sexy. A definite unplanned late night or early morning-after moment from the looks of her outfit.

I sighed and exited the link, slumping down on my sofa and staring across the room at the floor-to-ceiling bookcase where there was an entire shelf dedicated to the works of one Graham Forrester – the poem he'd left me after cleaning my shoe framed and set just so beside his novels.

I'd never admit it to anyone else, but I was a little crushed by this morning's drama. I'd thought we were becoming friends. Or at least friendly. But he'd chosen his horrible ex over a walk with me. Even after our lovely afternoon with his sister.

"You'll be in Seattle? Come join us. Meet my sister. See how charming I am? How thoughtful?" I flipped off his shelf of novels. "Dick."

I was still wallowing in self-pity and a pool of irritation when I got a text from Jeremy Lane, an actor I'd dated off-and-on a couple years ago. Out of the men I'd dated, he was the only one I'd thought I could make a relationship work with. He was kind and thoughtful, and hadn't seemed to be in the relationship for the attention being with me brought him, having his own huge fan base. But our busy schedules kept us apart and, in the end, it was just too hard.

"Hey you," his text said. "I'm in town for the premier of my new movie. You around? Wanna get dinner somewhere?"

My mind instantly went to Graham, but I shut that down in a hurry. I owed him nothing. Not one little consideration. And maybe an evening with Jeremy was just the balm I needed.

"I'd love to," I texted back. "Tell me where and when and I'll be there."

We met at one of our favorite spots, a lovely little Thai restaurant that served interesting beers and family style meals. We passed bowls and plates back-and-forth, catching up on one another's projects, sharing bad date stories, and doing a slew of "remember when's" until we were laughing so hard the family next to us couldn't stop staring. Or maybe it was because two very recognizable faces were sitting beside them in this tiny, decidedly not fancy establishment.

"We should go before someone realizes the two hysterical people in the corner are actually celebrities and start taking pictures," I said.

"Good call."

We climbed in a cab and then sat for a moment trying to decide if we wanted to head to a bar or call it a night.

"My hotel serves a decent glass of wine," Jeremy said.

I glanced at him, noting the sexy little smile he always got when he said one thing but was suggesting another. An image of Graham flashed in my mind again but I pushed it away. Whatever I'd thought could be happening with him clearly wasn't, and I was allowed a little no-strings-attached sex with a man I knew well and liked.

"I could go for a glass of wine," I said.

Ten minutes later I was wandering his suite at the Ritz-Carlton, the aforementioned glass of wine in my hand, Jeremy walking towards me with a hungry look in his gray-green eyes.

I found myself studying him as he stood inches from me, sipping from his glass and running the back of his fingers over the silk blouse covering my breast.

I sucked in a breath. He'd always been so good at drawing out sex until I was practically begging for it. Unfortunately, the sex itself had never been that great. It was good. Sufficient. He got the job done. But there was always something lacking, and the recollection of that now threatened to put a damper on a need that I didn't want to admit, even to myself, was due to a certain other man who had jilted me this morning.

In an effort to get Graham out of my head, I set my glass down and reached for Jeremy's belt. I didn't have time for foreplay today. I needed to forget. Now.

"What's the hurry?" Jeremy asked as I undid his jeans.

"It's been a minute," I said, sliding my hand into his briefs. Thankfully he was already hard and ready so I wouldn't have to put in much work.

I turned around and pulled up my dress, leaning forward and placing my hands on the table beside us. But rather than take the hint, he got on his knees and slowly ran his fingers up my legs, kissing the backs of my knees and gently running his hand over my thong that wasn't even remotely wet. Because I was not turned on. Because Graham Freaking Forrester's stupid face would not stay out of my head like I'd told it to.

"Jeremy," I said.

"Mmhmm..." he responded, his hands squeezing my thighs.

"I can't."

He paused as if he wasn't sure he'd heard me correctly.

"What?" he asked.

"I'm sorry." I straightened and pulled the hem of my dress down. "I can't. We're just... this isn't us anymore."

"Are you sure?" He motioned to his dick, which was out of his pants and red with readiness.

But it did nothing for me. In fact, I felt a bit repelled by the sight if it staring at me. Well, staring just left of me. And I suddenly wanted to cry.

"Yeah. Positive," I said.

In all future interviews, when asked about my relationship with Jeremy Lane, I would always say I'd love him forever, but we just couldn't get our timing right.

The following morning several media sites posted images of me hugging Jeremy outside the Ritz-Carlton. I ignored the texts that came in after, inquiring about what was going on, aside from Addie, whom I never ignored.

"Payback?" she texted, referring to the article about Graham and Nadia.

"Yes and no," I said. "FYI, nothing happened."

"You say that like I don't know you."

I sent her a heart emoji, turned off my phone, and tossed it onto my bedside table. I'd never heard from Graham the day before. Not one "sorry I stood you up". No text professing his bad friend behavior and promises to make it up to me. And I knew now, with the images of me and Jeremy out in the world, I wouldn't. Which wouldn't have been an issue if we didn't have a shoot for Vogue to do in a few days. Something I'd completely forgotten about in the past twenty-four hours.

"Shit!" I shouted at the ceiling, and then turned over and buried myself in my duvet.

CHAPTER 21

Graham

The Vogue offices were some of the nicest I'd ever seen, and I was more than a little intimidated as I followed a woman named Cass as she navigated the labyrinth of hallways with ease, finally delivering me to a large studio with dozens of people milling about, lighting being checked, and racks of clothing rolling here and there.

Lior was nowhere to be seen. But it was inevitable she would arrive at some point as we were due to do this photo shoot together. Unless... had she somehow gotten out of it as I'd so badly wanted to do after stewing for the past few days?

"You must be Graham."

I turned at the sound of my name and smiled at an intimidatingly put-together woman with laser-like, almost-sheer-black eyes.

"I am," I said.

"Lovely to meet you. I'm Risa Collins. I'm running the show today. And this," she tapped the shoulder of a petite blonde woman, "is Daniela, our fabulous designer."

"It's wonderful to meet you both," I said, shaking Risa's hand and then Daniela's. "Thank you for this opportunity."

"It's going to be good fun," Risa said. "Shall we get you in some clothes? Or..." She looked me up and down. "Possibly out of them. I'm not sure what we're shooting first – we have a lot of options. It's going to be fun." She waved someone over then who offered me a variety of beverages before I was passed off to someone else who took me to my dressing room.

A few minutes later I was standing listening to three more people staring at me in the mirror and discussing the hair on my head, the hair on my face and, much to my embarrassment, hair in other places too - when I heard a commotion on the other side of the curtained walls.

"Lior!" several people shouted.

There was laughter, more talking, and then I heard her voice, the low, sexy timbre I'd grown accustomed to in the past couple of weeks. If I wasn't so angry with her, I'd get out my chair and go say hello. But while I could forgive the photo with Marley showing up online, since it wasn't her fault in the first place, I couldn't get over how she'd seemed to respond to what had transpired three days ago when Nadia had appeared on my front porch.

Granted, it hadn't looked good when I hadn't texted her back. I wasn't able to go in to get a new phone until the following after-noon due to Brontë getting herself stuck in the shallow drainage ditch in the backyard – her back legs seeming to have gone out on her. I'd called a cab immediately and taken her to the vet who nodded sadly and gave B pets and me a pat on the shoulder.

"It happens," he'd said. "Near the end. Just keep an eye on her. Stay close near stairs or any surface that could send her tumbling."

After I'd gotten her home, I'd hurried out to replace the phone but the store was closed. Worried what Lior must be thinking, I'd jogged to her house only to find her not home. The following morning I found out where she had been when I saw what had been plastered all over social media.

"Jeremy Lane, the one that got away," one starry-eyed fan had said.

I'd turned off the new phone and sent it sliding across the kitchen table where it had hit the wall and fallen to the floor. I'd left it there for the next several hours, annoyed that rather than text or call me about what had transpired with Nadia, she'd resorted to childish tactics of trying to make me jealous. Or maybe she'd just decided she had more important, more famous men to hang out with.

The entire episode had just proved to me that I was right about her life. It was full of drama and it would never stop. And it was definitely not for me. Unfortunately, we still had this shoot to do, and so I'd taken a break from my fuming at home to come and fume while having my picture taken professionally with her for none other than Vogue Magazine. I couldn't wait to see what chaos this stirred up when the issue came out.

"Okay," the makeup woman said, giving my forehead a last pat of powder. "You're ready for clothes."

Ten minutes later I was dressed in the nicest clothes I'd ever worn, and was being ushered out to the set we'd be shooting on, the makeup woman, hair stylist, and the man who'd dressed me, all flitting around adjusting my shirt, smoothing my hair, and looking at my face with narrowed eyes.

"How's it going?"

Her warm voice had an edge and I turned in surprise to see Lior already there, lying on what looked like a large black brick, her dark hair like a river pouring over its side, the sight of her absolutely mesmerizing.

Someone was adjusting the white satin dress she was wearing so that it laid just so, and she was lying so still, her skin and hair so perfect beneath the lights, that she looked like a statue. A very beautiful statue.

"Well, I'm afraid to move in case I split these very expensive pants. And I'm positive my hair has never had this much product in it... ever."

For the briefest of moments it looked like she was going to

smile, but in the same breath her face went back to being stony-like, her honey-brown eyes looking toward the ceiling.

"Ok folks," a woman with a camera hanging from her neck said. "Let's get started. Graham, I'm Ava. I'm your photographer today. If I shout at you at any point, it's out of love." She winked. "Lior, you look perfect. Graham, I need you kneeling over her. Marcus." She waved another man over. "Show him what I mean, will you? We are maiden and brute, folks. Let's go."

After Marcus climbed onto the brick and knelt over Lior menacingly, it was my turn.

"Well, this isn't awkward," I whispered, trying to lighten the mood. It was going to be a very long day – made even longer if we didn't get along. But if she'd heard me, she didn't let on, her eyes cast away from me still, her body unmoving.

A few shots were taken and then we were given a new set of directions, which we took wordlessly.

While Lior kept her gaze anywhere but on me, mine couldn't seem to stop straying to her. Fortunately, we were kept busy with different poses, people adjusting our clothes, tending to our hair, and powdering our noses – or, in Lior's case, adding shine to her lower lip, which I found I couldn't stop staring at.

"Eyes up, Graham," Ava called out, and I felt my face warm as my eyes rose to meet Lior's. But hers were aimed at my eyebrows.

We did three more scenarios and then were whisked back to our dressing rooms to change. When we returned to the set, the black brick had been exchanged for a black throne and I was told to sit in my all-white suit. Lior, dressed in a plum dress with a leather corset over the top, leaned over me, one hand in my hair, pulling it to expose my neck, her other hand sliding inside the front of my shirt.

I could feel her breath on my skin and despite the anger I'd felt for her for the past three days, and the large audience, I found my own breath coming faster, my mind starting to short circuit as I wondered what it would feel like to have her tongue trace slowly up my neck.

"Okay," Ava said. "Now..."

As we got ourselves into the next pose, Lior's bare legs wrapped around me, my hand gripping the one thigh exposed to the camera, her eyes finally met mine.

"Not awkward at all," she said. "Hope Nadia doesn't mind."

"I'm more worried Jeremy will be annoyed."

"Oh, you don't have to worry about him. He's a pro and very considerate of my time."

"How nice for you."

"I think so."

"Lior," Ava called. "Lean in closer now, hovering your mouth over his. Good. Now give me a hint of tongue."

When they told us they got the shot and we were released to change into the next outfits, I stayed seated for a few seconds longer. I was angry, but I could see that she was too. And I didn't blame her. From her point of view, I'd stood her up for what looked like a romp with my ex. And then I'd never texted her back. I knew I could fix it all with a simple explanation. But I didn't like the way she'd handled her hurt feelings. It was something Nadia would pull, and that just wasn't okay with me.

Also, I now had a semi and badly needed it to go away before I stood and people saw. No matter that I was mad at her, the woman looked sexy as hell and her leaning over me in chiffon and leather, her breath hot on my skin, her tongue inches from my neck... it was cruel.

The day went on in much the same fashion. Lighting, makeup, clothing. Discussions about my facial hair – to shave the scruff or not to? Cut the hair? I'd been told by Fran that I could say no to anything I was uncomfortable with. But then I heard some of the ideas being thrown around and got curious – even excited. When would I ever get to do something like this again? And so an evolution of my look began and Lior and I posed again and again. We were Light and Dark. Death and Life. Lightning and Thunder. Love and Heartbreak. Lust and Chastity. Princess and Prince. Monster and Beauty. Black and White. Anger and Joy.

With each dynamic the color schemes changed. The scenery. The feel. The clothing. I was in all black. She was in all white. She was soaking wet, her dress sheer from the water and clinging to her skin. I stood above her, sinister, wind making my shirt billow behind me like a cape. My hair got shorter and more styled. Hers was blown out, pulled back, wild, wet and streaming rivulets of water down skin covered in goosebumps.

She was luminous in pink tulle kept in place by slender gold metal chains around her torso and the fabric undulated beneath the wind from a large fan. She looked sexy as fuck in cream-colored lace with stiff strips of vinyl encircling her waist and neck like an S&M tutu and collar. She emulated a dreamlike state in sky blue satin with chain link cuffs. But when she stepped from her dressing room in a red satin dress that stood apart from all the other designs as it hung to the floor from a wide black leather collar, and hugged her in places that made it very apparent she was wearing nothing underneath, I felt a surge of need I hadn't felt in ages.

Goddamn she was beautiful. The anger I'd held onto all day like a life raft dissipated in the wind from the fan and I stood across from her as we waited for the lighting to be changed, watching as her makeup was touched up.

A few minutes later, makeup done, she moved closer to me, still not looking my way.

"Hey," I said, my voice quiet. "I'm sorry for the other day."

"No worries," she said, studying her nails.

"Lior."

She looked at the nails on her other hand.

"Lior?"

She turned her hand over and traced the lines of her palm with one red and black fingernail. I started to laugh.

"What's it telling you?" I asked.

"That I have lousy taste in friends."

"I'm telling Addie."

She turned her face away but I caught the grin she was trying to hide.

"Can I explain what happened?" I asked.

"I think I got the gist."

"No, you don't. I was set up."

When she turned to face me, she looked upset.

"I'm telling the truth," I said.

She sighed and stared at me for a long moment before saying. "I believe you. Mostly because I know how her twisted little mind works."

"It's par for the course with her."

We were asked to move off the set while they tried out a new idea with props.

"I was just getting ready to come meet you when she showed up and marched her way in. It was a whole... thing. And then B peed on her shoe and she fell into me trying to get away from it and I dropped my phone in the puddle and while I was trying to save my phone, she ran upstairs and took a shower. Because apparently a shoe in pee means you have to wash your entire person."

Lior pressed her lips together, trying not to laugh.

"Well, that explains the wet hair," Lior said. "And the no response to my texts."

"While she was in the bathroom she apparently made some calls. I don't know if it was for you or for her boyfriend to see, but it was fucked up and I would've gotten in touch with you but then something happened with Brontë and I had to take her to the vet and... I didn't even get to the store to get a new phone until the next day. And when I did, well..."

"You saw the pictures of me and Jeremy."

I was quiet, watching a myriad of emotions play across her face.

"Is B okay?" she asked.

"Yeah. She's just old."

"I know you have a vet, but I could ask Addie for some ideas on how to make life a little more comfortable for the sweet girl. She has some interesting approaches sometimes."

"Anything to help would be appreciated. Thank you."

"You're welcome."

We grew quiet again, but I found I couldn't help myself. I was still curious. Still bothered.

"So, you and Jeremy Lane are dating again?"

"No, we are not."

"Was that just..." I trailed off, not wanting to sound presumptuous.

She didn't look at me for a moment, and then turned to face me, shoulders squared, eyes fierce.

"I was mad," she said. "But that wasn't for you. It was for me."

Jealousy snaked up my spine. Even though I already had been since the picture was posted, I didn't need an even more vivid picture in my mind of her and Jeremy Lane having sex.

She continued, "I felt... small. I just wanted..."

"I get it," I said. "I'm sorry if I made you feel that way."

She shrugged. "Of course, as these things go, I knew it was a mistake as soon as we got to his hotel. The picture they posted of me leaving was taken about ten minutes after I'd arrived." She started to laugh then. "Sorry." She held up a hand. "It's just... the media makes me out to be a maneater some days, and a sad sack that can't hold on to a man other days. If they knew how many of those dates were for show and how many of those men I've *never* slept with, their minds would be blown."

"But didn't you and Jeremy used to be a couple?"

"Yes. And that's another reason I said yes to going out with him. If I was going to go *there*, at least he was safe. And I needed safe, because I was feeling pretty down and lonely. And—"

But she stopped herself before she said more. And then we were called back to set, preventing me from asking what she had been about to say.

After some direction from the crew, we got into our first pose, me reaching up to her, her reaching down, her palm on my face.

"I'm sad you let them shave the scruff and cut off the waves," she said. "I like you that way. It feels more you. More authentic. Less..."

"Pretty?" I asked and she laughed.

"You are still very pretty, my friend," she said. "It's just less styled. Less perfect."

"Hold it there," the photographer said. The camera clicked several times. "Next position."

For our last scene of the day I wore a sheer black t-shirt with faux leather bands that wrapped twice around each bicep with another at the collar, and faux black leather pants. I was barefoot, my features had been played up with dark makeup, and my hair was slicked back.

I was Dark.

Lior emerged after me and I had to look away for fear that every thought in my mind would read on my face. She was devastating in a sheer shimmering white gown with bell sleeves and a faux white leather strip that ran down the center of her, from bust to mid-thigh where the dress then split, revealing the bare skin of her legs. She wore a long platinum wig, and the makeup around her eyes and at her temples sparkled.

She was Light.

"Are you blushing?" she whispered as we moved into our places. We were facing off, arms and fingers spread as if pressing each of our elements toward the other.

"I might be," I said, keeping my eyes on hers even though other parts of me were begging to skim downwards.

"But you've seen me in all states of dress today, Graham," she said, her voice low and breathy. "You've even seen me wet."

I knew she was alluding to earlier scenes we'd done when we'd both been doused with water, but the way she said it made it sound distinctly like she was referring to a different kind of wetness. And now I *was* blushing. And she... she was flirting.

CHAPTER 22

Lior

W hat. Was. I. *Doing?*

Flirting, apparently. Even though I didn't flirt. That wasn't me. I never gave men an opportunity to know I was interested, because that would mean giving up information, and I liked to keep my information private. "Don't show your cards too soon... or ever," was another one of my mother's mottos. It had served me well over the years when it came to men and friends who really weren't friends. And yet here I was, going against my own rulebook with Graham Hot-as-Fuck Forrester.

Dear floor, please open up and swallow me whole. I have lost my damn mind.

What was it about this guy? A half hour ago I'd been pissed at him. Sure, his explanation tracked. And sure, he was gorgeous, but I'd been around tons of gorgeous men. It was a byproduct of my career. Maybe it was because he was a writer. Maybe I somehow felt like I knew him. Like I'd seen into his soul through his beautiful prose and all-consuming stories. Or was it because of the time we'd spent together lately, and seeing him as an actual human being had endeared him to me? Was it all of those things combined and seeing him here today, in my environment, dressed and undressed, sexily unkempt and then shaven and cropped, had unhinged something I'd kept carefully locked down for years?

Fuckity fuck. Where was Addie when I needed her.

No, on second thought she'd be no help. She'd be rooting for this.

"Jerk," I mumbled to myself.

But oh... the sight of his body had done something to me. The feel of his skin against mine... My insides squeezed deliciously and I involuntarily tightened everything – primal need shooting through me like the lightning I'd been dressed as earlier. I hadn't had sex in a long time, despite what the public thought. If not for my trusty vibrator, I'd probably have closed up shop down there. And while my small arsenal of sexual toys had gotten me through, there really wasn't anything like human touch. I pictured Graham's hands... his long, capable looking fingers and—

"Lior?"

Fuck's sake, get a grip.

I took in a deep breath in an effort to clear my mind. Graham was outside my dressing room calling me and I was still only in my sports bra.

"Yup?" I said casually, poking my head out.

As bummed as I was that they'd sheared him, he looked like a god all clean shaven, his hair cut short around the ears and nape, the front swept casually to one side.

"Do you have plans after this or do you maybe want to go get a bite to eat?"

He was asking a lot of me. I'd just gone through the spectrum of emotions, capped off by spending hours seeing his body in all forms of undress – except completely undressed – and now he wanted me to sit across from him and pretend I hadn't and wasn't thinking naughty thoughts?

"As long as we go somewhere sweatpants acceptable," I said while inwardly berating my lack of resolve.

"Deal."

He disappeared again and I wanted to kick myself for showing up for the shoot dressed like a slob like I normally did. He looked gorgeous in faded jeans and a fitted black t-shirt. Maybe I'd keep some of the makeup on to offset my unkempt aesthetic? Or would anyone notice if I stole some clothes? I'm sure I wouldn't look strange walking the streets in tulle and chains – this was Manhattan after all.

Though Daniela might mind her designs getting ketchup dripped on them.

Finally dressed, I moved to the vanity and began wiping at my face, removing the shimmer and foundation and swapping white mascara for black. I added a touch of lip gloss, grabbed my purse and hurried out the curtain door to find Graham standing off to the side waiting for me. My breath caught at the sight of him.

As soon as we left the Vogue offices, hunger hit me hard. I'd snacked sparingly on nuts while shooting, too afraid I'd end up with food in my teeth. I needed to eat.

"Do you mind?" I pointed to the hot dog vendor on the corner. "I haven't eaten all day except for a few handfuls of almonds."

He stared at me for a moment and then started to laugh.

"How do you look like that and eat donut holes and hot dogs?" he asked.

"It's the official model diet. Didn't you know?"

"This explains so much. Okay. Let's get a couple of dogs and walk," he said.

And so we did, meandering north and talking in-between bites. When we finished, we popped into a corner bodega, each of us grabbing bottles of water before continuing on our way.

It was nice, just walking and talking with nowhere to be. No time limit. No one rushing the other. No agendas. And no paparazzi – my baseball hat, sunglasses, and baggy attire doing their usual camouflage act.

He told me about growing up in Oregon, his parent's divorce, his relationship with his mom, and how her death had knocked him sideways.

"She was my best friend," he said. "My dad is great. We're very close and always have been. But my mom was a special soul. She saw me like others didn't and always gave it to me straight rather than trying to hide things from me. All my friends loved her too. She was like our Yoda. If you had a problem, you came and talked to Carole."

I smiled. "She sounds a lot like Addie's mom, who was more a mom to me than my own was. Though, going to her for advice could be a crapshoot." I laughed, remembering the feisty opinions Mel had given us over the years. Most of it not to be repeated.

"What was your relationship like with your dad?" Graham asked.

"Amazing. He was just *good*. Decent. Kind and witty and quiet. He had this magnetism to him that made people gravitate to him. Including me. If he was in the house, I wanted to be in the same room, even if we weren't talking. His presence was large and soft and safe. After my parent's split, I wanted to live solely with him, but of course my mother wouldn't have it." I rolled my eyes. "The optics. And my father knew I'd benefit from living with us both." I made a face. "I'm still on the fence about that actually."

Graham laughed, but a moment later he sobered. "And when he died?"

We had just made it to Central Park and I motioned to Graham to follow me, finding a spot in the shade of a tree to take a seat in the grass. I thought about his question, pulling a blade of grass from the ground and sliding it between my fingers over and over.

"I was devastated," I finally said, my voice quiet. "He was the one I went to with questions, problems... all my crazy ideas. When I was at my mom's house, I would call him late at night and he'd just sit on the phone with me for however long I needed – even though he had to be up early for work. His death took my legs out from under me."

I grew quiet, remembering.

"When we found out he'd left the house to me, my mom wanted to sell it. I nearly launched myself at her. If Cal hadn't been there, she might've lost her fake eyelashes."

I grinned and Graham laughed quietly before reaching over and taking my hand, the warmth of his sending heat through my entire body.

"I'm sorry. I know it was a long time ago now, but I'm so sorry."

I nodded, my eyes filling with tears, and tightened my fingers around his.

"I'm sorry too."

We sat there quietly then, holding hands in the park, watching a myriad of people wandering, jogging, laughing, talking.

After a while we made our way out of the park and stood on the sidewalk contemplating dinner options and restaurants that wouldn't blink an eye at my outfit. We settled on tacos and margaritas, making our way to Vida Verde where we were seated on the colorful rooftop at one of their aqua-colored tables, surrounded by beautiful murals and plants. We immediately ordered chips and their trio of guacamole, a peach margarita for me, and a blue coconut margarita for him.

"You're going to have a blue tongue," I said.

"Why do you think I got it?"

We ordered three different kinds of tacos and shared, tried one another's drinks and swapped, and pondered for far too long if we should get dessert there or on our way back to Brooklyn.

"I made more cookies last night," I said.

"What kind?"

"Snickerdoodle."

"Hm," he said. "Tempting. I have Ben and Jerry's in the freezer."

"Flavor?"

"Flavors," he said, stressing the plural.

"Are you rich?" I whispered, my eyes wide.

"Terribly."

We giggled, finished off our second round of margaritas, and went outside to hail a cab.

"Ben and Jerry's?" Graham asked when we got in. "I should actually check in on Brontë. I've been gone a while."

"Ice cream and Brontë sounds perfect," I said.

He rattled off an address and we were on our way.

We could hear Brontë snuffling at the door as we stood on the front porch, Graham digging his keys out of his pocket. He unlocked the door but didn't open it.

"For the record," he said. "It was not my idea."

"What?" I asked, frowning in confusion.

And then he opened the door.

"Oh," I said, stepping inside, my eyes wide as I took it in. "Oh Graham. *No.*" I slapped a hand over my mouth and started to laugh as I slipped off my shoes and walked deeper inside, Brontë beside me. I knelt beside her, scratching behind an ear. "Is it... a mausoleum?" I whispered to her. "Is someone famous buried here? Is it a museum?" I stood and touched a finger to a small sculpture of... "Is this a boob?"

Graham snicked and waved a hand. "Have at it."

I did. Each room was white on white on white. It was bright. Glaringly so. Glass and acrylic and white stone and ceramic. I ran my hand over the back of a mid-century style white patent leather sofa, poked at a lamp shade that looked like was made of bubbles, and shivered from the cold white tiles under my feet.

"Did she hate color?" I asked. "Where do you find comfort?"

He looked amused as I moved on to the kitchen, poking my head into a powder room on the way. Brontë had curled up in her bed next to the acrylic kitchen table once she'd gotten a hello from me. Her space was the only comfortable looking spot I'd seen so far.

White dishes, white cups, crystal glasses, silverware with white handles...

"Graham," I said, my voice filled with... awe? Horror?

"I spilled spaghetti sauce in here once," he said. "That's the night I learned we don't cook red in here."

"You don't cook... red?"

"That's what she told me."

I pursed my lips, trying not to burst out laughing.

"It's... soulless," I said. "And you're so..."

"I'm so what?" he asked, his eyes meeting mine.

I took in a breath and let it out slowly. "You're so not."

The second floor wasn't much better, though Graham had clearly reclaimed some of the space since his ex had left. There were small white hand-weights piled in the corner of the home gym, new black weight plates and bars stacked on a black rack, and hand towels in shades of blue and beige folded on a shelf.

Her office across the hall, which was mostly cleaned out, save for a mirrored desk and fuzzy white chair, looked like a showroom for futuristic meetings.

The next door down housed his office.

"This and the bedroom are the only rooms I've really touched since she left," he said as I stepped inside. "I dropped all the furniture she chose at a local donation site and got mine from the storage unit I'd had to get. The only thing I haven't touched is the paint. But I'll get to it eventually. If I don't just up and move."

"I knew you had to be in here somewhere," I said as I walked around, touching books, plant pots and a beautiful fountain pen.

The walls were a green that somehow managed to be more cold than welcoming. But, beyond that, there was a beautiful old, weathered desk with a burgundy leather inlay that sat by the window, looking out over the street. On the white-washed wood flooring that covered the whole of the second floor, was a thick rug with a taupe on cream design. And there were books everywhere. On shelves, stacked on his desk, and piled on the floor.

On one wall was a bulletin board covered in notes, quotes, and photos. On the other walls were framed prints of men reading, writing, and typing on vintage typewriters.

"You love what you do, don't you," I said. It wasn't a question. It was clear to me as soon as I stepped into this room.

"I do," he said. "I've had stories in my head since I was kid. Making a living out of it is a dream come true, and I don't take one day of it for granted. I know there are so many people out there just trying to get that first deal. I'm very lucky."

"You're very *talented*. Don't downplay that."

He shrugged a shoulder. "Thank you. It's not always easy. It definitely makes me crazy some days, and I sometimes worry the ideas will stop coming. But I never want to stop. It truly is my dream job."

"Well, I hope you never do. I love your words."

We stood there smiling softly at one another for a long moment, something heated passing between us. I could feel my heartbeat, my body responding to being in such close proximity to his, moments from our photo shoot coming back to me. His skin against mine, his breath in my hair... We hadn't gone to the third floor yet where the master bedroom must be, and I had a feeling it was best we didn't. I liked him. I didn't want to ruin this tentative friendship.

"Ice cream?" I said.

He took in a long breath and nodded.

"Ice cream," he said.

And with that, we went back downstairs to raid the freezer and cool off.

CHAPTER 23

Graham

I was sitting outside in one of the two ugly, clear acrylic chairs, watching the world's most famous fashion model sitting on the patio with my aging dog and having a whispered conversation nose-to-nose while sharing her ice cream. I wasn't sure what this feeling was, but it felt dangerous and amazing all at once.

When the three of us had finished our dessert, I took the dishes to the kitchen and returned with two bottles of beer.

"This is none of my business," Lior said. "But I've had two margaritas so my manners have waned a little." She grinned impishly and took a sip of her beer. "Tell me about the girlfriends you had before Nadia."

I could feel warning signals going off in my brain. Abort! Abort! Heading into dangerous territory! Beer, talk of exes, a day spent seeing one another almost completely naked. This couldn't be going anywhere good.

Or, my nether-region thought, remembering her long, lean body in that last sheer dress, it could be going somewhere spectacular.

I propped my feet up on the white stone half-wall and she copied me. I could see B just over the top of it, while the arc of sunlight was about to disappear from the fence at the back of the yard.

"Must I?" I asked, giving her a pained look.

"That bad?" she asked. "Even the very first one out the gate?"

"She set the precedent."

"Oh dear. What was her name?"

"Elizabeth."

"And what did Elizabeth do to our young, impressionable Graham?" Lior asked.

"Taught me the subtle art of gaslighting."

"Well then."

"Yeah. For a while there, I really thought she liked me just as I was." I took a sip of my beer. "What a dummy."

"You're not a dummy. Manipulators are excellent at what they do."

"And you know this because..."

"His name was Jared." She wrinkled her nose and took another drink while I waited for her to continue. "He was an actor. Well, he was trying to be. At least professionally. Privately, he was doing a hell of a job, because I certainly believed the bullshit he was serving me. Anyways, I was just making it big, being invited to parties... all the things. He started talking his way into coming with me to these parties, many of which were exclusive. And then he got me to bring him on my shoots. I didn't realize what he was doing for a long time. We were together almost two years when one of my friends told me I should really stop letting him hit up the bosses for jobs. I was mortified. No one had ever told me that's what he was doing – and I was always so busy working and having fun with my friends, that I never noticed him going off to secretly schmooze and hand out resumes. It was humiliating. He'd been using me for years. And also quietly stealing money from me."

She stopped talking and let out a long sigh.

"And where is this Jared now?" *Because I'd like to have a nice long talk with the douchebag.*

"Surprise surprise. He never could quite get his acting career off the ground. I believe he moved to Arizona, got a corporate job of some sort and found a wife. Maybe has some kids?"

"Are you guessing or do you know."

She gave me a side-eye, smirking. "I may have looked him up once or twice."

I nodded. I'd had those moments too.

"Are you sad about not ending up with Jared?" I asked.

"There's still time."

I nearly spit out my sip of beer.

"Jesus," I said, wiping my chin. Lior laughed and dragged her fingertip down through the condensation on her bottle, reminding me of earlier today when they'd poured water on one half of us, so the clothes could still be seen in their dried form. It had been hard not to stare at Lior as the dress she wore clung to her body, rivulets of water running down her skin.

"I'm never sad about missing out on being with his dumpy ass," she said. "He is *not* aging well. I went to my ten-year reunion last year and..."

"Satisfying?"

"Quite."

I lifted my bottle toward her and she leaned over and clinked hers to mine.

"So, did Jared set a precedence for you in *your* dating life?" I asked, shifting my eyes away from her wet fingertip.

"Did he ever. I chose crap guy after crap guy. Guys who were only interested in what I could give them, whether it be through my fame or my money – or just because they liked how I looked on their arm or in their bed. Which led to some complexes... and a lot of mistrust."

"That sounds awful. But Jeremy Lane seems like a good guy."

"He is. We could just never get our timing right. It all became too exhausting and, to be honest, I had major trust issues that made me not always easy to be around."

"I wonder why."

"Yeah." She laughed. "Anyways, my therapy bill is justifiably large, as you can probably imagine." She gave me a lopsided grin. "So, who came after Elizabeth?"

"Allison." I practically growled the name.

She raised an eyebrow. "Uh oh. That doesn't sound good."

"Allison was actually less subtle than Elizabeth. More of a Nadia-in-training. One would've thought I'd learned my lesson after her but alas... I married the fully developed version years later." I finished off my beer and stood. "Another?"

She tipped her head back and finished the last of her bottle off. "Yes, please."

When I returned, she changed the subject.

"Do you travel much?" she asked. "Outside of work?"

We got into a long conversation about travel then. Where we'd gone, where we'd like to go...

"I'd love to spend a month or two in Italy," she said. "I love the language, the food, the feel of it. We did a shoot in Naples once and I felt like I was in a movie. The old women talking to friends from their open windows, mopeds speeding down narrow streets, music, and the smell of food everywhere... It's colorful and crowded and dirty and beautiful."

"I've never been but it sounds amazing."

"And the pizza!" Her eyes lit up. "There's nothing like it in the States. The mozzarella is so fresh and the crust just disintegrates." She closed her eyes, as if imagining it, and I smiled. She looked so comfortable sitting on my back deck, a beer in her hand, head tipped back, dressed in comfortable sweatpants and a t-shirt with a little cupcake patch on the sleeve.

"Do you let many people see you like this?" I asked quietly.

She opened her eyes and turned her head toward me.

"You mean looking like a slob?"

"That's not at all what I meant. I just mean... free, I guess. Uninhibited. Real."

"How do you know this is the real me?"

"I may have seen a few pictures on your social media page that resemble you in this state."

"Graham... have you been stalking my socials?" she asked, peering playfully at me.

"You mean social. Singular," I said. "And no. What gave you that idea." I grinned and she laughed.

"Usually just Addie sees me like this. And her family."

"I figured as much. I like this version of you."

"And I like you with a little scruff on your face and am sad you let them cut your hair."

We stared at one another, the alcohol loosening the firm structures of the walls we'd built to survive over the years, electricity crackling between us.

"Think you'd ever give me another shot at taking a walk together?" I asked, my voice quiet, afraid if I spoke louder I'd break the connection. And despite all my misgivings about her, I was enjoying this simple moment.

"That depends," she said. "Is Brontë coming?"

"Absolutely."

"Then yes, Graham. I'd love to."

CHAPTER 24

Lior

We met the following morning at our previously designated corner, Graham looking sexy in a pair of charcoal gray joggers and a white t-shirt, Brontë looking more chipper than I'd expected, her tail wagging, her face staring up at me as she waited for me to acknowledge her.

"Good morning, sweet girl," I said, kneeling and taking her face in my hands, staring into her clouded brown eyes and then whispering to her and kissing her nose. When I stood back up, she leaned her whole body against my legs.

"And good morning to you," I said to Graham.

He grinned "I see what the hierarchy here is. Good morning to you too. Ready?"

"Let's do it."

We ambled slowly, Brontë setting the pace, Graham immediately looking apologetic.

"It's not exactly a vigorous walk," he said.

"Good. I like a nice morning meander. Gives one time to take it all in rather than speeding by and missing out on the scenery."

He smiled, his chest expanding with a long, slow breath, and then exhaled, his entire demeanor relaxing. It wasn't a stretch of the imagination to figure out who had made him feel he needed to explain and apologize for things out of his control. Nadia had clearly done a number on him and, as his new friend, I decided then and there to make it my mission to be the anti-Nadia. I had a feeling Brontë needed some of that energy too, so every so often I reached down to give her a scratch behind her ears, a pet on her head, or say some words of encouragement.

"You're looking spry today, girl," I said as we stepped off the curb to cross the street.

"She actually does," Graham said. "It's weird. Like she knew before we left this morning that we were going to have company joining us and mustered up a bit of excitement."

"I'm flattered."

"I think I'm a little jealous."

"How come?"

"The leaning... the tail wagging. She normally only does that for me and Marley."

"Uh oh," I said, raising an eyebrow at B. "Are you flirting with me, Brontë?"

"Can't blame her," Graham said, his cheeks immediately taking on a pink hue. "I mean, who wouldn't flirt with someone who's being so nice?"

"That reminds me," I said, letting him off the hook as I dug into my pocket and pulled out a folded piece of paper. "These are some supplements Addie suggested."

"Supplements?"

"Yeah. She has a holistic side to her clinic, which people, and animals, love her for."

He looked over the list and then met my eyes with a smile. "Thank you. I'll buy every one of these."

I laughed. "I mean, don't go overboard. You don't want her to get an upset stomach. Addie suggested adding one to her diet at a time. The starred ones are what you should start with."

"Thank you, Lior. That was very kind of you to ask her."

I shrugged. "She loves her job. And she happens to be a fan of yours."

"We are very appreciative."

"You are both very welcome. Addie is a genius. It's why I keep her around. And she keeps me around for the free clothes I send her."

"I doubt it's just that."

"I do offer other benefits."

"Like?"

"Constant entertainment. You should've heard her howl with laughter when she realized that I, in her words, was the 'Meet-Poop Girl'. For fuck's sake, Graham... I will never live that down for the rest of my life."

I laughed as he once again blushed.

"I will forever try and make that up to you," he said.

"As well you should," I said, lightly smacking him on the arm. "My ego has been bruised."

"You mean shat upon?"

"'Tis in the shitter."

We tossed puns back and forth for the next block until he stopped and checked his watch.

"You up for a coffee break?" he asked. "Brontë and I have a regular spot we like to go, just up the road."

"And I'm invited?" I looked down at Brontë who had taken to leaning against me again as we'd paused.

"I mean, where will she lean if you're not there to support her?" Graham asked.

I grinned. Being chosen by someone else's dog was the highest honor, and I was not about to say no to a little more hang time with the old girl.

"Well, I certainly can't let her fall, so the answer is yes."

A few minutes later we pulled up to a cute café with a sign that read Mornin' Joe's above the door. Brontë planted herself next to one of two bistro tables set out in front of a large picture window. She wore an expectant look.

"I think B is ready for her cup of joe," I said, looking through the window at the interior. "I've seen this place but have never been in."

"You're kidding," Graham said, waving at an older gentleman through the window. "This is our spot. We come here nearly every day." He pulled out a chair and motioned for me to sit. "Since this is your first time, and is my and B's place, we'd like to treat you. Drink of choice?"

"Oatmilk cappuccino, please."

He nodded, handed me Brontë's leash, and went inside.

He returned a few minutes later with the gentleman I'd seen him wave to. The older man was carrying a tray with a small vase holding a single daisy in it, two steaming mugs of coffee, and a plate of pastries.

"Lior, please meet Joe. Joe, this is my friend Lior," Graham said.

"It's nice to meet you, Joe," I said, smiling at the leaf designs drawn in the foam of both drinks. "This looks amazing. I can see why Graham loves it here. Thank you."

"I never get a daisy though," Graham said, playfully glaring at Joe who then winked at me. "Joe owns the shop and employs the most amazing baker."

"How long have you been here?" I asked as Joe pulled up a chair from the table beside ours.

While we chatted, Graham sat and sipped his coffee, smiling as he looked back-and-forth between us, clearly pleased by the connection he'd forged. I noticed with amusement that Joe kept glancing his way, an obvious glint in his eyes. I could just imagine that the older man had thoughts about his friend Graham bringing a lady around.

After a while, Joe went back inside to help out the staff and the ever-growing morning line-up waiting for food and coffee.

"He's fantastic," I said, taking a sip of my cappuccino. "And he clearly keeps an eye on the two of you."

"This place became my little haven when the shit hit the fan last year. He knows when to talk and when to just sit in companionable silence. And he's got life lessons for days. The guy has seen a lot."

When we finished our food and drinks, Graham offered to walk me home.

"Brontë will be okay?" I asked.

"I think so. She's had a rest and a treat so she should be able to handle a couple more blocks."

"So, what's the rest of your day look like?" I asked as we walked.

"Still just trying to finish up this new book. I'll probably do a couple of sprints on that and then call it a day. I need to write my article for Around the Neighborhood, and I have some emails to respond to. How about you?"

We had reached my front stoop and I gestured toward the house.

"Do you want to come in for a bit? I don't have a pebble lawn, but B is welcome to lie down in the grass if she wants."

"Ha ha. Very funny." He looked down at Brontë who had taken to standing beside me again. "You sure we won't be interrupting anything?"

"All I've got planned is some research and I can do that later."

"Well then, we'd love to see where world famous fashion model Lior Flynn hangs her designer hats." He looked up at the faded baseball cap on my head. "Or... whatever."

I smacked him on the arm and then led the way up the front steps.

"This is... stunning," he said, stepping into the living room and taking in the tall ceilings, layers of patterns, artwork on the walls, my furniture that was both stylish and cozy, and the floor-to-ceiling bookcases. "It's not at all what—"

He stopped when he noticed I was smirking at him.

"Tell me, Graham Forrester," I said. "What exactly *were* you expecting my house to look like? Yours?"

His face turned red. "Maybe. My apologies."

"You should be." I grinned. "Though I did bring in a decorator once and she wanted to do exactly what Nadia did to your house. I didn't call her back."

"It's really lovely and warm."

"Well," I said, kneeling to give Brontë some ear scratches. "I have to admit that for the most part it came to me like this. My dad had fantastic style. It was our haven in the city when I was a kid. He left it to me when he died."

"But you were so young."

"Yeah. It sat empty for years. When I was scouted and realized it wasn't a fluke and I was actually going to do this thing, I moved to New York and opened the house back up. As soon as I had some real money coming in, I did a little remodeling and bought some furniture. It was a labor of love at a time when I felt pretty lonely."

"I'll bet it was cathartic too. Breathing life back into a place you had lived with someone you loved."

"It was." I stood and headed for the kitchen, patting my leg for Brontë to follow. "Come on girl, I have a yard for you to christen."

We stood on the patio and watched the old girl wander and sniff half-heartedly at the new surroundings, and then we went back inside, leaving the door open in case she wanted to rejoin us.

Graham went directly to the bookshelves and pointed.

"May I?" he asked.

"Have at it," I said. "Can I get you a glass of water or something? Juice?"

"I recall you mentioning something about homemade cookies last night... Tell me the truth. Are they really store-bought?"

My jaw dropped in faux outrage.

"I feel like you think I only know how to pose and smile."

"I know you can also do a sexy sort of death glare thing too."

I gave him the glare.

"I don't know if I should be turned on or scared."

"Shit, I must be doing it wrong again."

He laughed, asked for a glass of water and a cookie, and then laughed harder when I flipped my hair over my shoulder and did my famous runway walk in my baggy sweats all the way to the living room.

He was perusing my selection of books, pulling out classics, current titles, books in Italian and French, atlases, and a vintage guide for being a proper hostess. He ran a finger over a hand-sized globe, a small vase with a dried bouquet, a framed picture of me and Addie, and a miniature metal Space Needle statue, before moving on to the shelf dedicated to books on writing, and above it... his books, beside which sat the framed poem he'd written for me after he'd cleaned my shoe.

He pulled one of the copies of his books from the shelf and flipped it open. It was signed to "Elle".

"Uh oh," I said. "You've found out my secret."

"That you know how to be a proper hostess?" He pointed to the vintage book he'd noticed a minute ago.

I raised the plate of cookies in my hand. "I mean, that's a no-brainer. But no. I meant my secret about being a fangirl."

"You're a fangirl? Of me?"

"I am. Well, I was. Until—"

"The Meet-Poop," we both said and then laughed.

"Snickerdoodle?" I said, holding the plate out to me.

"Thank you," he said, taking one and then holding up the book. "How come you had me sign it to Elle? And when did I sign this?"

I blushed.

"It was a few years ago. I came to the event in disguise." I pointed to my baseball hat, then the pair of glasses on my coffee table. "And I didn't want to say Lior, just in case."

"So you said L, like the letter, and didn't correct me when I spelled it out."

I nodded.

"I owe you a new copy."

"I like my copy," I said, taking it from him and hugging it to my chest.

"Are any of the others signed?" he asked.

"Just one. I didn't want to come off as a complete stalker."

"*Are* you a stalker?"

"Nah. But I am a fan. Have been for years. Which was why I was extra mortified by that article."

"I'm really sorry."

"Don't be. It's funny now. Addie nearly bust her stitches laughing when she realized I was *the* Meet-Poop Girl. She will never let that go. And for that reason alone, you shall remain my mortal enemy."

"And here I thought we were getting along so well." He looked down at the cookie that was nearly gone. "Wait, is this poisoned?"

I took a large bite of the cookie in my own hand.

"Nope," I said with my mouth full.

He pointed at the shelf filled with books on writing.

"Are these yours?"

"The books on my bookshelf in my house?"

He laughed. "Sorry. You said the house used to belong to your dad so I thought maybe they had been his."

"That's the second time you've insulted me since coming inside my house," I said, glaring playfully at him. "Who's stepping in it this time?"

He dropped his head comically and then reached for one of the books.

"I love this one," he said, flipping through the pages that were heavily marked up by a highlighter. "I see you do too."

"It's my favorite."

"So... you write then?"

I chewed my lip, wondering how much I wanted to divulge to this man that not so long ago I'd thought was my enemy. I couldn't imagine he was like the users of my past. He certainly didn't have Jared-level vibes. But with my track record, that didn't mean much of anything.

But despite the warning bells going off in my head – *Don't trust! Turn back!* – I found myself reaching for the three-ring binder he'd yet to set his sights on, cursing myself as I handed it over, and wondering what the hell I was doing, because none of this was like me.

Lior Flynn never asked a guy into her house. Lior Flynn definitely didn't share her desserts – and certainly not the fresh-baked cookies she only made a dozen of at a time, because at some point her metabolism was going to fail her. More importantly, Lior Flynn didn't talk to herself in the third person. But Lior Flynn was freaking out right now because she'd just handed Graham Forrester a binder of articles she'd written herself.

His eyes widened when he opened it, and as my heart thudded in my chest, a light sheen of sweat rising on my upper lip, he took a seat and started to read.

CHAPTER 25

Graham

As soon as I read the first article I knew I was in trouble. Lior was a gifted writer. Insightful. Witty. And kind. Her words mesmerized, and I felt like I was falling down a rabbit hole I'd never find my way out of if I didn't leave now. Or at least soon... after I read one more of the articles she'd compiled in the binder now sitting in my lap.

When I finally looked up again, Lior was curled up on the sofa, absentmindedly petting Brontë who was lying on the floor in front of her.

"Lior," I said, sitting up, my eyes still on the last article I'd read. "These are good. *Really* good. Why aren't you using your name on them?"

She looked up from the book she was reading and then down at the binder.

"I have to keep them separate."

"Why?"

She gave B a last pet, set down the book, and sat up.

"Years ago, Addie and I came home from a high school party feeling sad and discouraged. The boy Addie liked had been chasing another girl all night, and I was on the back end of a major growth spurt and hadn't yet found clothes to fit my new gangly body. My jeans were too baggy and too short, my shirt hugged nothing of note, and I'd had an unfortunate run-in with my curling iron that evening that left a one-inch singe mark on my forehead. I'd been teased by Katee, one of the more popular girls, and we'd left early to drown our sorrows in a pint of Ben and Jerry's. Each.

When we got back to my house, my mother took one look at us and sat us down. Now, normally she'd have only commented on our ice cream consumption and let my stepdad Cal deal with our sad-sack selves, but for whatever reason, on this night, she imparted some wisdom, raising her hand to head height and circling it."

She demonstrated.

"I'd rolled my eyes, of course, and shoved a huge bite of Coffee Toffee Bar Crunch in my mouth. But she was adamant. She told us to exist up here." Lior kept circling her hand. "To rise above the bullshit. To never, *never* give anyone else the power to bring us down. We. Exist. Up. Here. We live up here. We don't lower ourselves to their level. We don't let them pull us down. We keep ourselves separate and never let them in where they can hurt us. We are better than that. We are better than all of them."

She dropped her hand and sighed.

"My mother, who I'd never understood and who kept me at arm's length distance, perhaps wasn't the empty shell of a person I'd always thought her to be. I'd realized in that moment that she'd become accustomed to hiding her feeling out of a need to survive in a world that was often cruel to women. She kept herself separate. She created walls. By existing *up here*." Lior raised her hand again. "Even with me. Her own daughter. Which of course took away what could've been a loving and nurturing relationship between us, and instead turned it into one where I was nitpicked and criticized for nearly everything I did and said. But still, that moment had made me see something. It had allowed me to know something about her. And though our relationship didn't change

– and in fact became more strained as the years went on – having that tiny bit of knowledge made me tolerate her when I might not have otherwise. That knowledge also taught me to keep part of me separate too. From her initially. And then to anyone not Addie. Because one day I would become as famous, if not more so, than she had been. And keeping a part of me for me has been my saving grace."

I nodded, but inside I ached for her. For what she'd lost by keeping parts of herself back. I understood it – having had to learn to keep some things private in this age of too much information, but the toll it had taken on her was obvious to me now. She was exhausted. She lived in a cage, albeit a beautiful one, but that didn't change the fact that it was indeed a cage.

"I get it," I said. "But it's a crime people don't know it's you."

"They might," she said, pulling at a thread on the armchair. "One day."

"Oh?" I set the binder on the coffee table and leaned forward.

She shrugged, not meeting my eyes, her wall trying to erect itself back into place.

"Your secret's safe with me, Lior."

She chewed her lip, a nervous habit I was endeared to now, and then shrugged. Almost to herself, as if she'd been having a conversation inside her head.

"I have a friend in Seattle that works for a major newspaper there," she said. "She's been trying to get me to come on board as a regular columnist for the past couple of years and I'm finally considering it. But it would mean changing my life somewhat. I've been thinking for a while now that maybe it's time to scale back modeling... but the thought of that is also hard. It's scary to think about giving up what I've built here."

"That's understandable," I said. "Big life changes are terrifying. But they can also be amazing. New chapter and all that. Would you move to Seattle?"

"That's part of what I'm considering. And what I was going to be researching today. Houses... neighborhoods..."

"Marley would freak out if you moved to Seattle. Maybe don't tell her. She'll never stop asking you to go shopping with her."

"I mean... that seems like something to go in the pro column." She grinned.

I hesitated telling her I'd been thinking of moving myself. To Seattle, no less. Partially because of Marley, but also because New York had lost a bit of its shine for me in the past couple of years. I yearned for new scenery, roads I'd never traveled before, a different muse to play with. And after my trip to see where Marley would be attending college, I'd found myself a bit smitten with Seattle. The views were incredible and I ached to see those mountains up close. Plus, Lior had told us it was only a couple of hours to the coast as well. Maybe I'd become a whole new me. Buy a little trailer and take road trips around the state. Learn to snowboard. Get a kayak and go looking for orcas...

"What's that look on your face?" Lior asked.

"Nothing."

"I just told you something very personal about me. *And* let you read my articles. Spill it, Forrester."

"Fine. But this is only a coincidence. I'm not a weirdo."

"Oh," she sat up straight. "This sounds intriguing."

"It's really not. I've just been considering a move to Seattle myself."

"Is it because strange women yell at you in the park in Brooklyn?"

I laughed. "That was actually a highlight. And it gave me something to write about in my weekly column." I gave her a cheeky grin. "But no. I just need something different. Something new that I can explore. I've started to feel..."

"Stifled?" she said, finishing my sentence.

I eyed her thoughtfully.

"Yes," I said. "Exactly that."

She nodded as if she understood.

"It's a beautiful state with a lot to offer." She peered at me. "I can totally see you there."

"Yeah?"

"As soon as you grow out your hair again."

"It's growing!" I said and rubbed my jaw. "And the scruff is back."

"I noticed."

Her cheeks reddened and for a moment neither of us said anything.

"Well hey," I said, getting to my feet. "I really should get home."

"Of course," Lior said.

We both stood at the same time and, in doing so, ended up standing inches from one another, the heat between us becoming something electric.

The quip on the tip of my tongue evaporated and I suddenly couldn't speak, her close proximity overwhelming. For some reason, despite all my misgivings, in that moment every logical thought left my mind and all I could do was stare at her lips inches from mine.

She exhaled, a tiny puff of air that felt like a surrender, and then her lips were on mine.

I had no idea who moved first, and didn't care. She tasted of snickerdoodles. Vanilla and sugar and cinnamon. And she kissed me so tentatively, with tiny laps of her tongue as if trying to figure me out mouth-first. It was maddening. And sexy as fuck. I wanted to press her against a wall and feel every inch of the body I'd glimpsed during our photo shoot before covering it with mine and having her so thoroughly, every wall she'd ever constructed would fall to pieces at our feet.

But a moment later I realized we were in front of the window. The window that faced the street. The window with curtains that were wide open.

"Shit," I said, releasing her and taking a step back as I tried to catch my breath.

"Definitely not the most flattering review I've had of my kissing," she said.

Her cheeks were bright pink and she was looking at my chest, not my face.

"Sorry," I said. "It's just—"

"It's fine. You don't have to explain. It was an ill-thought-out moment." She moved to the other side of the room, her entire demeanor turning defensive. "You should get going."

"No, Lior—"

"You don't have to say anything. I swear," she said. "It's not a big deal. I—"

I walked across the room and wrapped my hands around her arms gently. She stopped talking but still wouldn't meet my eyes.

"The window," I said. "The curtains are open. I'm sure there are people who know where you live. I wouldn't want to add more fuel to the media fire."

"Oh." The word was a whisper and she finally met my gaze, the tension leaving her body. "Thank you."

I wanted to kiss her again, but the moment, the heat, was gone. For now.

She bent to give Brontë a few pets, waking the old girl up, and then helped her to her unsteady feet and led her to the front door where she clipped her leash in place.

I pointed to the binder on the coffee table.

"Those are fantastic. Thoughtful. Smart... Insightful."

"Thank you, Graham. That means a lot coming from you."

I could see it now. The wall was back in place. But not fully. There was space for me now. A little cove of trust.

"I'm not done with them," I said. "I'll be back to read the rest."

"Okay."

I took the leash, my fingers brushing against hers.

"Do you think you might want to join Brontë and I for a walk again tomorrow?" I asked.

She hesitated for a moment, chewing her lower lip.

"Can we go to Joe's again?" she asked, looking at me with those molten golden-brown eyes.

"We'd be stupid not to."

CHAPTER 26

Lior

I didn't call Addie like I normally would. For some reason I didn't take what had happened between Graham and I as lightly as I'd pretended in my living room. I didn't have the bandwidth to tell her all the details and giggle like we had a million times before because there was something between us. It was obvious. But I knew he was hurting still from his last relationship, and I still wasn't sure I could trust myself to notice the red flags a man showed me, whether blatant or not. How did I know Graham, who had a book coming out early next year, wouldn't use my celebrity to garner more attention for it?

He didn't seem the type. But they never did.

And yet... that kiss.

"Fuck me," I said, staring at my reflection in the bathroom mirror.

My body was still buzzing from the feel of his tongue in my mouth and his hard body against mine. How badly I'd wanted to run my hands over his chest and reach down the front of his joggers and get a handful of him. I pushed off the counter and shook my head, as if the action would remove the thoughts from my mind. How the hell was I supposed to take a leisurely walk with him tomorrow and not think about that kiss the entire time?

Instead of sitting down to do the research I'd planned for the afternoon, I took the subway into Manhattan and did my best to forget things with a shopping spree that required a cab ride home and the driver's help getting everything inside. Afterwards, I changed back into my sweats and went for a jog, music blasting in my ears, eyes on the pavement ahead of me. I didn't stop until my shirt was soaked, taking a seat on a bench to catch my breath and pulling my headphones off, the quiet of the park a much-needed respite.

"Lior?"

I looked up and found myself staring up at Graham, his own shirt damp with sweat.

His blue eyes were steady on mine, holding my gaze, a current passing between us and shooting straight through my center, making me squirm with want.

"Hey," I said, my voice husky.

"Hey."

We stared at one another.

"Would you maybe want to get dinner with me?" he asked.

"I would."

More staring.

"I'll need a shower first," I said.

"Me too."

We stayed like that for a moment more, and then I stood and, without a word, we walked back to my house.

Neither of us said a thing as I let us in. We took off our shoes in silence and then he followed me up the stairs to my room where he paused to close the curtains before joining me in the bathroom.

I reached down to pull off my shirt but he shook his head and stepped toward me, placing his hands on either side of my face as he looked down at me and kissed me tenderly.

He moved closer, his body against mine, his lips parting my

lips, his tongue filling my mouth, and I could feel his need, the length of his dick hard and solid against my stomach.

I moaned softly and he backed me into the countertop, lifting me so that I was sitting on it, and pressing himself into me as my legs wrapped around his waist and he rolled his hips slowly, exquisitely, pressing against my clit as I sunk my nails into his back.

He moved back to remove my shirt, then his own, and then stared down at the white sports bra I was wearing that had become sheer with my sweat.

"Goddamn, you're beautiful," he whispered.

This time I shook my head, pressing my fingertip to his lips. I pulled the sports bra off and watched his eyes devour me.

He stepped away again, this time to turn on the shower, and then returned to help me off the counter, remove the rest of my clothes, and then his own.

Silently, we stepped into the shower and this time when he kissed me, he didn't hold back.

We explored one another within those glass walls like I'd never explored before, my mouth sliding down his body, his fingers finding all my hidden places. We barely remembered to get clean before he wrapped me in a towel and carried me to my room where he sat me on the edge of the bed and stared down at me, his own body naked and wet and glistening like a fucking god before me.

There was only a moment of hesitation when he realized we'd need a condom. But I directed him to my bedside table and we were off and running again.

Desire and need coursed through me as he stood over me. I hadn't wanted anyone like this in a long time. In fact, I'd never wanted anyone like I wanted Graham in this moment. There was something primal about the way I craved him. And it wasn't just that I wanted him. I wanted to be *had* by him.

Despite my job, I had never felt particularly comfortable in my body, shying away from being looked at by the men I'd been with. But with Graham I wanted him to look. To want. To *need*.

Unable to take it anymore, I unwrapped the towel and slid to the floor in front of him.

He was beautiful. Smooth and hard and ready.

"Lior," he said and then gasped as I took him in my mouth, his hips rocking slowly as he slid against my lips.

He pulled out suddenly and lifted me back onto the edge of the bed. I started to scoot backwards but he grasped my thighs, holding me in place, his eyes meeting mine as he knelt, and spread my legs, pinning them open as he began to lick me slowly from one end to the other.

And I watched. Something I'd never done before, my mouth open as my breath came fast, my body beginning to convulse as he lapped and sucked and licked.

Holy mother of pleasure.

A-fucking-men.

It was too much. Too many sensations. I tried to scoot away but he held me tight, sliding his fingers in me as he continued to lick, and my back arched and I shouted out, breaking the silence.

I collapsed to the duvet but he wasn't done with me. He climbed onto the bed and laid beside me, his fingertips grazing slowly across my collarbones to my neck, making my body light up from some sort of center source I couldn't tamp down now if I wanted to.

He was a magnet and I was moving toward him, unable to stop myself, my need to touch and be touched by him too strong. The warmth of his hands on me emanating throughout my body, goosebumps rising as if they too were desperate to get closer.

"Have me," he said, his voice husky.

My body nearly erupted at the words.

Have him. However, I wanted him. He was mine for the taking.

I pushed him onto his back and knelt beside him. He watched as I wrapped my hand around him, feeling his thickness, the heat of him, the pulsing beneath the skin. I watched his face as I stroked him and then leaned down, licking up and around him before taking every inch of him in my mouth until I felt him at the back of my throat.

"Fuuuck," he groaned, digging his fingers into my hair as he thrust into my mouth. "Lior."

He pulled me gently from him and I looked up to see the need in his eyes. Grabbing the condom from the bedside table I straddled him and took one of his hands.

"Touch me," I whispered.

He grasped my hips with both hands and began drawing circles around my clit, making me move above him, hovering inches above his dick which was practically begging to be taken. I lowered down a fraction of an inch, letting the head of him just barely press against my opening.

He moved fast, flipping me onto my back and looming over me before grabbing the condom from where I'd left it on the pillow beside us. I heard the rip of the wrapper and then he was kneeling between my legs, his eyes on mine as he entered me slowly, spreading me, filling me, pushing... taking. I grasped onto him, pressing him further into me, pulling him down to me so that his chest was against mine.

"Kiss me," I said.

"Kiss *me*," he said.

And I did. I kissed him with an abandon I didn't know I had, letting go of the worry that he was just here because of who I was, and just taking what I wanted from him as our bodies, slick with sweat, found a rhythm all on their own.

He pulled away and got on his knees, pulling me with him, one hand on my waist as he held me where he wanted me, the other between my legs, his thumb rubbing me into oblivion.

I writhed, but he held on tight, watching as he pushed inside me over and over, the friction building until I came apart and, a moment later, with a final thrust, he let go, his entire body tensing as he came hard and hot inside me.

Spent, he pulled me to my side and laid with me, our bodies still connected in the most intimate of ways.

"Well," he said. "I think we might need another shower."

I laughed against his chest.

"I went for a run to get you out of my head," he said, his voice soft. "And then there you were." He twisted a lock of my hair around his finger.

"Funny. I went for a run to get *you* out of *my* head."

"How did that go for you?"

I leaned back and let my eyes move down the length of his body.

"Pretty good, I think. You?"

He leaned over and gave me a soft, slow kiss before moving away and staring into my eyes.

"Best run I ever had."

CHAPTER 27

Graham

We fell asleep and I woke an hour later to Lior's hand on my chest and my body and brain battling it out.

I'd just had incredible sex with a beautiful woman I actually liked. She was funny, kind, sexy as hell... Every inch of her body intertwined with mine felt more right than any other had. Ever.

What had we done?

"Are you freaking out right now?" Her voice was sleepy.

"Not even a little bit."

"Liar." She chuckled.

"It's only a modicum of freaking out. Not a full-fledged meltdown."

"Is it okay if I have a full-fledged meltdown?" she asked and I looked over to see tears peeking from beneath her lashes.

"Lior?"

"Did we ruin our friendship?" she asked, her voice small, her eyes still closed.

I sighed, relief and something else filling my body. I was glad she was worried about the bond we seemed to be forming too. But was that also disappointment I felt? Was I upset that she hadn't said she wished we could be more? Surely we'd crossed a friendship boundary somewhere in between her taking me in her mouth and me burying myself between her legs.

"Actually," I said. "This is how the ancients, way back in olden times, sealed their friendships. I've seen videos of the drawings they did on walls of caves."

She pressed her lips together, trying not to laugh. But it didn't hold.

"You're dumb," she said, hauling herself up so that she was sitting and taking the sheet with her.

I sat beside her and took her hand.

"I think our new friendship is still intact," I said, unable to meet her eyes. "We just went a little off-track. We veered off-course."

"Just a little bit."

"Minor veer. More of a smidge." She laid her head on my shoulder, her dark hair trailing down my arm, and I tried to stay focused. "I think as long as we're both okay with it—"

"We can veer off course again?" she asked and I laughed. But just the thought of being inside her again made me hard and she noticed before I was able to sufficiently cover it up.

But this was not to be. While Lior was definitely not a Nadia, she had her own brand of drama swirling around her. And I just couldn't put myself through that. Not for anyone. It was too hard. Too invasive. Too much.

"I'm not sure that's a good idea," I said, my dick swearing silently at me. "As badly as I want to... As good as it was— "

"It was really good," she said and I smiled.

"You lead a kind of lifestyle too much like one I was part of not that long ago. A lifestyle that brought me a lot of pain and trust issues and anger."

"And I," she said. "I can't see red flags when they're being waved inches from my face. You seem lovely. Witty and sexy and

—" She lifted her head and rested it on the headboard. "But I don't trust myself to make good decisions. And so here we are."

"Here we are."

We were quiet as we sat staring at the rumpled bedding, the depressing thought that not being together was actually the healthy decision hanging between us. Despite all the signs that we could be really good together. But if there were ever two people who should not read into signs – it was the two naked people sitting on Lior's bed.

"So, what now?" she asked.

"I suppose I should put my pants back on and get back home to Brontë," I said, trying to lighten the mood. "Do you still want to meet us for a walk tomorrow?"

"Yes, please."

I slid from the bed and started to walk to the bathroom where I'd left my clothes nearly two hours ago. Feeling suddenly self-conscious, I turned to look back at Lior who was watching me with something so intense in her eyes I immediately got hard again.

"Graham," she said, her a whisper.

My name in her mouth was all it took. She let the sheet drop from her breasts and I reached down and yanked it away from her entirely, exposing the length of her body. A guttural sound I'd never heard before rumbled in my throat as she bent her legs, pulling them up, and then spread them for me. Friendship could wait another few minutes.

"So," I said, when we were once again finished and a tangled mess of sweaty limbs. I kissed her bare shoulder and gave her a grin. "Tomorrow morning then? Same corner?"

"You got it, pal."

"Can't wait, buddy."

I threw my sweaty clothes on and then she donned a robe and walked me to the front door, careful to stay out of view from anyone that might be walking by on the sidewalk.

When I awkwardly turned to say goodbye, her hands were covering her face.

"Don't make it weird," she said, her voice muffled through her fingers and I laughed but felt relieved. We really were on the same page.

"Have a good night, Lior."

Her hands slid from her face and I felt my heart give a tug. *Dammit.*

"You too, Graham. Give B a hug from me."

I hurried down the front steps and turned to wave. She waved back and then shut the door. With a long sigh I walked back home to my white-on-white home and my sweet old dog, wondering what the hell we'd just gotten ourselves into. Because despite what we'd both said, there had been some pretty clear fireworks between us, and I knew, at least for me, it was going to take a lot to forget them.

We met the next day, as agreed. And, after some initial awkwardness, returned to our usual banter as we took a slow, ambling walk followed by a quick coffee at Joe's, before Lior had to hurry off to get to a job. But not before crouching down on the pavement beside Brontë and having a private conversation with her. I watched my old girl's tail give the sidewalk two resolute thwacks, and then Lior gave her a last kiss on the head, waved goodbye to me and Joe, and walked away.

"I like that one," Joe said and I eyed him with surprise. He'd never said that about Nadia. Not even in the beginning when she'd been on her best behavior, tolerating my love for the cozy little coffee shop before slowly removing herself from our mornings here in favor of a slicker cafe a couple blocks over.

"Yeah," I said, not offering up anything more. But I could feel the old man's eyes watching me.

"A woman who gets down on your dog's level is a woman you want to keep around."

"Don't think I don't know it, Joe."

"What's the hesitation then?"

"I think I need therapy."

"Don't we all."

"I have a habit of picking a certain kind of woman. I'm worried Lior—"

"She isn't that type."

I laughed. "You just think she's cute."

"Cute," he said, waving his hand. "Cute is not a word one uses for women like her."

I sighed and nodded.

"I know, Joe," I said. "I know that all too well."

A group of five entered the cafe and Joe pushed up from his seat.

"Best get back inside. See you tomorrow?"

"That you will."

Alone again with Brontë, my mind returned to Lior. To her body pressed to mine. To the sound of her breath when we'd grown still, our voices and bodies quieted. There was something about her that made me want to take a sledge hammer to my concerns – both my penchant for manipulative women and her lifestyle in the limelight. I knew she had demons to contend with too though. And so friends we would be, as long as we didn't keep veering.

"Timing," I said to Brontë. "It's a bitch."

CHAPTER 28

Liar

I checked the time on my phone. Eight a.m. I looked down the street, a little smile on my face in anticipation of seeing them come into view.

Meeting Graham and B had quickly become my favorite part of the day over the past two weeks. After the initial awkwardness, post-veering, we were able to fall into a comfortable routine of walking and talking about how we'd spent our evenings and what we had on for the day ahead.

But each day, the moment I saw him and his eyes met mine, his lips moving in a conversation with Brontë that I couldn't yet hear, my heart sped up and a yearning filled my body so powerfully, I was surprised I didn't orgasm right there on the sidewalk.

I checked my watch again and pulled my hat lower over my eyes. They were a minute late, which sometimes happened so I didn't sweat it. I wondered if Marley had called him. Classes were in full swing, autumn had arrived, and every couple of days he told me how she had called on her way to class to tell him some funny incident from the day before, not wanting to forget it, in case he could use it in a story.

"She's been doing that since I got published," he'd told me on one of our walks. "Telling me tidbits from her day she found interesting in case they might make it into one of my books."

"And have any of them?"

"The mom having a meltdown outside her car after dropping her kid off?" he said, waiting to see if I recognized the moment.

"A Day of Firsts," I said, naming the book it had come from with a laugh. "Really? That came from Marley?"

"My stepmom, Lisa, had dropped her off at school one day and they'd watched another mother completely lose it and—"

"And then drop her fancy coffee cup in a puddle?"

"Yep."

It was now eight oh-three. I frowned, leaning to try and see further down the street, but there was still no sight of Graham or Brontë. I wondered if I'd forgotten him say he'd be late today. Or maybe...

I chewed the inside of my lip. There had been a moment the day before when we were at Mornin' Joe's. He'd said something sweet and I'd reached out and squeezed his hand. It was brief and totally innocent, but perhaps he'd been put off by it. Despite our moment at my house two weeks ago, we hadn't veered off the friend path again, save for some heated looks that had caused us both to blush and look away, and a bit of sexual tension. But neither of us had even hinted at crossing the line again, and he'd even gone so far as saying outright that he was glad we'd decided not to indulge in a friends with benefits scenario, which had hurt my feelings just the tiniest bit. Partially because he'd felt the need to warn me off. Partially because I had, in my bed at night, trusty vibrator in hand, entertained the thought.

Eight oh-seven. Fuck.

I was sure he'd said "See you tomorrow?" yesterday as we left the coffee shop.

"What do I do?" I whined out loud. Two women glanced over their shoulders at me as they passed by. Should I text? Potentially coming off as a girlfriend tracking her boyfriend's every move?

Should I just take the walk myself and go home? Or should I stop by his house. Perhaps he and B were just getting a late start and I'd end up running into them on the way?

I nodded. Yep. That's what I was going to do. But I'd text on the way. In a totally nonchalant way.

My text went unanswered and my ambling turned into strides, my eyes trained straight in front of me as I hurried toward Graham's house. Was I hurrying because I was worried something had happened to him or B? Or was I rushing because that post by his ex still haunted me sometimes? Either way, there was no sighting of him or Brontë by the time I took the steps two at a time to his front door and rang the bell.

I counted the seconds as I waited for the door to open. I was at one hundred and eighty-three, and clearly moving in to stalker territory when I heard the deadbolt slide open and sucked in a breath at the sight of Graham's drawn face and red eyes.

"Graham?" I said, and then a feeling of dread filled me and I took a step forward. "Brontë?"

He swallowed, his eyes filling with tears, and stepped backwards, opening the door wider and allowing me inside.

"Is she...?" My voice trailed off.

"Not yet," he whispered, and took my hand, leading me to the kitchen where his beloved dog lay on her bed, her big brown eyes staring straight ahead.

"Oh," I said, my voice soft as I let go of Graham's hand and dropped to my knees in front of her, my own eyes now filled with tears too. "Hey girl." I took her face in my hands, kissed her nose, and then rested my forehead against hers.

There was the faint sound of her tail thumping twice against the tile floor.

Graham kneeled beside me, his shoulder leaning against mine, his hands replacing mine as he cradled his long-time friend's head. I wrapped an arm around his back, the other hand petting Brontë, whose breaths were shallow, her eyes now at half-mast.

"You're such a good girl, Brontë," I said softly. "Thank you for being so nice to me and letting me hang out with you guys. Even after the terrible way I acted when we met. I've had the best time getting to know you, sweet girl. It's been an honor."

Graham's body shook beside me.

"You're the goodest girl," he said. "I love you so much. Thank you for hanging in with me, even when I made you live with that whiny monster who wore way too much perfume." He sniffed. "And the time that terrible dog groomer shaved your hair... you were such a good sport about it, even though I knew you were embarrassed. And the way you followed me around and laid on the bed beside me for weeks after grandma died was worth all of Nadia's screaming and threatening about hair on the comforter."

Tears streamed down my face.

"I love you, B," Graham said. "Thank you for choosing me. I'm going to miss you every day, sweetheart."

There was silence, and then Brontë sighed... and was gone.

Graham's body shook in a silent sob and I wrapped both arms around him and held him as he grieved. We sat for a long while like that, leaning into one another and just being.

After a while I excused myself to call the veterinarian's office from the phone number listed on a business card on the refrigerator, knowing he was in no shape to have the conversation that was needed.

Thankfully they provided a service for such occasions, and I was reassured they'd be there within the hour. We could come along, if we wanted.

We did.

It was agonizing watching Graham leave his friend behind at the vet's office, and when the cab pulled up to Graham's house, I didn't even bother to ask if I should stay, I just paid the driver and got out behind him.

"What can I do for you?" I asked after closing the front door behind us.

We stood in the entryway and he couldn't have looked more like he didn't belong in this stark house that was devoid of warmth... and his dog.

He shook his head. "I don't know," he whispered.

"Do you even want to be here? Is there a friend I can call? Or I could get you a hotel room. I have a guestroom you could hole up in for a while. The hostess is nice but she only serves donut holes for breakfast."

He didn't even smile. I wasn't sure he'd even heard me as he looked through me, then toward the kitchen where the corner of one of Brontë's beds could be seen.

"I wouldn't be in your way?" he asked, his voice husky with emotion.

"Of course not."

He packed his laptop, a few notebooks, a book that was dog-eared at least two dozen times, and a duffel bag of clothes.

"All good?" I asked, pulling the strap of his messenger bag over my shoulder.

"All good," he said.

We walked the few blocks to my house in silence, and then I left him to get himself settled in the guest room on the second floor while I made us both cappuccinos and texted Addie, who still didn't know about what had happened between Graham and I.

"How is he?" she texted back.

"He looks as though he's lost his best friend."

"He has. Give him a big hug from me."

I served the coffee in the living room with a container of donut holes, receiving a small grin in return.

"I think you have a problem," he said, and popped a chocolate dipped one in his mouth.

"And now you do too," I said, going for a powdered sugar.

We spent the next few days in a quiet little fog, sometimes talk-ing, sometimes sitting in companionable silence, him working or reading, me reading or making notes for an article I'd been hired to write for Elle magazine.

Rather than go on our usual morning walks, we headed straight to Mornin' Joe's instead. Like us, Joe was devastated to hear the news of Brontë, and looked with concern at Graham who was a shell of himself.

When I had to leave for a job in London for a few days, I texted Marley, who had been in contact every few days since we met in Seattle, and asked her to check in with her brother.

"Just try and distract him," I said. "Especially in the evenings if you can. I think that's when it's the hardest."

Some nights I cooked, some nights he cooked, other nights we called for takeout. We consumed a lot of television, watched a dozen or so movies, and sat at opposite ends of my sofa reading. But I could often tell he wasn't distracted as much as he pretended to be, his eyes often taking on a far-off look before filling with tears.

And we talked. He told me about his best friend from school who he'd lost touch with when married to Nadia.

"She didn't like competition," he said. "Even from Cooper, who I've known since I was eleven."

"Have I mentioned I don't like her?" I asked.

"This may come as a surprise to you, but you are not the only one."

On a particularly warm October evening, we took our plates of food outside and sat on a blanket in the grass, our beer bottles tipping over, and Graham laughing when a spider crawled across my garlic bread, causing me to scream and chuck it into one of the potted plants. He retrieved it and ate it (the bread) much to my horror.

It was nice to hear him laugh.

"See you in the morning," I said a couple hours later as I started up the stairs to the third floor.

"Goodnight, Lior," he said. But this time, instead of going to his room and quietly closing the door like he had for the past week and a half, he stood watching me from the doorway.

"You okay?" I asked.

He walked toward me and I descended the stairs and stood at the bottom, waiting. When he reached me, his eyes met mine and he wrapped his arms around me.

"Thank you," he said.

I nodded, overwhelmed by his scent, the weight of his arms around me, and the feel of his body against mine.

He started to pull away and then stopped, staring down at me, his eyes moving over my face until they reached my lips.

He exhaled, gave a small shake of his head, and then kissed me.

My reaction was instantaneous, my entire body clenching with desire as his tongue filled my mouth and his erection pressed into my stomach. We were pulling at one another's clothes until he was naked and I was wearing nothing but a sheer pink bra.

He moved me back onto the stairs and knelt between my legs, biting my nipples through the fabric of my bra and slipping his fingers inside me as I wrapped my hand around him.

"I need you," he whispered.

I repeated what he'd said to me not so long ago.

"Have me," I said, and then led him to the guest room.

He fell asleep shortly after and I gathered his clothes from the hallway and left them hanging over the chair in his room before grabbing my own and going upstairs to my bed. When I came down the next morning, he was sitting at the kitchen island, his phone in his hand.

"Brontë's ashes are ready," he said, his voice soft. "I can go get them anytime."

"Do you want me to go with you?"

He nodded.

The beautiful sea green urn Brontë came home in was placed on the mantle of Graham's living room. On one side of it, propped against the wall, was an imprint of her paw in clay that had a small hole at the top, a white ribbon running through so it could be hung on a Christmas tree if desired. Her collar lay on the other side.

Graham stood staring at the display for a long moment before turning to take in the rest of the room, his gaze landing on the empty dog bed.

"Do you want me to take it?" I asked. "And the others?"

He sighed with his whole body, his eyes filling with tears as he shook his head.

"No," he whispered. "I'd like them around. At least for a little while longer."

I nodded.

"I think..." he started and then trailed off. "I think I'm going to go lay down for a while."

"Do you want me to stay?" I asked. "Or do you need some time alone."

He walked to where I was standing and wrapped his arms around me, squeezing me tightly to him, his body rising and falling with his breath. We stood like that for a long time, leaning into one another, our hearts beating together.

"Why don't I give you some space," I said, loosening my hold and taking a step back as I stared up at him. "Time to get used to —" I looked around the room, so empty and quiet without Brontë here. "This."

I didn't want to leave him. He looked so lost without his friend. But I also knew where we stood with one another and we were treading on dangerous territory. If he stayed at my house any longer, he might grow so comfortable he forgot to leave. And I'd forget to ask him to. And then we'd both potentially find ourselves in the kind of predicaments we were trying to avoid. I wasn't willing to risk our friendship with stupidity and want.

His arms tightened, pulling me close again, but not like before. This time it was brief. An understanding.

"The past couple of weeks have been amazing," he said. "No

one has ever taken care of me like that before. I know I said it last night but, thank you."

"That's what friends do for one another, Graham."

"Yeah." His voice was soft.

"Shall I bring your duffel over later? I can just leave it on the porch for you."

But even as I said it, a current of panic ran through my body. This felt like a relationship ending. And while I knew that was silly to think, we were friends and friendships didn't end like this, I was still worried. Especially in light of what happened the night before, which neither of us had had the opportunity to mention, due to the phone call he'd gotten first thing this morning.

"Sure," he said. "Thank you."

He pulled me to him again, burying his face in my neck.

"Thank you," he whispered once more... and then he let me go.

CHAPTER 29

Graham

T he following morning I heard a knock on the door. When I opened it, a to-go coffee cup and a small paper bag from Mornin' Joe's sat on my front porch. I stepped outside, looking up and down the street, knowing it would only be from one person. But somehow she was already out of sight.

I took the gift inside, taking a sip of the coffee as I walked to the kitchen, and then placed both items on the counter and peeked in the bag. Inside was a chocolate croissant – the smell of butter and bread and chocolate intoxicating. I pulled it out and a napkin fluttered to the floor. When I picked it up, I noticed it had writing on it.

"From your friendly neighborhood porch fairy," it read in Lior's familiar handwriting, a little pair of wings drawn on either side of the word 'fairy'.

The following morning it was a vanilla bean scone. I sat on the white sofa in my white living room, pulled the scone out of its bag, and took a large bite, a small chunk falling free and landing on the cushion beside me. As I picked it up, I noticed a small triangle of blue between the cushion and grabbed it, pulling until my missing dress sock hung from my thumb and forefinger. I smiled.

Brontë.

My mind was flooded with dozens of memories. Since the day I'd brought her home she'd decided "burying" clothes was going to be one of her favorite pastimes. More often than I could count I'd heard Nadia stomping through the house shouting, "Where did you put my bra, Brontë?" Bra, top, shorts, favorite gym towel, underwear... I'd never forget the time Nadia threw a party after the renovations on the house were done and one of her influencer friends pulled a lacy hot pink thong from one of the matching white armchairs.

"Whoooo!" she'd shouted, swinging it around her finger. "Someone's sex life is on fire!"

I set my scone on the coffee table and then lifted each of the two couch cushions and chuckled at what I found. The head of the rubber chicken toy I'd thought she'd eaten several months ago when I'd found its headless body at the foot of my bed. A pair of my boxer briefs, a sock, and a kitchen towel.

I removed the items and put the cushions back and then turned to the armchairs.

"What other surprises have you left behind for me, old girl?" I asked aloud in the empty room, a small smile on my face.

I laughed as I lifted the cushion from the first chair. Beneath it was one of my flannel shirts.

"How on earth did you get this entire thing under there?" I whispered, pulling the wrinkled garment free. I held it to my nose and breathed in the scent of my sweet old dog. She must have rolled around with it before tucking it safely away.

Moving to the second chair I saw the corner of a familiar bit of fabric sticking out. I couldn't place why it was familiar until I pulled it free completely and then I laughed again. Harder this time. Until tears ran down my face and I had to sit in the chair I'd just pulled the shirt from.

Oh this shirt. I stared down at it and shook my head. It was Nadia's. A prized possession from her early days as an influencer.

She'd hunted high and low for this shirt when she'd packed up her stuff. And for weeks she'd come back looking for it, barging in the front door, asking if I'd found it. She'd made me look everywhere. Behind the washing machine, under it, in every nook and cranny of every closet... even in the attic. But neither of us had ever thought to look beneath the cushions.

I shook it out now, getting a good look at it. It had been in pristine condition as she'd kept it in a sealed bag when she wasn't wearing it for an anniversary video. Now half the collar was detached from the body of the shirt, the distinct imprint of dog incisors indented in the fabric.

"Good girl, B," I whispered, and then wadded the shirt up. Perhaps a little fire in the fire pit tonight was in order.

Just thinking of sitting out back made me wonder what Lior was up to. But I quickly pushed her from my mind. The entire way to the vet's office to get Brontë's ashes I'd wondered if I'd been stupid to take her up on her offer to stay in her guest room. It had been lovely. She had been warm and kind and gave me space, but was also available when I needed to be distracted.

And then that last night happened. I still didn't understand why I'd stood there staring at her. It was as if for a moment all the sadness I'd been feeling had cleared, making way for a yearning I couldn't tamp down.

Have me, she'd said, repeating my own words back to me and lighting my body on fire. And I'd had her. Repeatedly. Until we were both exhausted and draped over one another.

But though it had been incredible, it had left me feeling even more conflicted about us and our situation. I'd been adamant that more than friendship couldn't work with Lior. Her line of work coupled with her level of fame seemed an automatic no-go for me. But we'd hung out together loads of times now and, other than a couple of doubletakes by women at the coffee shop, she hadn't once been stopped for a photo op or an autograph. Unlike Nadia, she didn't invite it. She made a concerted effort to be invisible by wearing hats, sunglasses, no makeup, and more stained tops I'd ever seen on any one person.

Had I been wrong? Had my assumptions been based more in my fears than her facts? Was it possible being more than friends could actually be... possible?

But even as I thought it, my brain began to reject it.

Lior Flynn, the woman who had taken me into her home for two weeks without hesitation, was still *Lior Flynn*. And while the bubble she'd been able to create, most likely for my comfort, had been nice, it wasn't sustainable. She could hide from the press, but she couldn't escape them forever. They would turn up, just like they had when we'd been in Seattle with Marley. Sneaky, intrusive, and unwanted. And while I got my own bit of press here and there when a new book of mine came out, once the excitement had passed, I was left alone again. Lior would never be left alone. Not only because of who *she* was, but because of who her mother was as well. And I could just imagine the scrutiny I'd get by being connected to her. Who was this guy and why had she chosen him? I'd gone through it once with Nadia. With Lior... it would be ten times worse.

I sighed. As much as I'd love for it to happen, we were not to be. And part of me must've known that when I let her leave the other day. As much as I'd have liked her to stay, I couldn't hang onto her. We could be friends, but we had been treading in dangerous territory by my staying for so long. One of us had to keep things on track. I hated that it was me.

The next day the bag from Joe's contained a large piece of coffee cake. The day after, a brown sugar pecan brioche. I was going to need to start running again if she kept this up.

I picked up my phone.

"Good morning, Neighborhood Porch Fairy," I typed. "Thank you for the coffee and treats. But if you continue on this path, I will not be able to do much more than roll down any given path, as I will have turned into a cinnamon roll. Though, even as I typed that, I think I've decided there are worse things. Anyways. Thank you. You are very sweet."

I hit send and then immediately wished I could take the latter part of the text back.

You are very sweet? Come on, man. Do better.

I was embarrassed for myself, but also... I didn't have much more to say than that at the moment. I was grieving and I could only hope she'd understand.

I placed the bun on a plate and sat at the kitchen table, my laptop open in front of me. My agent had asked if I needed to extend my deadline, understanding the trauma of losing Brontë. But the book was the only thing getting me out of bed in the morning, and so every day I got up, drank and ate the treats left for me by Lior, and got to work. I didn't set a timer. I just put my head down, my fingers on the keys, and got to it. I was now at the final chapter.

The cursor blinked at me, waiting. I knew what was going to happen. What I wanted to say. What I wanted to leave the reader with. But I wasn't ready to let go of this story just yet. It was the last book I'd written while Brontë was alive, and it was a story of resilience, kindness to oneself, and realization. It was, in a way, my story. And while I knew how it would end, I was still torturing myself over how my own story would go forth after the book was done. I was considering taking a break. Maybe even a vacation.

My text alert went off and I opened the message from Lior, smiling at the litany of pastry emojis, followed by a bandaged heart and a simple, "Thinking of you."

I set the phone back down, shut the laptop, and took my coffee and pastry out onto the back patio and sat in one of the stupid, clear plastic chairs Nadia had purchased and put my feet up on the edge of the copper fire pit, a small, charred remnant of the shirt I'd watched burn stuck to the inside of the drum. Maybe I'd have another fire tonight. I'd found a pink ankle sock with an avocado print "buried" in my office chair last night.

Taking a long sip of coffee, my eyes fell on the red rubber ball B had once liked to gnaw on and nose around the house before picking it up and dropping it at my feet in a slobbery mess. Sadness bloomed in my chest, but instead of my eyes welling like they had so often this past couple of weeks, I just smiled, got out of my seat, and retrieved the ball, tossing it up in the air and catching it, and then laughing as it squeaked, startling me as it always had.

I set the ball on the mantle inside the circle of B's collar, and then went upstairs to work out.

* * *

The following day, after the morning knock on the door, I opened it to find Joe standing on my porch with a coffee and paper bag and gave him a confused smile.

"I'm here on assignment," he said, holding out the cup and bag. "Lior had to leave for a job. For the next three days I'll be your porch fairy."

I was positive the man blushed as he struggled to get the last two words out. I laughed at his obvious discomfort.

"Thank you," I said, taking the food and drink. "You really don't have to. Though you do make a very cute fairy."

"She threatened me," he said.

"Lior threatened you?" I grinned, trying to imagine this.

"Said she'd spread rumors that I secretly put edibles in all my pastries and that's why people thought they were so good and couldn't stop coming back for more."

"Hm," I said. "It's not a bad idea."

"The rumor or me actually doing it?"

"Both?"

"That's what I told her." He grinned for a moment and then sobered. "You doing okay?"

I shrugged. "As well as can be expected. I'll be back by the coffee shop soon."

"Good. Bring Lior. I like her." He tipped an imaginary hat then and shuffled down the front steps, leaving me to stand there, his parting words doing laps around my brain.

"Yeah," I murmured. "Unfortunately, I think I do too."

I stepped inside and closed the door, taking my treats from Joe to the kitchen table. I opened my laptop again and perused a local news site while I ate. On the front page was a video of Lior walking through the airport last night, her head down, dark hair flowing out from beneath a knit hat, people standing and pointing and taking pictures as they shouted her name in an attempt to get her to look up.

I closed my eyes, my heart heavy as I came to the decision that I needed to take a step back from our friendship. Because if we were both being honest, it was more than that. And more than that would lead to heartbreak. Possibly for her. But definitely for me.

CHAPTER 30

Lior

"Look here, Lior." Click. "Chin up." Click. "Chin down." Click. "Nice. Lighting?"

I straightened my body out while the lighting was changed, glancing at the clock on the wall as I did. We'd been at it for three hours and I ached deep in my bones. Not from the physicality of holding my body at weird angles for long periods of times, but from the mental and emotional toll.

As soon as I'd arrived I was shoved into a jumpsuit that was about an inch too short in the torso and rode up painfully, practically slicing my clit in two and making me have to hunch my shoulders to accommodate my tender parts. But hunching wouldn't show off the clothes. Thirty minutes later, my nether regions numb from lack of blood flow, I was allowed to change.

"Lior?"

I moved back into a pose.

"She needs powder. And what is happening with her hair?" the photographer asked.

The makeup and hair team moved in and I was powdered and brushed and then left on my own again beneath the hot glare of the lights.

The cameraman dropped the camera down.

"You look thick through the middle. Can you turn and twist more that way?"

That way. As if I knew what "that way" meant. But as I so often did, I tried to read his mind, moving my body accordingly. Thankfully I'd been doing this a long time now and rarely got it wrong.

"Excellent," he said.

Several dozen more clicks of the camera and I was off to change into my next outfit.

"You have gained weight?" the woman helping me slip into a pair of pants asked in a thick French accent.

I gave her a tight smile. "I have not."

"Oh. We get your measurements beforehand but... it is tight."

I knew for a fact, from having worn this designer's clothes before, that they often arrived slightly smaller than what my measurements were. I also knew I was not big by anyone's standards and this was just what they did to us females. They tried to make us feel as though it was us, because surely it couldn't be the one who sewed the garments.

"You can measure me again," I said, careful to keep my voice from taking on a tone that would be taken as rude. "Do you have a scale to weigh me on?"

Her smile was quick as she backed away to grab the blouse I'd be wearing for these next shots.

"Ah. No," she said. "I'm sure it is just a mistake."

I buttoned the pants, holding in my breath a little as I did and then donned the blouse she held out. Standing still, I let her fuss about me, tucking and pulling until everything looked just right, and then I was under the lights again, feeling the scrutiny of the photographer from behind the lens.

Click, click, click. Turn, pose, hold, hunch, arch, hold, tilt head this way, that way, look there, now there... hold.

"Bring in the male model," the photographer said, and a young man I recognized as the new face of Chanel's fragrance for men stepped into the light.

He was handsome, of course, in a brooding way, his pale skin in contrast to his dark hair, his eyes a piercing pale gray. He smiled and I smiled back and reached out a hand.

"Lior," I said.

"Jean-Michel," he said, sliding his hand slowly into mine. I resisted the urge to wrinkle my nose. "And I know who you are," he said in a thick French accent. "You are a legend. An industry great. Though your time of course is nearing its next phase."

I'd have bristled at basically being called old, but this wasn't the first time it had happened. As soon as I hit twenty-nine the whispers had started. Younger women were coming up. I didn't mind it. This is how the business worked. And there was only so long I could take the sort of scrutiny I'd received for the past decade. I'd nearly reached the end of my rope. The feelings I had tamped down time and time again were starting to rise uncontrollably. Staying "up here" like my mother had taught me, wasn't working so well anymore. The tight-fitting lid that sat snug on my box of emotions was starting to tear at the corners. Kind of like my nether-regions in this new pair of pants.

We were called to action and set our poses. Stare into each other's eyes, hold. Look over your shoulder at him, hold. Lips nearly touching. My back to his front. My lips touching the skin of his neck. His hand low on my stomach, fingers spread. Hold. Hold. Hold. I felt him growing hard against my ass and anger rose inside me.

Click.

I threw his hand off me and marched to the changing area.

"One more for—" the photographer started.

"No," I said, and disappeared behind the curtain.

When the stylist slipped in behind me, I was already calling my agent, not paying the slightest attention to what time it was in New York.

"If I get one more boner pressed against my ass, I'm suing," I said to her voice mail. I disconnected and turned to the stylist. "What's next?"

She stared at me for a long moment as if wanting to say something, and then turned to the rack of clothes. A long, diaphanous green dress was held out to me.

"Do you want... I can leave," she said, her voice quiet.

Tears welled in my eyes and I threw my head back. I would not ruin my makeup over that twat of a man. I sniffed, dabbed at my eyes, and gave her my most famous smile.

"I would love your help, Marceline. Thank you."

She nodded, giving me a sad smile, and then helped me out of one outfit and into the other. As she laced up the back of the dress I heard her whisper, "I'm sorry" and then she disappeared out the curtained door.

Two days later I was on a flight home, exhausted mentally and emotionally, moments from my three-day shoot wreaking havoc with the walls I'd firmly put in place years ago. I was angry. Violated. And sad. I was so sick of people thinking I was a thing to be used, dealt with, and thought to be problematic when I stood up for myself. I was tired of men like Jean-Michel, who treated me like a prop they could handle any way they wanted – including pressing the erection they couldn't control up against my ass as if I had been standing there waiting for it and should feel honored.

"Fucking men," I muttered under my breath, ignoring the curious look of the woman beside me.

I was done. I wanted nothing more than to get to the safety of my home, crawl into my bed, and sleep for the next several days.

I wondered if lobotomies were still in fashion.

When the cab pulled up to my house and I saw Graham sitting on the front steps, I wasn't sure which emotion to pick from the many threatening to burst from my skin.

Was I happy to see him? Yes. Was I annoyed by his "You are very sweet" text? Also yes. I understood he was hurting, but seeing as there had been something between us, a little more than "You are very sweet" felt warranted.

Shoving down the tears I desperately wanted to cry, I pasted on a smile instead as I got out of the cab.

"How did you know when I'd be home?" I asked, hauling the lone backpack I'd taken on my trip over my shoulder and noticing the coffee and bag from Mornin' Joe's in his hands, despite the fact that it was four in the afternoon.

"That's my secret and I will not tell."

I peered at him. His voice was light but there was something in his eyes. Something not right.

"Well," I said, my voice bordering on business-like. "I'm happy to see you." Could he sense that wasn't exactly true?

And then, horror of horrors, I burst into tears without warning.

"Holy shit." He got to his feet and started towards me. "Lior?"

I shook my head and hurried past him to unlock my door and get inside before someone saw me. He followed, locking the door behind us and tailed me to the kitchen where I was wiping at my face with a hand towel covered in a spider motif.

"Did something happen?" he asked. "I mean, obviously, but... Are you okay?"

I put the towel down and leaned my elbows on the kitchen island, covering my face with my hands.

"I think I've finally had enough," I said, my voice muffled.

"Tell me what happened."

His face went from concerned to furious as I told him about Jean-Michel and the comments made by the photographer and the stylist about my body. He listened as I recounted the shoot that happened the following day. The makeup artist, different from the one the day before, used a cream on my face that made me break out in hives, and everyone seemed to be annoyed with me as if I'd somehow caused it. When the rash finally calmed (after I downed some Benadryl and was covered in cold packs someone had run out to get) the hair stylist burned me with the curling iron so bad I had a blister that the makeup artist then tried to cover up – which was so painful I cried, messing up the intricate eyeliner job she'd already done. By the time I was ready for the shoot, I was shaking from nerves and lack of food because no one had thought to feed me in all that time and the only snack I'd brought I'd eaten two hours before.

My agent was out of town and had terrible WiFi, so she didn't get my messages until I was on the plane home. She apologized profusely and promised to rip them all a new one.

"We'll never book with them again," she swore.

But I wasn't sure I wanted to book with anyone again. Ever.

"I think I'm done," I said to Graham.

"I think I want to meet this Jean-Michel dickhead," he said, reaching across the island and squeezing my hand. "What can I do for you?"

"Nothing," I said, sliding my hand from his and standing up straight. "I'm fine."

"Lior. You've taken care of me like no one ever has. Let me do something for you. Please."

I pointed to the bag and coffee cup from Joe's sitting off to the side and he grinned and slid them to me.

"What else," he asked. "Do we call for takeout or make something here. Is there anything in your cupboards besides donut holes?" He got up from the stool he'd been sitting on and started opening cupboards. "Do we need to make it a movie night? What have you got going on tomorrow? We could do a movie marathon. Is it finally time to watch all five Sharknado movies?"

Despite myself, I started to laugh. "It will never be time to watch *any* Sharknado movie."

"You are a snob, Lior Flynn. Let it be known."

Again, despite the lightness in his voice, there was something off about him. Was I noticing it because I felt off too? He was obviously still sad about Brontë, as he should be, but I didn't think that was it. There was something about the way he wouldn't hold my gaze and was constantly looking away from me or around me, instead of really at me like he usually did. Before I could think about it further though, he had raided the drawer filled with takeout menus and was waving them in my face.

"Pick your poison, Flynn."

"My choice?" I asked, eyebrows raised. What I really wanted was to just crawl into bed fully clothed and pull the covers over my head. Maybe forever.

"Your choice."

Fuck it. Graham was here and he was trying to cheer me up. I'd deal with my emotions and his inability to take me as I was tomorrow. I squeezed my eyes shut, thinking about what I wanted.

"Um. You're not doing this right," he said.

"I totally am," I said and opened my eyes. "I want dumplings and steamed veggies from BK's, panang curry from Chantanee, fries from Five Guys, and a milkshake from Shake Shack."

His eyes were wide. He slowly started to nod, a smile stretching across his face.

"Impressive," he said. "Let's do it."

It took over an hour for everything to arrive. We set it all on the coffee table family style and turned on a new series both of us had been wanting to watch, leaving a couple of feet between us on the couch.

When the first episode was over, he turned to me.

"Do you really think you're done with modeling?" he asked.

I stared at him for a moment, noticing a light in his eyes that hadn't been there when he'd arrived.

"I don't know if I can put myself through it anymore," I said, my voice flat. "The whole plane ride home I recounted so many moments of feeling like shit over the years. Of being at the mercy of these people all in the name of making it big. And now I *am* a name and I'm still dealing with it. Assholes that think they can press their dicks against me or whisper innuendos or expect me to go out with them just because they're good looking or famous. As if I don't have a mind of my own."

"What would you do if you quit? Would you take that job for your friend in Seattle? Have you been looking at houses still?"

I hadn't been. To be honest, there had been a glimmer of hope after we'd had sex that first time that maybe we could figure this thing out between us. Maybe we could actually trust one another. Maybe he wasn't someone who would ever try and make me be what he wanted and use my fame to gain something for himself. And maybe he'd learn that there were upsides to my fame as well as the chaotic downsides. It wasn't all bad. And if I'd learned to live with it, he could too. But the way he looked now, I had a feeling for him there was only one answer. If we were ever going to make a go at something more than friends, I'd have to step away from the limelight. And while I was pissed over what had happened at this most recent shoot, was I really ready to give it all up?

CHAPTER 31

Graham

I couldn't sleep, my mind going over the events of the evening repeatedly. From my decision to tell Lior I thought it best we didn't see one another for a while, to her turning up at her house looking like she was going to cry – and then actually crying. And *then* she dropped the bomb that she might quit her chaotic life, giving me hope. Only for her to then get distant and say she was tired and needed to get to bed after I perhaps seemed a little too excited that maybe there was a chance of us getting together if she dropped out of the spotlight.

"Maybe I was wrong," I said out loud. "Maybe she's not into me that way and it was just about sex."

I rolled over and looked toward Brontë's bed. But she wasn't there to give me one of her looks of wisdom, and now I had something else sad to think about.

I slept fitfully, giving up around five and trudging downstairs to make coffee before the sun came up. Opening my laptop, I sat and stared at the last line I'd written. I had one, maybe two pages to go and I was done with the draft. It was my best book yet. The critics and my readers might not agree, but I knew it. Because this book was personal, and I'd poured my soul into it.

I took a sip of my cappuccino, and then placed my fingers on the keyboard and started to type.

Two hours later I'd finished the story, addressed the notes I'd left for myself within the manuscript, and printed it off. For Lior. I knew she was dying to read it and I wanted her to be the first person to get their eyes on it.

Checking the time on my laptop, I picked up my phone and sent her a text.

"Race you to the corner." And then I waited.

And waited.

A half hour later she still hadn't responded.

"Must still be sleeping," I said, feeling empathy for her. She'd been in a state when she'd gotten home the night before. She was probably going to need a day or two to recover. I got to my feet. I'd bring her a cappuccino and coffee cake from Joe's again. I'd be *her* porch fairy.

But when I arrived an hour later and rang the bell, my freshly printed manuscript in a large manilla envelope under my arm, a to-go coffee cup in my other hand with a bag hanging from my wrist, she didn't answer.

Putting the coffee down on the stoop, I checked my phone to see if she'd texted back and I hadn't heard.

Nope.

"What the hell," I murmured, looking up at her windows. But all the curtains were closed as if she was still asleep.

I rang the bell a third time but after another five minutes passed, I gave up. I shoved the manuscript through the mail slot and headed back home, sipping the cappuccino as I went. As I climbed the steps to my house, my cell phone rang. Marley.

"Hey Marzipan. Shouldn't you be in class right now?"

"I'm in-between classes, Dad."

"Very funny. What's up?"

"I was just curious if you were coming to Seattle too."

"Too?" I asked, sliding the key in the deadbolt and unlocking the front door.

"With Lior."

"Lior's going to Seattle?"

"I'm assuming she is by the picture she posted on her socials earlier this morning."

I dropped the bag with the coffee cake in it. The cake bounced out and landed beside the potted plants I'd shoved in the corner of the porch. With a sigh, I picked up the cake and tossed it in the bag. It definitely wasn't edible now.

"I didn't see the post," I said, going inside and heading for the kitchen trash.

"Oh. So, then I guess that means you're not coming."

I sat down at the kitchen table and opened my laptop, clicking on a new tab and quickly typing in the website Marley was talking about and finding Lior's most recent post, which had gone live at six this morning.

"How do you get that she's going to Seattle from that?" I asked, looking at the image she'd taken of her legs and shoes in what was obviously an airport and then reading out loud what she'd written. "Off to see the Wither?"

"Don't you two talk all the time? It's a long-standing joke she has with Addie."

"It is?"

"Oh my gawd, G. Seriously?"

"Sorry. She failed to tell me that one."

"They dressed up as Dorothy and the Wizard of Oz when they were in like, second grade or something. And there was a kid in their class with a lisp. He kept calling Addie the Wither."

I laughed, picturing the two of them, and then sobered. She hadn't told me last night that she was planning to go to Seattle. What had happened between then and this morning?

"Is Addie okay?" I asked.

"I don't know," Marley said. "Seriously. I thought you guys

were friends and talked all the time now. Has something happened?"

"I... Honestly, Mars. I have no idea."

We got off the phone a minute later when she realized she was about to be late to class and I sat at the table staring at the picture on Lior's social media page. What the fuck was going on?

The call came several hours later, Lior's name lighting up the screen of my phone.

"Hey," I said.

"Hey."

"You okay?"

"Yeah. You?"

"I mean, I'm a little confused right now. Did you know you were going to Seattle today and just forgot to mention it last night?"

"No. I didn't. At least, not while you were still there. I think I decided somewhere around midnight."

"Okay." I frowned. "Why?"

"I needed Addie. I... needed advice."

"About?"

She didn't say anything for a minute and then: "You. Us. My job. Seattle."

"Are you still thinking of quitting modeling?"

"Not exactly."

I was quiet.

"But what about what happened at that last shoot?" I asked.

"It wasn't the first time."

"Right but.... you said you were sick of it. And rightly so."

My text alert sounded but I ignored it.

"This job has also been a part of my life for a very long time. It has a lot of perks I enjoy. Travel—"

"You said you never even see the cities you're working in."

"Clothes," she continued as if she hasn't heard me.

"You hardly wear anything but sweats."

My text alert sounded again.

"Money."

"Don't you have a fortune by now?"

She was silent again and I knew I'd overstepped.

"Sorry," I said, ignoring two more text alerts. "I'm just... well, I'm confused too. You were so upset last night. Why would you keep doing something that makes you so miserable? Besides the travel, clothes, and money. It just doesn't seem worth it to me."

She sighed. "Graham, why were you at my house when I got home yesterday?"

An uncomfortable feeling washed over me.

"What do you mean? I thought it would be nice to see you and bring you a treat after your flight."

"No. There was another reason. I could see it in your eyes. Tell me the truth."

I got up from my chair and started up the stairs to my bedroom as several more texts came in. I glanced at the screen. Fran. She could wait. I had a feeling I was going to need to lie down for the rest of this phone conversation.

"Fine," I said. "I was going to tell you I thought it would be best if we didn't see each other for a while. Your job breeds drama and chaos. I'm always on edge when we go anywhere, even though you're a pro at blending in. But it wouldn't always be like that. I know that the moment we get dressed up and you aren't covered by a hat and sunglasses, people will start hounding us and I just can't live a life like that again. It's intrusive and crazy-making." I paused, my heart beating hard in my chest. "I like you, Lior. I—"

I cut myself off, afraid to say more.

"You what?"

I ran a hand through my hair and sat on the edge of my bed as my phone went off again.

"I have real feelings for you," I said. "I'm sure that's obvious. And I'm sure on paper we're a great match. But the fact is, I hate what your job brings. And I know you're still hurting from past relationships and don't trust yourself to be in a real one because of how you've been treated before. Which is understandable, but also hurtful to be put in a category with those guys. I'm a good person and would never do what other men have done to you. I just think that neither of us is in any condition to be in a relationship right now. And while I love being your friend, we've veered more than once into more-than-friend territory. I think it's a recipe for one or both of us to get really hurt."

I stopped talking. No sound came from the other end. Had she hung up? I looked at the phone but the counter was still adding seconds.

"You may not be a user," she said, her voice low. "But you want to change me. Or— maybe you don't want to change *me*, but you want something *about* me to change. And I get it. The lifestyle is a lot. But I've been in so many relationships where the guy tried shoving me into a perfect-partner-shaped-box so that *they* felt comfortable. Pushing me down, trying to make me conform to rules *they* thought I should live by until I couldn't breathe." She paused and I heard her sniff. When she spoke again, there were tears in her voice. "I'm so tired, Graham. I'm tired of trying to be what everyone else wants so that everyone else feels secure. I'm tired of having to do the thing that makes others feel good and safe and happy. Yes, I am sick of certain aspects of this job, but it's also the only thing I've done for years and I'm really good at it. I have status and success and a career I can be proud of. It's not easy to just let that go. Even for someone I have feelings for. And I do have feelings for you. Great big ones. But I'm not going to overhaul my life just because *you* were married to some snotty little twat who abused your kindness. That's not fair to me, and I would never ask that of you. I too am a good person. And I'm furious that you refuse to even try giving me a real chance."

She hung up then and I stared down at my phone, her profile picture staring up at me, along with a dozen or more text alerts I continued to ignore. I'd taken the photo of her at the bistro table in front of Mornin' Joe's. She was sporting a jaunty foam mustache and winking into the camera.

I looked over to Brontë's bed.

"Well. I fucked that up," I said, and then startled at a clatter downstairs.

Shoving my phone in my pocket, I hurried down the stairs, stopping on the last step when I saw the mail had come and was sitting on the doormat. There was the usual bills and ads, and then something thick in a padded manilla envelope. Probably a manuscript I was waiting on, for an author hoping for a blurb.

I scooped up the pile and took it to the kitchen, ripping open the large envelope and pouring the contents out onto the table.

And there it was. Vogue magazine.

On the cover for all the world to see was me and Lior Flynn. I was bare-chested with only a pair of black jeans on, and she was standing in front of me in a sheer pink dress, her hands gripping my thighs, my arms were wrapped around her torso, covering her breasts.

We looked sexy as fuck, and my soul ached for her.

My phone pinged with another text alert. And then another.

And then another.

Now I understood what the commotion was about. I set my phone on the table and went upstairs, closed my bedroom door, and got under the covers.

CHAPTER 32

Liar

"I don't understand," Addie said, frowning at me from across the kitchen island in her kitchen. "I thought you guys were just hanging out every so often. No big deal. That's what you told me."

I had arrived at her clinic at noon after renting a car and driving straight there to see her. She'd been in the middle of an exam and popped her head out to wave at me and tell me when she'd be home. From there, I went to her house, let myself in with my key, turned off my phone, and laid on the couch where I fell asleep until she arrived home several hours later.

"I know that's what I told you," I said, not meeting her eyes and fidgeting with the frayed cuff of my flannel shirt. "I may have undersold the situation a bit though."

"Undersold it how much?"

I puffed out my cheeks and then exhaled.

"We've had sex."

"WHAT?!"

She tossed a wadded-up napkin at me and I batted it way, my face hot with embarrassment.

Glaring at me, she turned on her heel and disappeared. When

she came back, she had a bottle of wine in one hand and two glasses in the other.

"Move it, Flynn," she barked at me, nudging my knee with her leg. "I want details."

An hour later she was caught up and the bottle of wine was nearly empty.

"You love him," she said.

"I *don't* love him."

"Well, you sure feel something for him. Why didn't you tell me?"

"I don't know. I guess... I was afraid. Not of you but, saying the words out loud. Because that would be admitting to it and— I just couldn't."

Addie leaned back on the couch and swirled her wine, studying me.

"I know you've had a rough go of it with men," she said. "I get it. My track record isn't something to shout from the rooftops either. We choose dumbasses and assholes. It's like a gift. Behold!" She threw her head back and arms wide, the wine in her glass nearly spilling over the edge. "The almighty queens of bad decisions and regret!"

I laughed.

"But—" she said, dropping her arms and turning serious again. "I don't think for one minute you *didn't* know those men weren't right for you. I think you thought you could change them. You were self-sabotaging from the get-go."

I thought about that for a long moment, remembering how many times I'd wondered how to fix them, or us. I'd bend myself backwards, tie myself in knots and get angry as I tried to make something work that just didn't because they weren't willing to change. They weren't willing to do the work to make *us* work. Because for them, it was working just fine. According to them, I was the one with the problem. How many times had I heard that?

And then it hit me.

I had accused Graham of doing the same thing to me. Of trying to make me change. But he hadn't. He'd never asked me to change *me*. He just got excited that my *situation* might change. Sure, he was an ass for not wanting to give us a chance, but could I really blame him for that? My life could be a lot. The attention. The photographs that came seemingly out of nowhere... It was invasive, and a job in itself just to avoid it. And he knew what that was like. He'd lived it. He knew what he could and couldn't handle. What he *would* and wouldn't handle.

He had set boundaries. Healthy boundaries.

What was that like?

And I— I was still the same young girl inside. Scared of being rejected and projecting my own actions on someone else.

I looked at Addie, nodding.

"Okay," I said. "I get that."

"Graham is a good guy, Lior. I think you know that. I think you know you can trust him too. So, what's the real problem?"

I peered at her. "Have you been reading books on how to psychoanalyze pets again?"

"Maybe. That's not the point. Tell me what the real problem is."

"I don't trust myself?"

"Nope."

I glared at her.

"I..." I bit my lip, trying to find the answer hidden somewhere in my brain. "I don't know!"

"Lior, my love. You have mommy issues."

I stared at her, frowning in confusion, and then shook my head.

"No," I said. "That's..." I shook my head again, my brain whirling.

"You were cast aside by your mother, a woman who uses her looks and celebrity to get what she wants," Addie said. "She's a user. A manipulator who made you feel less than by putting you down and picking you apart every chance she got, making you feel small and not worthy. And so you tried to change. I watched it unfold almost daily, babe. You tried so hard to gain her approval, and she just wouldn't fucking give it to you." She sat up and put her empty glass on the coffee table and then moved closer to me. "Your first crush. Whatshisname. Remember how he always asked you for money at lunch? And you always gave it to him, even though that meant you wouldn't have enough for your own lunch, so you ended up eating half of mine."

"Sorry," I said.

"It's fine. I lost those last few pounds of baby fat that year and finally fit back into that pair of jeans I loved. Anyways. You gave him the money because it made him pay attention to you. You knew he'd come back again. He needed you. Every single guy you dated, with the exception of Jeremy, used you. Made you feel like you had to do something or change something about yourself to make yourself worthy of their time and affection. Just. Like. With. Your. Mom."

I couldn't see now, my eyes were so filled with tears.

"And here comes handsome Graham Forrester," Addie continued. "Decent guy. Not too hard on the eyes. Doesn't need anything from you. Doesn't even actually want anything because he's been so fucked over by his ex, he's afraid of his own shadow. But you two collide on a fate paved in dog shit, and neither of you can get out of your own way to figure out that you've found something pretty fucking special."

She reached for my hand.

"Your mom is a classic narcissist, my friend. And I'll never forgive her for what she's done to you. Never."

I drained my glass and set it beside hers on the coffee table.

"What do I do now?" I asked.

Addie tilted her head and I laughed.

"One really does look like a puppy when they do that," I said.

"See?" she said, her eyes widening before getting serious again.

"Look, I obviously don't know what's going to happen with Graham. He has his own set of issues that he needs to deal with and he's numero uno on my wink wink shit list right now for making my girl cry, so my fangirl status has dropped a few rankings. You guys will figure this thing out, or you won't. What I do know is, you need to start thinking about *you*. Really considering *you*. What *you* want. Not what anyone else wants. And not what would make Lillian Flynn proud. Fuck that chick. That last photo shoot you were on was bullshit. It was not the first time and it won't be the last. You need to decide what you want to put up with. You've complained a lot the last couple of years about the hours, the travel turnaround time, and the ridiculous standards. You've also been contemplating next steps for a while now. Maybe it's time. If not to completely step away, to at least dip your toes in something else that could be the starting point of a whole new chapter. Something that uses that fantastic brain of yours and makes you feel worthwhile inside. Like maybe that job for Avery? And only then, and after some more therapy focused on how your mother screwed you up, should you think about having a romantic relationship with anyone."

I nodded, considering what she'd said.

"So... is it an in-person course on psychoanalyzing your pets, or just a book," I asked. "Because it is well worth the money and I'd like to invest in you. I think you're going places, kid."

She threw a pillow at me. "Jerk."

I laughed and placed the pillow on my lap and reached to take her hands in mine, my eyes filled with tears.

"I hear you," I said. "Thank you. You've given me a lot to think about. I know I have a lot of work to do, and I will. I promise."

"Good. Because despite that ugly mug of yours, I think you're going places too."

I made a face, gathered our glasses and the empty bottle, and headed for the kitchen.

"More wine?" I called over my shoulder.

"Let's mix it up," she said. "There's sangria in the fridge."

I snorted laughter as she shouted that she'd be right back, she was going to check the mailbox.

As I headed back to the living room with two glasses of sangria, I could see Addie standing stock still in the entryway, staring down at something in her hands.

"Everything okay?" I asked.

She walked to me, took the glass from my hand, and held out a magazine. Frowning, I stared at her for a moment and then looked at what she was holding out.

And there we were. Me and Graham. On the cover of Vogue magazine.

And we looked hot as fuck.

"Figure out your shit, Lior," Addie said. "Or I will never let you live down letting *that* one go."

She sank onto the sofa and took a long drink of her sangria.

"Now, give it back," she said. "I need to see what you two got up to."

We sat side-by-side, slowly taking in each photograph, me telling her details from the moment, her threatening to take the spread to bed with her. When we got to the last one, she flipped back to the beginning, taking them all in again while I sat beside her, remembering every second of how it had felt to touch him that day. And how it had felt to touch him more intimately later.

My body and soul ached for him.

"Hey," I said, getting to my feet. "I think I'm going to make an early night of it. Can I take you out to dinner tomorrow night after you get off work?"

"Of course."

She was looking at me with concern but I waved her off.

"I'm okay," I said. "Just a lot on my mind and those pictures are painful to look at right now."

"I'm sorry," she said, closing the magazine.

"No. It's okay. You have at it. I just can't anymore." I went around the back of the couch and landed a kiss on the top of her head. "If you take it to bed with you, please feel free not to tell me."

"You're no fun."

In the morning Addie found me sitting at the kitchen island with my laptop in front of me and a notebook open beside it.

"Forgot to do your homework last night?" she asked. "I'm telling mom."

I stuck my tongue out at her.

I could feel her watching me as she went about making toast and pouring herself a cup of coffee from the pot I'd made.

"So whatcha doin' over there," she asked, standing across from me at the kitchen island.

"Real estate homework."

"Oh yeah?" She rounded the island and sidled up next to me and looked at the list I'd made. "These all look promising." She picked up my pencil and started crossing things off. "Except that one and that one and... that one."

"Hey!" I said, laughing and taking the pencil away.

"They're too far from me."

"I know, but I still want to look at them."

"Is my part of the beach not classy enough for you?"

"Your part of the beach is plenty classy. I just want to know all the options." I tapped the pencil on the notebook. "I also emailed Avery this morning."

"And?" she asked, her eyes wide.

"It was four a.m. I haven't heard back yet. But I did tell her I was in town and if she was available, I'd love to take her to lunch and chat."

Addie threw her arms around me.

"Now all you need is a good therapist, your mom to pull her head out of her ass, and Graham to come to the realization that he can't live without you."

"And my bestie to get her head out of the clouds," I said,

shaking my head. "That feels like a very tall order. Maybe I just fix me and let the chips fall where they may."

"I've never understood that saying," Addie said. "Any chips falling are landing in my mouth."

I laughed and then stopped abruptly, my mind going to Graham. I'd gone to bed last night with him solely on my mind. He had the potential to be the best thing to ever happen to me in the love department, but I'd once been told by Ty that you can't hang on to someone based on their potential. That was right before he told me his latest boyfriend had dumped him for a man three decades older because he had a yacht and Ty could only offer dinners out at nice restaurants.

"I'd have dumped me too," Ty had said with a sigh.

"I think... I have to let him go," I said to Addie. "At least for now. I'm not the only one who needs therapy to work through the trauma others have inflicted. And I can't wait around expecting him to figure it out. I need to focus on me now. Not just my career, but my life and what I want it to look like."

Addie hugged me again.

"Good," she said. "That all sounds amazing." She checked the time then and gave me an apologetic look.

"Go," I said. "You have other pets to psychoanalyze. I get it."

I spent a week at Addie's, reveling in our morning verbal sparring sessions before she hurried off to work, luxuriating in walks on the beach, coffees from my favorite café, hours spent walking through homes for sale, and feeling at peace in the evenings as we rehashed our days over dinner.

I took no pictures and spoke to no one but her, other than a few texts to thank my agent Jen, Risa Collins, Daniela, and a handful of friends who had congratulated me on my Vogue cover and spread. Including Marley, who I could tell knew something was up between me and her brother, but didn't push and took me up on my offer of a video chat in a couple of weeks.

There was no word from Graham. And I didn't send him a message either.

By the time I left, I'd signed a year-long contract with Avery and the Seattle Tribune as a weekly columnist for the arts section starting in January, put in an offer on a house, and scheduled a therapy appointment.

"Take care of you," Addie said, giving me a hug.

"I will. Take care of you too and, I'll see you soon!"

When I returned home several hours later, there was a note to retrieve a package at the post office, a pile of mail, and a large padded envelope waiting for me. Leaving my suitcase at the base of the stairs, I took the mail to the kitchen, opened the container of donut holes that expired today, shoved one in my mouth, and ripped open the manilla envelope, assuming it was a copy of Vogue sent from one of many sources. But the pages I pulled out were not filled with glossy, high-resolution photographs. They were covered in words. Graham's words. It was his latest book.

A note was paperclipped to the title page, dated the morning I'd left for Seattle.

"Be gentle," he'd written.

"Yeah," I whispered, sliding onto the stool beside me and turning to the first page. "You too."

* * *

I was deep into chapter five when my phone rang, my agent's name illuminating the screen.

"Hey, Jen," I said,

"Amalfi and Armani," she said.

A job. It was tempting but—

"I know you're scarred from that last shoot and probably need a break," she said. "But you're going to want to do this one."

"Tell me," I said, rubbing my eyes and preparing to say no.

"Allegra is shooting it."

I sighed.

Allegra Giordano was a magician behind the lens. She'd done my very first magazine shoot, which had catapulted me into the limelight. Not long after, tragedy struck her family and she put down her camera and hadn't returned since. I'd always said I'd do anything to work with her again. Her images were works of art, and her grace and understanding of both the female form, and condition, enriched each photograph.

Jen was right. I wanted this one.

"Send me the details," I said.

CHAPTER 33
Graham

Vacationing alone, I'd decided, was an acquired skill. This realization hit as soon as I sat down to dine by myself at a restaurant my first night in Amsterdam.

I hadn't been planning on taking a vacation, but after the spectacle from the Vogue cover and spread, and my last conversation with Lior, I'd barely left my house and was craving freedom and anonymity.

The Vogue attention was to be expected and I didn't blame Lior for that drama. I'd brought it on myself and, from the emails I'd received the evening before – from both my agent and my editor – it was doing wonders for my book sales.

That coupled with the conversation had me feeling rattled and caged though. I was angry. And... I was scared. Was I willing to risk something that seemed so right? So destined? So Brontë two tail thumps approved?

So many times I'd had to stop myself from going to Lior's house. But what would I say? I had set boundaries for myself for a reason. And while Lior was no Nadia, I knew what I could and couldn't handle. I knew what I did and didn't want in my life.

I needed to stand my ground. Honor what I felt. Take control of myself and my emotions. One slip and it'd be all over. Back to square one. Back to my bad habit of overlooking the red flags.

Not that any of it was an issue anymore. Because then the kicker came. The thing that pushed me over the edge and had me skimming my favorite vacation site for last-minute-trip ideas.

Per the accompanying article, Lior was on the Amalfi coast for an Armani campaign. So much for moving on from modeling. A picture showed up in the papers with a bold "New Couple Alert?" headline. In the photo was Lior and Colin Graydon, action star, romcom leading man, and newly minted dramatic actor that was rumored to be in the Oscar running for his portrayal of an alcoholic politician in his last film. He was standing with Lior, his arm around her back. Sort of.

I tried to get a better look, enlarging the image on my screen. Was his arm actually around her body? It was hard to tell. I went to another site and the photo was there as well. Just as grainy. Clearly taken from a distance by an onlooker.

"Fuck," I whispered, typing in the name of a popular social media page and then her name. Twenty-five thousand, two hundred and fifty-three mentions. Awesome. People were freaking out at the thought they were a couple.

I found a back-and-forth of people analyzing the photo.

"Is his arm really around her?"

"His arm is totally around her. Are you blind?"

"It's such a sweet, respectful embrace."

"I think he's just reaching around her. See that drink at the edge of the photo? He's totally reaching for it."

I went back to the photo and looked for the mentioned drink. It was half out of frame. But it was there.

"Oh my god," I said out loud and tossed my phone to the end of the bed. It bounced off and landed on the floor. I covered my face with a pillow.

This. This was the kind of drama I didn't want. The kind my exes had all encouraged, and had in fact thrived on. I was convinced they subconsciously manifested it. Or maybe even consciously. The consistency of it had been exhausting. It had worn me down. I'd felt myself getting smaller and smaller until I was relegated into this little pocket of their lives, only good for photo ops I wasn't in, merely acting as photographer as they posed with food, drinks, friends, and different beautiful views around whatever city we were in. My only role became supportive boyfriend, which was a role I was happy to be in – until it became me supporting the weight of their needs, unending wants, and inflated egos.

It was a paparazzi photo that led me to the realization that my wife wasn't on a girl's trip like she'd claimed, but on a private yacht in the Mediterranean with the man she'd apparently been sleeping with for months. Somehow the paparazzi caught wind of it and were able to get photos using a drone. There was no is-his-arm-around-her-or-not questioning. It was obvious they were together as she was straddling him, topless on a sun chair on the deck of the boat.

I hated the paparazzi. I hated what and who it made me question. Especially if they had it wrong. But there was no way of knowing for sure. Trust? Yeah... hard to do that when there were pictures making their denials outright lies.

I'd pulled the pillow from my face and put it behind my head. In truth, I'd never once seen Lior encourage or fan the flames of her fame. At least, not while I was around. She'd made a conscious effort to keep it at bay. But did that matter? The truth was, she was famous. Whether she encouraged the circus that sometimes happened or not, her fame was the issue. *My* issue. And I had no business faulting her for doing her job well and being beloved for it. It went hand-in-hand with the job and her level of success.

Lior wasn't the problem. I was.

"Fuck," I'd whispered.

And so, with the picture of Lior and Colin Graydon burned

into my brain, I'd decided it was finally time for that vacation I was always saying I was going to take.

If I could just get past the dinners out alone, I figured I'd be okay.

I glanced at the families and couples sitting around me, laughing and talking over shared meals and drinks sparkling under the overhead lights.

There was an older man and woman one table over, sharing that secret sort of smile one shares with a lover. I imagined what Lior might say if she were here. If she'd notice the elegance of the couple. Or maybe the woman's beautiful sapphire-colored dress and how she kept touching her ear. A nervous habit? Were they on a first date?

I looked at the empty chair across from me, wishing Lior were there. Missing her messy buns and stained sweatshirts. But before I got too deep into my feelings, I recalled the image in the newspaper and was immediately angry.

"You can run, but you can't hide," I whispered and raised my hand to the waiter to indicate I needed another drink.

* * *

My first therapy appointment was at four p.m. on my third day in Amsterdam, where I'd been meandering the streets, staring down canals, marveling at the picturesque city that at once felt large but quaint, and taking pictures of all of it. I'd seen sunrises from bridges while drinking my morning cappuccino, and sunsets while enjoying a beer from one of the many pubs.

I'd found the therapist, Novi, through a friend of a friend when joking over text that I'd be in Amsterdam and if they knew of anyone I could see while I was there to let me know.

And now here I was.

"What brings you to me today?" she asked in a beautiful accent.

I had low expectations that I could be healed in the few sessions I'd set up, but it was a step in the right direction and, if I felt it was helping, I'd find a therapist in Brooklyn to continue my self-help journey.

Novi looked to be around my stepmother's age and had a no-nonsense feel to her as she waited for me to answer the question.

"I'm taking a solo vacation. A me-only vacation. I thought bike rides through fields of tulips and drinking bottles of wine by myself could only be enhanced with a side of therapy."

The pleasant smile on her face didn't move. Maybe humor was frowned upon in Amsterdam.

"I think I'm addicted to narcissists," I said.

She nodded and her smile transformed into something I recognized. Empathetic. I inhaled and let the breath out slowly, my body sinking into the sofa I was seated on. I suddenly felt less alone. She'd heard this tale before.

"Narcissists usually have a few stand-out traits," she said. "They are *very* charming. They love to talk about themselves and their accomplishments. They need a lot of praise, aren't very empathetic, and don't usually have a lot of long-term friends."

She had ticked each point off on her fingers and I had nodded along as she stated each one.

"I assume some if not all of that resonates by the way you've been nodding your head?" she asked.

"You assume right."

"And you've found yourself with people like this... more than once?"

"Three times. The only women I've been in serious relationships with have had those traits."

"So then we need to ask the question... why do you think you're choosing to be with people with those traits?"

I shook my head. "I don't know. I had a great childhood but I was never particularly confident and really quite shy, preferring books and movies to socializing. I was a good-looking kid, but because I was shy I didn't respond in kind to female attention and I started to get labeled as weird. And then gay. And then a dork. And then a loser. But during my junior year of high school I found a love of three things: running, working out... and Elizabeth Bristol. She was on the school's gymnastics team and often in the gym in the mornings. She started talking to me and I was hooked. She drew me in, asked questions about me, seemed interested as I prattled on about the book I was reading, asked what I'd thought at the time were insightful questions, and made me feel seen. Finally. I blossomed under her attentions."

"Did something happen?" Novi asked.

"She wanted all my time. I didn't realize it at first, but I was suddenly abandoning books for gymnastics meets and movie outings with my parents to do whatever she wanted to do."

"That's not out of the norm when you get in a relationship though. Making sacrifices is something we all do."

"True but... this was different. I even knew it then, but she had a way of pulling me back in when I started to retreat."

"She was a snake charmer," Novi said.

"Indeed."

"And how did you feel when her attention was on you?"

"Seen. Special. Popular."

"And those things were important to you why?"

"Because I'd never felt those things by my peers and it felt good."

"And then what happened?"

"She started having excuses as to why she couldn't hang out with me. And then I'd find out she'd been hanging out with other friends. Other guys."

"And that made you feel?"

"Hollow."

"Who broke up with whom?"

"She dumped me after four months. I was crushed and didn't date anyone again until college."

She made a note and then looked back up at me. "And what was she like?"

"Elizabeth 2.0. She strung me along for two years."

"She strung you along? Or you hung on?"

I was silent. Fuck.

My experiences with both were nearly identical and it was embarrassing to realize my compliance. My desperation. My basement-level self-worth and the way I'd sought the high I'd gotten from the beginning days of the relationship. The attention and love and feeling of being seen.

But Nadia had been the master. And now I could see it so clearly. The way they'd seen not me, but my weakness.

And sure, what they'd done wasn't okay by any means, but the truth of the matter was, they weren't to blame for me staying in relationships that weren't healthy.

I was.

I went back to my hotel room after and laid on the bed, staring at the ceiling, thoughts circling my mind as I revisited the things Novi had said and asked in our session.

My alarm sounded and I turned it off and lay for a moment more before swinging my legs over the side of the bed and grabbing my laptop. My article for Around the Neighborhood was due the following day and I needed to finish it up and send it. But when I opened the document – my eyes skimming the paragraphs I'd written the day before about a new brunch spot with a great selection of vegan pastries – I found my usual enthusiasm for finding little gems like this lacking.

My finger wandered to my email app and I clicked it, then opened an email my editor at the newspaper had sent a week ago. Subject line: The city demands an update.

I rubbed my eyes and then scrolled down to the screenshots she'd attached. Image after image of emails readers had sent to the paper. To me. Accumulated over the past couple months ever since the incident in the park with Lior. Apparently people were invested. They wanted to know if I'd seen the woman again. If perhaps she'd seen the article and emailed me an apology. If she knew about B's passing. If I could describe her so people could be on the lookout.

In my mind, I pictured her that day, seeing now what I hadn't seen then. The looks of confusion, anger, and angst like a kaleidoscope on her pretty face, changing as some invisible hand turned and turned.

I stared at the article nearly done. Nearly ready to read over and send off. And then I opened a new document and started anew. Not for my readers... but for me. And for Lior. Maybe we'd never talk again, but in case she still read my articles, at least she'd know I was sorry. She'd know that I'd seen how I'd failed both of us by giving up before even giving us a chance.

Lowering my hands to the keyboard, I began to type.

"Sometimes, friends, shit happens."

CHAPTER 34

Lior

"Well," I said to Addie. "What do you think?"

"It's gorgeous," she said.

We were standing outside on the master suite balcony of the house I was about to purchase. I had returned to Seattle to sign the contract eight days after I'd left. Addie had insisted on meeting me there so I'd asked for an evening appointment to allow us to leave from the house straight to dinner and drinks to celebrate.

The house was stunning, with the same cozy feeling my brownstone in NY had, but airier and with a paler color palette and views across the water.

"You're gonna need a car," Addie said as she peeked in the master suite walk-in closet.

"Oh yeah," I said, wrinkling my nose. I rarely drove these days. Didn't have much opportunity to do so. In New York I took the subway or cabs, and when I traveled, it was normally for work and a car was provided. "That's scary to imagine."

"When was the last time you drove?"

I narrowed my eyes, trying to remember.

"Welp," she said, laughing. "That's terrifying. I'll get you a bus schedule."

After showing her the house, I sat down with the realtor and signed all the things. An hour later I had my own set of keys. I immediately removed one and handed it to Addie.

"Shall we go celebrate?" she asked.

"Absolutely."

We walked down the hill to the main drag and wandered up the road to Cactus, a local favorite with fun salads and interesting cocktails.

"How do you feel?" Addie asked, taking a sip of her drink. "Excited? Nervous? Ready to take on Seattle?"

She looked prettier than ever, even with the red scar across her cheek where she'd been stitched up after her accident. Her hair was longer than it normally was, and instead of her usual ponytail, it was loose and flowing over her shoulders.

"I don't know," I said, peering at her. "Why do you look so good? Have you been having sex without telling me?"

She laughed and tossed her hair back over her shoulder.

"I think it's just the scar. It makes me look like a badass. Adds to my mystique."

"Your veterinarian cat lady mystique?"

"Exactly."

"You still verbally sparring with Mr. Vet?" I asked, referring to the veterinarian who had helped out with her practice while she was recovering.

She rolled her eyes. "Oh my god. He's so obnoxious. He's set up a run/walk along Alki Avenue for people to come with or without dogs, and at the end there's going to be an mobile adoption bus."

"And that's bad why?"

"He just wants to run around shirtless and show off his abs."

"Again I ask... that's bad why?"

She glared at me. "It's gross, that's why."

"But if it gets pets adopted."

"Who are you and what have you done with my friend?"

"I think you like him," I said. "You never get like this with the guys you actually date, who are certified losers by the way. But men who challenge you... Remember Tom Williams?"

"I'm not listening to you," she said, lifting her menu up to block my view of her. "And you're wrong. I think he's a chauvinistic pig."

"Mmhmm..."

An ice cube came flying over the top of her menu and went down the front of my shirt, making me squeal. The menu lowered.

"Mmhmmm..." she said, mimicking me. My drink had no ice cubes so it was even funnier when the tiny slice of cucumber I threw stuck to her collarbone. "Any news from you-know-who?" she then asked, removing the food from her skin and popping it in her mouth.

I glared over the top of my menu. We hadn't talked about Graham in days. Maybe even weeks. Definitely one week.

I'd gone from sad and numb to angry and numb, and was now back to sad, grief hitting me like a wave as I'd stared at my bed a few nights ago, realizing I'd never roll over to find him sleeping beside me ever again. The pain hit me like a punch to the gut and I'd folded in on myself and cried into my duvet. My therapist told me it was normal, but as far as Addie knew, I was managing just fine.

"Why are you trying to ruin my good mood?" I asked.

"Sorry," she said. "I was just curious. You two have really just cut ties, haven't you. Usually people linger but—"

"I guess we're just grown-ups," I said, avoiding her gaze across the table. "Also, my therapist is amazing. I have a mantra and everything. Came up with it myself." I smiled like a little kid, proud of taking her first steps.

"Tell me what it is."

"No."

"Tell me!"

I put down my menu and folded my hands on top of it.

"No more Graham," I said. She nearly spit out her sip of drink as she burst out laughing.

"Lior. That's—"

"Helpful? Healthy?"

"Sure." She gave me a placating smile and I felt relief as the waitress came over.

We put in our orders and then moved on to other subjects, namely me moving to Seattle.

"What's the timeline?" Addie asked.

"The movers are scheduled for November twelfth."

"So you'll be here for Thanksgiving?"

"I'm always here for Thanksgiving."

"You know what I mean. A resident of Seattle once again."

"I will."

"Well then," she said, raising her glass. "Cheers to that."

The next week was spent choosing items I wanted to take with me to Seattle. Pink couch? Yes. Deck furniture? No. Books? Duh. Bed? My mind was immediately filled with images of Graham, sleeping, naked, on his knees between my legs. Fuck. The bed needed to be worshipped, mourned, and then burned. I'd get a new one for new memories to be made in... with all the pets I'd adopt from Addie's nemesis's adoption events. I'd be a cat and dog lady and my home would become unsuitable for guests. It would be perfect.

I walked through the house with a clipboard, several sheets of paper organized by room, and three highlighter pens with coordinating stickers. Pink for move, orange for donate, and yellow for sell. It took me three days. When I was done, I decided I was glad I had another visit with my therapist the next day. I was at the end of my emotional rope. Leaving this space, again, was harder than I thought it would be.

"Lior," she said, her voice warm as she ushered me into the familiar, cozy space that was her office.

"Hey Hestia," I said, sinking into large beige couch that took up one side of the room.

Hestia Galanis was a godsend. I'd found her by accident early on in my career when we were both attending the same gallery opening. She'd walked into the bathroom where I was tearfully wiping at the skirt of my brand-new Alexander McQueen minidress that was dripping with olive oil from the messy hors d'œuvres I'd waited a second too long to put in my mouth. She quickly taught me about soap and oil while removing a handkerchief from her purse.

"Use this instead," she'd said. "It won't leave pieces of paper towel on the fabric."

Ten minutes later I was standing under the heated hand dryer and the stain was barely visible. When I'd asked if she was a magician, she'd laughed and said no, she was a mother and she was Greek.

"We use a lot of olive oil in our cooking. I have to get it out of my clothes at least three times a week."

She'd then pulled out a slender packet of makeup remover towelettes for the smeared mascara under my eyes.

"You're amazing," I'd told her after dabbing the black streaks from my skin. "Do you do anything else besides mother and cook with olive oil?"

"I'm a therapist."

"Do you have a card?"

That was nine years ago. She'd been helping me maneuver through life – whenever I managed to get in to see her – ever since. But it had been months since I'd seen her last, and we'd been doing a lot of catching up the past few weeks.

"Did you sign on the house?" she asked.

"I did."

"Congratulations! It's a big step and I'm proud of you. You are moving forward, Lior. Does it feel that way?"

I made a face and she laughed.

"Well," she said. "I am here to tell you that you are. What else?"

"I turned down a modeling job. One I would've taken previously but knew I'd be miserable if I did it."

"Wonderful. That's more progress. And have you talked with your agent?"

"I have. I let her know that I want to scale back. We had a nice long talk about it and she was lovely."

"Well done. Now... how can I help you today?"

"Tell me how to not end up with people who use me or want to change me?"

"I cannot do that. Tell me why."

"Because I haven't done the work."

"And because you've been existing..."

I raised my hand, mimicking the motion I was taught by my mother.

"Up here."

CHAPTER 35

Graham

T he airport was crowded when I got home, but my usual apprehension that came with big crowds was softened by the sense of calm I'd inherited from traveling, therapy, and doing some really tough reality checks with myself over the past two weeks.

I wasn't bothered by the couple fighting in front of me, as we all waited in line for a cab while the rain poured down. Nor did I care about the cacophony of noise as travelers made their way in and out of the state. Something in me felt lighter. As if I'd unpacked my crap overseas and left it behind. There was still work to do. Still thoughts to shed that had become habitual and harmful to my enjoyment of life and trust in myself. But I was getting there, and that's what I'd been telling myself like a mantra every night.

A cab pulled up and I climbed in. The drive through town made me smile. The trees had shed their leaves, their skeletal bodies exposed and glistening with the rain streaming down them. The streets were littered with brown mounds of fallen foliage that one would track inside their house on their shoes for weeks and months on end. And despite it all, people milled about, hurrying to catch up with friends, catch a train, or hurry home from work.

"You been somewhere nice?" the cabbie asked as we sat at a red light.

"The Netherlands."

"Never been. Was it nice?"

"It was lovely."

Traffic moved along at a snail's pace but I found I didn't mind. I loved New York in the fall and, thanks to my trip abroad, therapy, and texts with Marley, I felt my time here was coming to a close. I no longer felt the fear that had been clinging to me. Or rather, the fear I'd been clinging to with both hands for years. I didn't feel as tentative or stuck. There was an openness inside me that was palpable, and that I couldn't remember ever feeling before. It was freeing. Comforting. And it made me curious.

"Hey," I said, leaning forward, and then proceeded to give the driver directions that would take me past Lior's house on the way to mine.

Perhaps it was a bad idea. But I tried to think of it in a different light, as Novi had been teaching me to do.

"See how a situation can serve you," she'd said one day after I'd come back from a couple days visiting The Hague. "Don't count it all as bad. Count it as learning something about yourself."

"And if it makes me feel like shit?"

"Then don't do it again," she'd said with an uncharacteristic wink.

It had been weeks since I'd seen Lior and, while I didn't plan to stop, I just wanted to drive by. I wanted to see how it would feel. Was she home? Were the lights on? Would it look as though she had company? How would I feel if she did? How would I react? Would I be angry? Sad? Resigned?

My pulse sped up as we rounded the corner onto her street and I mentally braced myself for what I would see – and then physically braced myself as the driver swerved around a garbage bin that had fallen over into the street.

"It's been windy while you were gone," he said. "You're lucky you were out of town. Me and the missus lost power a couple of times this past week. You'll probably have blinking clocks all over your house when you get in."

I nodded, barely listening, because Lior's house was four away... three... two...

All the lights were off, aside from the porch light. And then I saw it.

"What the fuck is that?" I said.

"What's what?" the driver asked, hitting the brakes.

"Don't stop!" I said, moving away from the window in case she was home and somehow saw me in a small cab window through the rain. But then I leaned forward again, my eyes glued to the sign posted on the column at the bottom of the stairs leading to her front door.

A 'For Sale' sign.

Lior was moving.

All the air expelled from my lungs. I leaned back against the seat and closed my eyes. I had no idea where she was going. Seattle? Somewhere else? Europe? But I wasn't privy to that information because I'd let her go. And she... she was moving on.

I paid the driver and dragged my suitcase up the front steps to my house. The stormy weather had knocked two of the three potted plants onto one another, and there was a small pile of wet newspapers shoved into the corner – the newspaper boy's attempt at keeping them out of the elements. I'd deal with them later.

For the next week I wandered my house feeling more than ever like I didn't belong in it. With Brontë gone and Lior not around to soften the bright white and hard edges with her warmth and laughter, everything felt off kilter. Even more now than when I'd first lost them.

"You look terrible," Marley said. We were doing a video call so she could show me the clothes she'd picked out for a job interview. She didn't need to work, our dad and her mom were able to provide for anything she might need, but she'd never had a job and thought it might be fun to earn a paycheck. Mostly, I was pretty sure, because some of her roommates had jobs and she said the responsibility of it made them seem more mature.

"Don't be in a rush to grow up," I'd told her. "Take advantage of this time to just learn."

But Marley had gotten it in her head that a job equaled fun. Who was I to burst that bubble?

"Are you sick?" she asked.

"No," I said.

"Are you sad because of Lior?" I'd finally told her we were no longer speaking. She'd said she'd suspected as much, but didn't say why. I wondered if the two of them still talked, but I never asked.

"No. And yes. But... Look, I'm just sad, okay? It's been a rough few weeks and I've had a lot on my mind."

"I thought you said the vacation was cathartic."

"It was. And then I came home and nothing here has changed. Brontë is still gone and—"

"And?"

I knew she was fishing for me to talk about Lior, but I would not satisfy her need.

"And it's a lot," I said.

"I'm sorry, G."

"Thanks, Mars."

"You could move here. Then you wouldn't have to be in that house anymore."

"I mean, I could move down the street if I was just trying to escape the house."

"You know what I mean."

"I do. And I am thinking about it."

"Really? Like for real real?"

I laughed.

"Yes," I said. "For real real. Now, can we get back to the reason for this call?" I pointed to the two outfits lying across her dorm room bed.

"Oh right." She stood and picked up two hangers with dresses hanging from them. "Sensible? Mature? Classic?"

My mind suddenly went to Lior. Had she already moved? Was it on her social media account and Marley wasn't mentioning it to spare my feelings?

"G!" Marley shouted to get my attention again.

"Shit. Sorry." I glanced at the clothes she was holding up. "Very nice."

She rolled her eyes, tossed the outfits back on the bed and sat down again.

"Graham?" she said, her big blue eyes staring through the camera at me.

I was in for it now. I prepared myself for the lecture that was coming.

"Yes?"

"Why don't you just call her?"

I'd thought the same thing a hundred times. Probably more. I'd thought it moments after she'd hung up on me, that entire evening, and every day since.

The problem now was, I'd waited too long, and she was clearly moving on. She was moving god knows where and there was the potential that she wasn't going alone. She could've met someone, had a whirlwind romance, and was now moving in with the guy. I'd fucked up. I couldn't call her now. It would be selfish, and cruel to both of us.

I didn't say all that to my sister though.

"I think I missed my window," I said. "And now I have to accept that, and move on as well."

Marley was quiet for a minute.

"Whatever happened to your friend, Cooper," she asked.

"Nadia happened."

"Of course." She shook her head. "Do you still have his number?"

"If he hasn't changed it, then yes."

"You should call him."

"And say what? Sorry I ghosted you for a horrible woman not worth a tenth of you?"

"For starters, yes." She sat down on her bed and looked at me with eyes too wise for an eighteen-year-old. "You need friends, G. I mean, I love that we're close and can talk about stuff, but you need people your own age, with a little more life experience, to give you advice."

Truly. The psychology course she was taking was already paying for itself.

"Yeah well... I'm not sure he'd be excited to hear from me at this point. It's been a long time."

"I think you should give yourself more credit and give him the chance to make his own decisions."

"I thought you were supposed to get less annoying the older you got," I said, running a hand over my face.

"Once again, you were wrong." She gave me a toothy grin and I laughed. "Call him. Apologize. And then put your stupid house up for sale and move here. You don't have to stay forever. It might just be good for you to have a change of scenery for a while. You can decide what you want to do next after that."

There was a burst of noise on her end as her roommate and two other young women came into the room.

"I have to go," Marley said, leaning closer to the microphone. "I love you, G. Call Cooper!" she yelled, and then she was gone.

Before I had a chance to overthink it or talk myself out of it, I was scrolling through my contacts to Cooper's number. I hesitated for only a second before I hit the call button. He answered on the second ring.

CHAPTER 36

Lior

The house was a disaster of boxes and booby traps.

I tripped over the rug I'd rolled and slid under the coffee table the night before, the end of it sticking out just a little too far. Coffee splashed onto my Adidas joggers and I stared down at the wet spot on the taupe-colored fabric, then kept moving toward the kitchen.

Glancing around at the happy space, my chest ached. I had loved this house for so long, it was hard to say goodbye. Part of me wanted to hang onto it. I could come here in the winters... spend Christmas... put my tree in the main floor window like I always had, and like my father had done before me. I could rent it out. Maybe I'd have kids one day and they'd want to live here.

I recalled the many long weekends Addie had spent here before she'd opened her clinic and got so busy. How we'd take the subway into Manhattan and shop all day, and then come back and order take-out and watch movies until we passed out on the couch covered in bits of popcorn and Sweetarts. She was the only person I had let into this space. Well, her and Graham.

My breath hitched, caught on a memory of him in my kitchen giving me that smile of his.

Goddamn that smile.

I felt my wall going up, trying to shut the pain out. "Up here" I heard my mother's voice call from the deep recesses of my mind.

I shook my head, pushing her voice and the wall away and letting the pain rush through me. It was okay to hurt, Hestia had told me. Hurt leads to healing.

"Pain is how the injury lets itself be known. Tears are it being cleansed. And then the tender scab will cover it and it will slowly begin to heal. Don't pick at it, don't cover it up. Let it breathe and do its thing. It will heal quicker that way."

Tears slid down my cheeks and I let them drip onto my t-shirt. I hated how much I still missed him. He'd barely been in my life, only present for a moment, but he'd made his mark.

"Maybe he was the thing you needed," Addie had said the week before when she'd called to ask for a grocery list of items she could put in my kitchen before I arrived – so I didn't have to immediately run to the store and shop.

"What do you mean?" I'd asked.

"To break through these walls you've had up for so long. Maybe he was the impetus to a better quality of life. He opened you up and—"

"Well, that's a bit personal don't you think?" I'd said, cutting her off.

She snorted loudly in my ear. "You're disgusting." She snickered some more. "And stop trying to distract me. Look, maybe thinking of him in those terms is a good way to help you get over him."

"I thought you were still holding out hope for us." Even though I'd told her not to. Repeatedly. And she'd ignored me. Repeatedly. Telling me she knew better.

"Oh, I am. I have a bet going with Alexandra."

At the mention of her much more austere partner at the clinic, I laughed.

"Alex is too classy to bet on my love life," I said.

"That is where you're wrong, my friend."

"Fine. But if you win big, I expect a big gift."

"If I win, I imagine you will be getting a big gift. Didn't you hint that Graham is well-endow—"

"Addie!" I'd blushed profusely as we'd both laughed.

I checked the time now. The movers would be here in an hour. There was so much to do still, but I also needed to finish my latest article. A piece for Harper's Bazaar. I sat on one of the four kitchen stools and opened my laptop. But I was too distracted. Rather than look at the document, I started to scroll. First a social media site, then a fashion blogger's website I followed, then an online home goods store for items for the new Seattle house. Each click was more unsatisfying than the last. Because I knew what I really wanted. I wanted to read Graham's Around the Neighborhood articles.

It had been weeks since I'd read one and my fingers itched to type in the newspaper's website.

"Don't do it, dummy," I whispered as I began tapping each key in turn until there they were, all the ones I'd missed, lined up down the right side of the screen.

I moved the mouse down and clicked the oldest one, reading, smiling, hearing his voice in my head. Then I moved on to the next one. And the next.

When I reached the latest article, I was already a mess. Sniffling. Tears welling in my eyes. I missed his humor. His thoughtful observations. When we used to take walks, or go out to eat, or talk on the phone, or spend any time together at all, he had a way of noticing things exactly like I did. He saw the absurd in the mundane. The sweet in the ugly. The silliness in the elegance. He was kind and decent and sexy and...

"Perfect," I said, and then wiped away a tear and clicked on one last article.

I knew from the first word that the article would be about me. Though he never named me, what he did do was something entirely different than all the other articles he'd ever written for the paper, explaining to his readers what had really happened that day. What was going on behind the scenes of a woman who had publicly lost her shit. How we never know what it is to walk in someone else's shoes. And when those shoes step in poo? Well, sometimes we falter. And sometimes we need a little grace.

I could barely read as he explained in vague details my plight that day. How he'd actually been so distracted by my eyes at first that he hadn't realized he was being yelled at. How we ran into each other later. And then again. And then again.

"Destiny?" he asked his readers. "I don't believe in coincidence so why now, after years of living blocks from one another, were we constantly in one another's paths?"

He talked about Brontë's clear approval of me. Her traitorous double tail thumps and leaning. How I'd taken care of him during her last day and passing.

He talked about it all. Briefly. Poignantly.

And then it ended. Elegantly as always with a sweet quip, a final thought, and a tender goodbye.

Carefully closing the laptop and shoving it aside, I laid my head on my arms and cried. Big, body-wracking sobs, the pain of this loss pouring out of me. The angst of the men I'd allowed in before, the lows I'd allowed myself to hit, the terrible words used against me by my mother that had sat in my body for years. I cried over all of them. I cried until I couldn't anymore. And then I lifted the hem of my shirt, wiped my face, and sat looking around the packed-up kitchen.

"Time for a new chapter," I whispered to the room.

There was a knock at the door and I spun to see the top of the moving truck out front. Sliding off the stool, I went to let the movers in.

I kept out of the way as much as possible, packing up the rest of the books that were still lining the bookshelves in the living room and watching from the window as the movers loaded my bed, which I'd decided not to burn after all, and the rest of my bedroom furniture into the truck.

As I emptied one shelf and moved to the next one down, my eyes caught sight of Graham's name. There they were. All seven of his books and the manuscript for the eighth that would be coming out next year. It was his best yet. I'd stayed up late the night I'd gotten it, and then finished it the next morning over coffee and donut holes. When I'd finished, I'd started all over again from the beginning. It was an intricate work of art as lives intersected and broke before crossing again, the bonds too strong to sever forever.

I closed my eyes, letting the emotions flow through me. When I opened them again, a flash of light blinded me and I raised my hand to block it while peering through the brightness to see what it was. The sun coming through the window was glinting off my little silver Space Needle statue. I stared at it and then had an idea. Picking it up, I held it in the palm of my hand, turning it over and over, my mind and heart racing in unison.

Maybe it was a stupid idea, but I didn't care. It was my move.

Wrapping my fingers around the little statue, I dodged the moving guy carrying my desk across the entryway to the front door.

There was one pair of shoes left in my foyer. My favorite old white sneakers, which I'd planned on my wearing on my flight to Seattle.

But I was going to have to wear something else, it seemed.

CHAPTER 37

Graham

It was strange taking walks without B. I found myself looking down for her or catching myself starting to warn her about big steps coming up or tree roots growing through the pavement. Near the end, she'd started to stumble over these things and now I always watched out for them.

It took two weeks of walking alone to work up the nerve to walk by Lior's house. I had no idea if it had sold and the quick glimpses of her social media page had shed no light on where she was, or what she was doing. It was as though she'd disappeared. I hated it.

My phone buzzed in my pocket and I pulled it free, smiling when I saw Cooper's name lighting up the screen, followed by his text.

"I can feel your indecision from here," he texted. "Just walk by already!"

I laughed.

When I'd called my old friend a few weeks ago, I'd been terrified thinking he either wouldn't answer, or would – and would rip me a new one before hanging up and never speaking to me again. But what I got instead was:

"I understand why you stopped talking to me. That girl had issues and you were standing by your woman like any good man would," he'd started. "What I *don't* understand is, you've been free of her for over a year and you're just *now* calling me? Dude. That's fucked up."

I'd grinned at the amusement in his voice, my shoulders relaxing.

"Coop," I'd said. "What can I say? I'm sorry. I was embarrassed for disappearing like I did."

"As you should be, man. We could've had some epic nights out drinking."

I laughed. "Goddammit. I've missed you. Hollywood still treating you okay?"

"You don't read the news either anymore?"

I covered my face with my hands and groaned.

"Tell me everything I've missed."

We'd talked for hours, taking a break so I could have dinner, then reconvening an hour or so later. By midnight my time, we were all caught up. He knew how Marley was doing, that she was in school in Seattle, how the folks were and all about Lior, my therapy, and the possible move in my future to the Pacific Northwest. In turn, he told me about the movies he was producing, as well as the one he'd co-written that was currently in production, the woman he was dating, and what his two brothers were up to.

"I needed this, Coop," I'd said as we said goodbye for the day. "Thanks for picking up."

"You think I would've missed the chance to give you shit?"

We'd talked or texted every day since, which was why he knew about my burning desire to walk by Lior's house.

I looked down at the text again and typed back, "Shouldn't you still be sleeping?"

He sent a laughing emoji ahead of his response.

"What is this sleep you speak of? I'm up by five, sometimes

four-thirty every day these days. Stop distracting from the assignment. Just do it."

"FINE."

He then sent a dozen thumbs up emojis and one of a hand flipping the bird. I grinned and tucked my phone back in my pocket.

"Here goes nothing," I mumbled under my breath, looking down out of habit for Brontë. It would've been so much easier if she were with me. At least we could commiserate over whatever we'd found later at Joe's. Now I'd have to go it alone, with no good girl to talk to about it after.

I walked the three blocks slowly, trying to distract myself by taking in the scenery. A preschool class wandered by in adorable chaos. An old woman sat on her stoop, giving the stink eye to any who dared cross her path. A young family with one baby in a stroller, and a slightly older child in the dad's arms, laughed as they walked by. And then I was there, standing across the street from Lior's home. My eyes immediately went to the third floor where her bedroom was, then moved down slowly until they landed on the for sale sign... and the bold "SOLD" notice that had been tacked across the top of it.

"Well," I said to the ghost of Brontë. "I guess that's that."

I headed to Joe's next – a dull ache in my chest as I entered the café – gave him a halfhearted wave as he helped a customer with something from the pastry case, ordered my usual, and took a seat inside by the window.

The man himself delivered my coffee, taking a seat across from me as a light snow began to fall outside, the first of the season.

"Still strange seeing you here without the old girl," he said and I nodded and took a sip of my coffee.

"I find myself looking down to talk to her constantly when I walk."

"I remember that after our last dog passed. I swore sometimes I still heard her bark even years later."

I gave him a sad smile.

"Ya know," Joe said. "I haven't wanted to ask but today it seems I've left my filter at home." He grinned mischievously and I laughed.

"Go ahead," I said. "I can take it."

"Whatever happened to the lovely Lior?"

I sighed and sat back in my chair.

"It's a long story. I wouldn't even know where to begin," I said and then shook my head. "Except it's really not. I had trust issues I hadn't resolved, and she was trying to figure out what she wanted to do next with her life and—"

"That didn't include you?"

"We never even got to *that* conversation. And to be honest, I wasn't being very fair to her. I hated the attention she got from her job and being so famous. It scared me. And that made her think I was trying to change her. Which, I swear I wasn't. I just... I've been with people before who liked the drama. It created so many issues and put me in uncomfortable and awful situations."

"Well Graham, I do think you have had enough drama for a lifetime."

"I have. So it was hard to trust what she was telling me because trusting women has only brought me misery."

"I'm sure you know this, but not all women are as self-absorbed as that last one was. My wife sure isn't. And Lior? I could tell immediately that she was a good one. The way she looked at you..." He sighed. "Nita used to look at me like that. Now she just rolls her eyes at me."

He chuckled and I smiled.

"Also," I said. "She's moved."

"And they don't have phones where she's gone?"

I narrowed my eyes at him. "Maybe."

"Bet you could find out. If you really wanted to."

I shook my head. "I messed up."

"You had things to figure out," he said, waving a hand.

The front door opened and a group of women came noisily

inside, shaking the snow from their hair and coats as they made their way to the counter. Joe stood and put a hand on my shoulder.

"Lior didn't strike me as the kind of woman who wouldn't give a second chance to someone she cares about. And Graham, that woman cares about you."

I sighed. "I care about her too."

"Feelings like the ones I saw between the two of you don't just disappear, my friend. Not even when someone dies. Give her a call."

"I don't think it's that simple, Joe."

He tapped the table with his knuckle,

"But it could be," he said, and then spun around to help his customers pick out pastries.

I took the rest of my cappuccino in a to-go cup and walked slowly home, enjoying the way the snow tamped down the noise of the city and made everything look clean and bright.

I thought about Joe's words. About Marley's. Even Coop had encouraged me to reach out.

And then I erased all of them and thought about the only two people that really mattered in all this.

Me and Lior.

"Screw it," I said, startling the young man I was passing on the sidewalk.

As I climbed the stairs to my front door, I pulled out my phone and immediately tripped on something on my front porch. A rolled-up newspaper. Ever since returning from my vacation, I'd avoided the newspapers piling up and the plants desperately in need of water. It almost looked like an abandoned house. I'm sure my neighbors were pleased.

Pocketing my phone, I knelt down and gathered up an armful of old newspapers. I unlocked the front door and hurried inside to deliver them to the small blue receptacle in my pantry, then filled a watering can and returned to the porch. As I watered and rearranged the pots, I stopped and stared in confusion at the shiny item tucked beneath the leaf of the furthest plant.

"What...?" I said, reaching out a tentative hand. As soon as I touched it, I knew.

I smiled as I lifted the little metal Space Needle statue that had sat on Lior's bookshelf, and then frowned when I noticed it seemed to be caught on some sort of string. But as I pulled it higher, I realized it wasn't caught. It was tied. To one half of Lior's favorite pair of sneakers. The half I'd once cleaned for her after she'd had the misfortune of stepping in B's droppings and had yelled her pretty head off at me.

"Maybe it *is* that simple," I said.

CHAPTER 38

Liar

I stood wrapped in my favorite cardigan, staring at the view outside the French doors leading to my balcony. Even with a sky full of clouds, it was a beautiful scene: the Puget Sound dark and moody, ferries making their journeys to one island or another.

My phone beeped with a text and I opened it to find a photo of Addie's male cat.

"Gomez misses you," the text that followed read.

A moment later another photo came through. It was the backside of Gomez's wife as she walked away.

"Morticia does not," Addie texted.

I sent a heart followed by a hand flipping the middle finger emoji.

"Dinner tonight?" she replied.

"It's a date."

I hurried to get dressed, determined to stay on the schedule I'd set for myself. I'd found keeping a routine helped me be more productive, more organized, and I felt better at the end of every day because I'd ticked things off a list. It had been my therapist's idea, and Hestia was never wrong. I'd hated having to let her go,

299

but she'd given me a referral to a great therapist in Seattle and we already had our first appointment scheduled. I still had work to do and I would not fail myself again.

After throwing my hair into a ponytail, I ran downstairs and slid my laptop into my messenger bag and headed for the front door, admiring my surroundings as I went.

It had taken the moving truck six days to arrive. I'd stayed with Addie until it did, busying myself with shopping trips to find new furniture and rugs to replace the things I'd donated or sold. By the time my belongings arrived, I knew where everything would go and stood and pointed while Addie sat at the kitchen island drinking the champagne she'd brought over to celebrate.

That was just over six weeks ago and I still couldn't believe I was here. I woke every morning smiling at my surroundings, and got into bed each night tired in a way that felt peaceful, rather than anxious.

And while I thought about Graham every day still – wondering if he'd found what I'd left yet – I didn't let it consume me. I didn't check his socials to see what he was up to. I just let him be, because he'd made it clear that day, and every day since, that it was what he needed. Maybe one day he'd show up with my shoe and a bashful smile. Maybe one day it would arrive in the mail, having been sent by my agent, along with a note of confusion as to why she'd been asked to send a scuzzy old shoe to me.

Whatever happened, it was out of my control. It wasn't something to have power over. And so I let it be.

A few minutes later, bundled against the wind in a white Burberry knee-length puffer coat with a coffee stain on the cuff, and a wonky knit cap made by Addie (a new hobby of hers I was *not* encouraging), I entered my new morning coffee spot, Ampersand.

"Hey Maya," I said, greeting the dark-haired high school girl who only worked Saturdays.

"Hey Lior," she said shyly, despite the fact that this was the fourth time she'd seen me and the last time I'd come in I'd told her I was a regular now and she was just going to have to resign herself to chatting with me. She'd blushed and rang me up for my usual cappuccino and veggie egg scramble without another word.

I set up shop on my favorite stool at the far end of the cafe that faced the main strip and the water beyond, pulling out my laptop and notebook, and opening the article I was currently working on. I was enjoying my new job immensely. It was more challenging than the odd article here and there that I'd written on a whim. I had to be prepared for this. I had to have more than one idea at a time to pitch in case Avery didn't like the first one, two, or ten. There was research to be done and sometimes people to interview. But it was all about the fashion world, something I knew a lot about, and it was always highlighting a different side of it. A designer, the delicate balance of fame and normal life, and the mental health aspect of being in a job where people are constantly critical of your body, your face, your hair.

I'd even interviewed my agent for a piece, asking what she looks for in a client and what will get someone fired from her roster.

"Here you are," Maya said, placing a coffee and the scramble next to my laptop.

"Thank you," I said, turning to smile. But she was already hurrying away. I grinned and returned to my laptop. I'd get her to talk to me eventually.

As I'd done off and on for the past few weeks, I took a picture of my set-up with the cloudy skies beyond and posted it to my social media account with the comment, "No rest for the wicked". And then I got to work.

An hour later I was still going and had switched to tea, poor Maya having to leave the safety of the counter to serve me again.

"Thank you," I said as she set the steaming cup beside me. "Oh, I didn't see any donut holes in the case today. Do you have them hiding somewhere?"

"We do. Would you like one?"

"I'd like a half dozen." I grinned. "For now."

She laughed. "What flavor?"

"Surprise me."

I was typing away when footsteps returned and something was placed beside me. I paused to pop a donut hole in my mouth. But the item my hand landed on wasn't what I was expecting.

I stared at the white shoe, confused for a moment. And then I saw the small silver Space Needle sitting beside it, attached by a shoe lace.

My heart pounded as I slowly turned around, and I felt as though I were going to burst out of my skin at the sight.

Graham. He was here. More gorgeous than ever with scruff on his face, his hair tousled and sexy... and he'd brought my shoe all the way to Seattle.

"You know," he said, eyeing the plate of donut holes he'd clearly just taken from Maya and placing them next to the shoe, his voice strumming my heartstrings into a sappy lovesick melody, "you really should leave some of these for the other customers."

I grinned.

"It's proper coffee shop etiquette," he continued.

"Oh yeah?" I asked, grabbing one and taking a bite.

"Yeah," he said, his pale eyes taking in every inch of my face before meeting mine again and settling there as if perhaps he had nowhere else to be.

"Wanna share?" I said, sliding the plate toward him.

He pulled out the stool beside me, sat down, and then took my hand in his.

"Don't mind if I do."

Epilogue

"How do you think it went?" Graham asked.

I smiled down to the dog at the end of the leash I was holding. He looked very handsome with his new collar, bought for the occasion, and sporting a black bandana around his neck.

"He did very well," I said, stopping to give our boy a pet. He immediately jumped up on me.

"Fitzwilliam," Graham said, his voice a gentle warning. "*Down.*"

The puppy ignored his dad and I laughed as Graham made a face.

The three of us were walking down Alki Avenue, me in a stained white Nike tracksuit, a gift from the company after a photo shoot I'd done for them two weeks before, and Graham sporting the purple UW sweatshirt he'd bought for the last football game we'd attended with Marley.

Our new puppy – brushed and primped – was prancing ahead of us, proud of his own first modeling moment today.

We'd adopted Fitzwilliam, named after none other than Fitzwilliam Darcy, Jane Austen's most adored male lead, three months ago from an adoption event put on by Addie's veterinary clinic. He was a purebred Bernese Mountain Dog that had been given up because the previous owner was allergic. The dog was gorgeous, with tan and black around his eyes and a white stripe down his nose. He was also one hundred percent dork. He suited us perfectly.

As part of Graham's local column in the Seattle Post, *Seattle Big and Small*, he'd recently interviewed Fitzwilliam about his adoption experience. A local magazine, inspired by the sweet and silly column, asked for an expanded version... and a photo shoot with the "aspiring model, who is following in his mother's footsteps". We'd just finished the shoot, which had included stoic poses with the Puget Sound and Cascade Mountains as a backdrop, and some racier photos of him frolicking on the beach.

"You're going to be a star!" the photographer assured him afterwards, giving him a mom-and dad-approved treat.

"Dammit," I said suddenly, stopping and staring down at the front of my sweatsuit jacket where I'd just spilled coffee. Again.

Graham laughed. "Why you wear anything but black I'll never know." He lifted my hand, my fingers interlaced with his, and kissed the back of it, ignoring the two teenage girls walking by, their phones lifted as they took pictures or perhaps even videoed us. It rarely happened in Seattle, but when it did, we didn't care where it ended up. We had nothing to hide.

Since seeing that shoe and the little Space Needle statue beside my laptop in the Ampersand Cafe two years ago, we'd experienced a lot together. My shock that he'd really come was quickly replaced by elation. I'd slid from my stool, as if in slow motion, and sank into his arms, fitting against him just like I'd remembered... perfectly.

He rented a cottage five blocks from my house and for six months we dated. There were long walks along Alki, cozy evenings at both his house and mine, books discussed – both his and ones we purchased from local indie stores like Paper Boat Booksellers and Edmonds Bookshop – and road trips up and down the coast, something neither of us had ever done but found we loved. We discussed buying a camper and seeing more of the country. Maybe we'd even get a dog.

Addie and Marley were frequent visitors to our homes, the two getting along so well, their smug smiles at being right about us so annoying that we threatened to disown the pair of them if they didn't tone it down. They promised to give us a break, so long as they both were named maids of honor at the wedding they knew was in our future. A few months later we made good on that promise in a small ceremony in Tuscany, a place we'd both always longed to see properly. It was a family affair, with our parents, Marley, and just a few close friends joining us for big Italian style dinners at the villa we'd rented. There were morning cappuccinos on our private balcony, and long walks through the countryside and neighboring towns. We returned home tanned, happy, and excited to begin our life together.

Graham was working on his ninth novel by then, a love story that moved through different times and worlds, and I was working on my own book. After being hired by Vogue to write a monthly column the year before, as well as keeping up with my job for Avery in Seattle, I was approached by one of the big five publishers to write a book about my time as the world's leading fashion model. It was to include the good, the bad, and the ugly. There would be photos and, adjoining them, my memories surrounding the photo shoot. Like the time I was straight up told I was too fat and put in a girdle beneath the clothing. At the time, I was five eleven and one hundred and twenty pounds. I looked malnourished because I was. The book would debut later this year. Graham was already planning a party for when it hit number one on the New York Times Bestseller List.

"Because it will," he kept saying with confidence.

Life had slowed again since finishing the book, and I was

happy to have my time back as I considered what I wanted to do next. Graham was encouraging me to try my hand at fiction.

"Maybe something dramatic?" he'd asked the other night when the subject had come up again.

"I've had enough drama," I said.

"A thriller? A murder mystery?"

I peered at him. "I might need to do some research for the latter."

He made a scared face.

"How about a happy little romcom then?" he offered up next. "About a sloppy model and the sexy novelist she meets while stepping in poo?"

I laughed. "No one wants to read a book that starts with poo, my love."

"You never know. I'd be into it."

I wrinkled my nose and shook my head. "Toilet humor is gross, babe. Try again."

But the idea was intriguing. Maybe I would write a novel one day. And maybe it would be a love story after all.

"Grocery shopping after we get home?" Graham asked now, giving my hand a little squeeze and pulling me from my thoughts.

My parents were coming for dinner tonight, a monthly routine that had started after I'd finished the first draft of my book and shyly, with Graham and Cal's encouragement, asked my mother to read it. She showed up on our doorstep a few days later with tears in her eyes. She hadn't changed much since then, but she'd changed a little... and that was a start. The dinners were helping. Surprisingly, I looked forward to them. But maybe that was because of the pitchers of sangria or margaritas Cal was always bringing.

I nodded and squeezed Graham's hand back, only to be distracted by Fitzwilliam who had paused in front of me. *Oh come on*, I thought, as he suddenly squatted in the middle of the walkway.

"Fitzwilliam," Graham groaned.

As I pulled on the leash to try and shuffle the offending pooper away from the pedestrian traffic and onto the grass, I looked to my husband in desperation.

"Please tell me you remembered to bring the bags?"

He frantically patted his pockets.

"Ah shi—"

Acknowledgments

This was a silly idea that came to fruition during a morning walk when I passed a gentleman walking his dog. So first and foremost, thank you to whoever you are – even though you will probably never know this book exists, and that it exists because of you. It was such fun to write. And I hope that goodest boy is living his best life.

When I told this story idea to my boyfriend, he didn't balk once. If anything, he tried to make it sillier. That's how you know you've found a good one. The fact that he's an ace editor as well was also great for me. Dan Hanks, my adoration runs deep. My love... deeper. Thank you for your support, laughter, and editing skills.

To my beautiful and hilarious kids who kept asking how the meet-poop was going, thank you. You get me. I am weird. I am your mom. I am proud. I hope I make you proud too.

So many of my friends could not believe I was actually going to put a book out there with such an absurd title. But they showed up for me anyways. Supporting me. Laughing along with me. Reading for me. Kate Quinn, Jamie Pacton, Sarah Daley, and Emily Ohanjanians. You are amazing humans, phenomenal writers, and I appreciate you every day for being my own personal cheerleading squad. Thank you.

My readers. I feel like I've asked a lot from you in picking up this book. If it's a physical copy in your hands... bless you. If you have toted this thing around in public, daring to display it... 100 points to you for your bravery. Truly though, it is an honor to be chosen. To have you spend your precious hours with my characters. All I want is to tell stories, and you being here, with this book in your hands (or in your ears), is a privilege and an honor.

THANK YOU.

Stay tuned for Addie's story... Coming soon!!